Louis Becke, Walter Jeffery

The Mutineer

A Romance of Pitcairn Island

Louis Becke, Walter Jeffery

The Mutineer
A Romance of Pitcairn Island

ISBN/EAN: 9783337019464

Printed in Europe, USA, Canada, Australia, Japan

Cover: Foto ©Andreas Hilbeck / pixelio.de

More available books at **www.hansebooks.com**

THE MUTINEER

E MUTINEER·

A ROMANCE OF
PITCAIRN ISLAND

BY

LOUIS BECKE

AND

WALTER JEFFERY

LONDON

T. FISHER UNWIN

PATERNOSTER SQUARE

MDCCCXCVIII

CONTENTS

PART I

viii

CONTENTS

PART II

PART I

CHAPTER I

THE HEART OF A SAVAGE

IT was night at Tahiti, in the Society Islands. The trade-wind had died away, and a bright- flood of shimmering moonlight poured down upon the slumbering waters of a little harbour a few miles distant from Matavai Bay, and the white curve or beach that fringed the darkened line of palms shone and glistened like a belt of ivory under the effulgence of its rays. For nearly half a mile the broad sweep of dazzling sand showed no interruption nor break upon its surface save at one spot ; there it ran out into a long narrow point, on which, under a small cluster of graceful cocos, growing almost at the water's edge, a canoe was drawn up.

Seated upon the platform or the outrigger, and conversing in low tones, were a man and woman.

The man was an European, dressed in the uniform of a junior naval officer at the end of the last century. He was or medium height, with a dark, gipsy-like

2   1

complexion and wavy brown hair, and as he drew the woman's face to him and kissed her, her skin showed not so dark as his.

The woman, or rather girl, was a pure-blooded native, wearing only the island *pareu* of tappa cloth about her loins and a snow-white *teputa* or poncho of the same material over her gracefully-rounded shoulders. The white man's right arm was round her waist, she held his left hand in hers, and with her head against his bosom looked up into his face with all the passionate ardour of a woman who loves.

For a few moments the man ceased speaking and looked anxiously over his shoulder at a number of white tents, pitched in a grove of breadfruit trees some few hundred yards away.

As he looked, the moonlight shone upon the musket barrel of a sentry, whose head could just be discerned above the beach as he paced slowly to and fro before the tents.

Bending her head of wavy, glossy black hair, the girl pressed her lips softly upon the white man's hand, and raising her face again, her eyes followed his, and as she noticed his intent look, a curious, alarmed expression came into her own lustrous orbs.

"What is it?" she murmured. "Does the soldier see us?"

The man smiled reassuringly and shook his head; then still clasping the girl's waist within his arm, he gazed earnestly into her beautiful face and sighed and muttered to himself.

"Mahina," he said hesitatingly in the Tahitian

tongue and speaking very softly, " you are a beautiful woman."

The girl's lips parted in a tender smile, her eyes glowed with a soft, happy light, and again she took his hand in hers and kissed it passionately.

" My white lover," she murmured, " would that I could tell thee in thine own tongue how I love thee. But the language of Peretane [1] is hard to the lips of us of Tahiti; yet, in a little time, when thou hast learned mine, thou wilt know all the great love that is in my heart for thee, and then thou shalt tell me all that is in thine for me."

The man drew her slender figure to his bosom again ; although he spoke her tongue but indifferently and she knew little of his, the ardent love which shone in her eyes and illumined her whole face, made her meaning plain enough. For a minute or so he remained silent, then again the girl's eyes sought his and her hand trembled as she noted the troubled, anxious look deepening upon his features.

" Kirisiani," she said, stroking his sun-bronzed cheek, "what is in thy mind to make this cloud come to thine eyes ? "

" Mahina," he answered in English, " the time is near now for us to part "; then seeing that the girl did not quite comprehend, he repeated his words in the native language.

" And wilt thou leave me who loveth thee, to sail away with the white *Arii*, [2] thy enemy ? "

" How can I help it ? Am I not the King's officer ?

---

[1] Britain. [2] An officer, a captain, or chief.

Did I yield to my love for thee and let the ship sail without me, then in mine own land I should be held up to scorn as a false man, and those of my name would be shamed."

The girl slowly bent her head and put her hands over her face ; then came a sudden, silent gush of tears. For a while she sobbed softly, as only women sob when some bright dream of love and happiness passes away for ever. Then with a quick movement she freed herself from the man's encircling arms, flung herself upon her knees on the sand, raised her tear-dimmed, starlike eyes to his, and spoke.

" Yet thou knowest we love thee ; and if thou wilt remain with us my people will take thee to their hearts, and thou shalt become a chief among us. For see, I, Mahina, am of good blood, and there is no other woman in the land that loves thee as I do. And thou shalt have as many slaves as Tinā, our chief, and like him, be carried upon men's shoulders wherever thou goest, so that thy feet shall not touch the ground."

The man took her hands from his knees and, passing his arms around her, tenderly lifted her up to her seat again. Then with his forehead resting upon his hand he sat and thought.

" No, Mahina. It cannot be as thou desirest ; for I am the King's servant, an *Arii*, and it would be death to me were I to yield to my love for thee and flee from the ship like one of the common sailors. Some day I may return—when I am no longer serving in a King's ship."

He was on the point of rising and bidding her return

to her home in the native village which lay some distance back from the cluster of tents, when she sprang to her feet and stood before him with one hand pressed to her panting bosom.

Barely eighteen years of age, her tall, slender figure, as she stood in the flood of moonlight, showed all the grace and beauty of perfect womanhood. Unlike the generality of the Polynesian women (who possess in their youth a faultless symmetry of figure rivalled by no other race in the world, yet too often have somewhat flattened faces), her features were absolutely perfect in their oval regularity and beauty, and through the olive skin of her cheek there now glowed a dusky red, and her lover saw that her frame was shaking with over-mastering passion as she strove to speak. Only once before had Fletcher Christian seen her look like this— when some of her girlish companions had coupled his name with that of Nuia, the sister of Tinā, the chief.

"Mahina," said her lover, stepping forward and essaying to take her hand.

She drew quickly back, and made an almost threatening gesture.

Christian paused irresolutely, for the look of scorn and fury in the girl's eyes daunted and shamed him. Then he spoke.

"Mahina, this is folly. Why art thou so angered with me?"

"Thou false white man!" she answered, and the strange, hoarse break in her young voice startled him —its melody and sweetness were changed into the jarring accents of rage and wounded pride; "touch me no more," and here a quick, sobbing note sounded in her throat. "Am I nothing to thee? Is all my beauty so soon dead to thee, and wilt thou put such shame upon me?"

"Nay, Mahina, but listen——"

"Why should I listen to thee, now that thou art about to cast me off? Dost thou think that I am a Tahitian woman, to be played with till thou hast tired of me; and then be given, with a laugh, to some other white man on the ship—as I have seen done? Did I not tell thee once that though I was born in this land of Tahiti my mother's mother came from the far distant island of Afitā—the island that springs up like a steep rock from the blue depths of the unknown sea? And by her was my mother taught to despise these dog-eaters of Tahiti; and as my mother was taught, so she taught me."

For the hundredth time since he had fallen under the spell of the girl's beauty and succumbed to the witchery of her ways and to the sound of her melting voice, her white lover again felt that her presence would overcome his resolution to part with her and · return to his hateful duty; and for the hundredth time he struggled to resist a fascination he knew was fatal. So, not daring to look into the danger-depths of her now tear-dimmed eyes, he spoke again with seeming calm, but yet his face paled and flushed and paled again at the sound of his own cold words. He loved her, he said, but how could he escape from the ship? The punishment would be death.

"Death," she said; "nay, not so, my lover, but life

for us both. Listen to me, and I will show thee that we shall never part again. And heed not the hot words of anger that leapt from my heart"; and then with all the eloquence of her passionate nature she unfolded to him a plan of escape, and as she spoke her eyes and hands and lips came to the aid of her soft, low voice.

"Mahina," and he turned from her abruptly and walked to and fro upon the sand, with working face and clenched hands, "let this end, girl; I cannot do as you wish."

"Ah," and again the tender voice became harsh and the red spark came into the dark eyes, "then there is some painted woman in thine own land whom thou lovest—a woman such as is she whom we saw on the ship—and it is for her thou hast cast me off."

"Why, you pretty fool," said the man in English, with a laugh, as he took her hand, "are you like your mother—offended at a silly jest? Did not you cry with the other girls, '*Huaheine no Peretane maitai*,'¹ and when you were told that it was but a figure of wax did you not laugh with them?"

"Ay," replied the girl, and her voice had a sullen tone, "but how know I that this image, which thou sayest was made by one of the sailors of the ship, is not the image of one thou lovest in Peretane? And my mother hath told me that this image of the woman with the hair like the sun and eyes like the ocean blue is carried on the ship as a spell to keep the white men's hearts hard to us women of Tahiti."

¹ "The Englishwoman is good" (to look at).

"Nay," said the man, in Tahitian, "I tell thee no lies, Mahina; 'twas but a silly jest of the sailors. The thing was the waxen head and shoulders of a woman, and the sailors, to make the people laugh, made unto it a body and wrapped it in garments and made pretence that it was an Englishwoman. Thy countrymen knew it was but a jest—but thy mother, who, lacking keen vision, for she is old, was foolish enough to believe in it; so when she placed presents of mats and food at its feet, all who saw laughed at her; and because she was angered at this hath she told thee this silly tale."

"Then, if the thing lives not, how is it that the man who showed it to our people carries it with him?"

"Thou silly little one! know that in my country there be men who are workers and dressers of men's and women's hair, and such images as that which thou hast seen are placed outside their dwellings so that men may know their trade. And this man on the ship dresses and curls and whitens the false heads of hair that some of us wear by placing them on the head of the image—for then is his task easy."

"Ah," she said in a whisper, "forgive me; but tell me that thou wilt not leave me."

"No, no, Mahina, tempt me not again; it cannot be. Good-night. Go to thy mother's house—and try to forget me." Then, not daring to look into her agonised face, he hurriedly embraced her and walked quickly towards the tents.

"Go," said the girl, as she sank down with her black mantle of hair falling over her shoulders, "go, then, and see Mahina no more. It is because I am not white that thou leavest me here with hunger in my heart for thee." And as she heard the sound of his footsteps over the loose pebbles some distance away, followed by the sentry's challenge, she lay prone upon the sand and wet it with a flood of anguished tears.

CHAPTER II

SCARCE two cables' lengths away from the dark fringe of palms which lined the white, shimmering beach, the *Bounty* lay motionless upon the placid, reef-sheltered waters of the quiet little bay, her hempen cable hanging straight up and down from hawse-pipe to anchor, fifteen fathoms below her forefoot. From the cabin windows a light in the captain's berth shot a dulled gleam upon the darkened water under her cumbrous stern, which the bright rays of moonlight had not yet touched, for though the moon was full it was not high, and the ship lay head to the south-eastward, with her bows toward the verdured slopes of Orohena Mountain, whose mist-capped summit towered seven thousand feet to the sky. Aloft, the ship's black spars stood silhouetted against the snow-white canvas bent in readiness for her departure ; for in a day or two her long stay at Tahiti would come to an end, and the bows of the little barque would be turned southward for her voyage to the West Indies.

In the great cabin, the chief entrance to which was

from the main deck, the moon-rays sent a stream of light through the open doors, and showed a strange sight to see on shipboard.

Instead of being fitted up like a King's ship, or indeed as a merchantman, the whole cabin space was filled with young breadfruit plants. Reaching fore and aft from the cabin doors to the transoms were five tiers of stout shelving, built to receive the pots in which the plants were placed ; while sloping upwards towards the after part of the quarter deck from the transoms themselves were five tiers more. Nearly all the plants were fully-leaved, and a stray moonbeam now and then pierced its way through them to strike against and illumine the dark mahogany doors of the rooms on either side of this strangely furnished cabin.

Nearly nine months before, the *Bounty*, of 215 tons burden, had left Spithead for Tahiti under the command of Lieutenant William Bligh, who had been sailing-master with the great navigator Cook in the *Resolution*. The ship which Bligh now commanded was specially fitted to convey specimens of the bread-fruit tree from Tahiti—the Otaheite of Cook—to the West Indies, in the hope that the tree would there take root and flourish and furnish as bountiful a food supply to the negroes of those islands as it did to the light, copper-coloured people of the isles of the Pacific.

Of the forty-six persons who sailed from Spithead in the *Bounty*, all, save Fletcher Christian, the senior master's mate, and a guard of four men who were on shore, were at that moment on board ; and all, except the anchor watch, were deep in slumber.

Walking to and fro on the forepart of the upper deck was Edward Young, a square-built, dark-complexioned man of twenty-two, and midshipman in charge of the watch. For nearly an hour he had thus paced the deck, glancing now at cloud-capped Orohena, six miles away, and now at the white tents of the shore party with the dark figure of the sentry in the foreground. Presently he stopped and looked intently towards another part of the beach where, an hour before, he had seen two figures seated upon a canoe which was drawn up on the hard, white sand; they were gone, but his quick eye discerned the smaller of the two disappear among the coconut groves towards the village of Papawa, while the taller person walked quickly over to the largest of the four tents and entered it.

"Ah," he said to himself, and an amused smile flitted over his sallow features, "Master Fletcher and Mahina, as I thought. He's badly love-smitten with that girl . . . no wonder he doesn't grumble at doing duty over the breadfruit plants on shore, with such a woman as that to sit by his side and charm him with her sweet prattle. . . . Better to be at that than doing this cursed dog-trot up and down in the moonlight . . . and yet 'tis dangerous . . . aye, as dangerous for him as it is for me to linger among these people so long."

He sighed, and then baring his left arm, looked at a name tatooed upon it lengthwise; then with an angry gesture of contempt, pulled down his sleeve, and resumed his walk to and fro.

"Dangerous! Aye, indeed it is! Else why should
I, a King's officer, and as proud a man as Fletcher
Christian—whom I call a fool—commit such folly as
this? What would my fine uncle say did he know that
I had gone so far as to promise this girl, whose name
is on my arm, never to leave her. And though I do
leave her, is it less dishonourable for me to beguile her
with lies because my skin is white and hers is brown?
Well, in a week or so, poor Alrema will have to learn
to forget me."

A cool breath of air touched his cheek, and looking
shoreward he saw the plumèd palm-tops swaying
gently to and fro; then again a smart puff rippled
the glassy surface of the water between the ship and
the shore and swept seaward; and Young saw the
black wall of a rain squall come fleeting down from
the dark shadow of the mountain.

Calling to the watch to stand-by, the young officer
picked up his oil-skin, which one of the men brought
him, put it on, and waited for the squall to strike the
ship. Quickly it loomed down upon the line of palms,
the black cloud paling to a misty white as it drew
nearer; then it rustled, then fiercely shook the waving
branches and drenched them with an ice-cold shower
ere it hummed and whistled through the *Bounty's*
cordage and sent her sharply astern, to tauten up her
cable as rigid as an iron bar.

"Pretty stiff while it lasts, Tom," said one of the
anchor watch to a messmate, as, ten minutes afterwards, the tail end of the squall passed and the bright
moonlight again played upon the soaking decks.

" Damme, but I'd like to see a stiffer one come along
and part the cable, eh ? " ·

As the droning hum of the squall ceased and the
palm branches hung pendulous to rest again, a woman,
nude, except for the narrow girdle of leaves around her
waist, raised herself from the foot of a coconut tree
behind which she had crouched, and looked at the
ship. In her right hand was an open clasp knife.
She leant her back against the tree and gazed steadily
at the *Bounty* for nearly a minute, then with an angry
exclamation cast the knife from her into the sea.

" Fool that I was ! Why did I not cut the rope
through ? Even though the young *Arii* had seen me
he would not have raised his hand to harm me, for he
too would gladly see the ship cast away and broken
upon the reef, so that he need not leave my cousin
Alrema."

An hour later, when daylight broke, Edward
Young, after calling the ship's company, again went
to the bows to take a look at the cable. It was his
last duty before reporting to his relief that all was
well, and then turning in. As he peered over the low
bows of the vessel he saw the hemp cable stretching
away down into the clear depths of the calm water.
In a moment his sailor's eye saw that all the strands
of the cable but one were parted.

His sallow face turned white, then flushed again,
and quickly walking aft he knocked at the door of
the state room occupied by Lieutenant William Bligh.

" Who is it ? " inquired a sharp, imperious voice ;
then ere the young man had given his name the cabin

door opened and a man of medium height, little more
than thirty years old, stood facing the midshipman.
His features were clear cut and refined and of
singular whiteness—remarkable in one whose occu-
pation was the sea—and his complexion contrasted
strikingly with the jet black of his hair.

"The cable is nearly chafed through, sir, or the
strands have parted. There was a strong squall just
before daylight and the ship strained very heavily upon
it. I think——"

"Keep your opinions to yourself. You are a damned
careless fellow, and not fit even to keep anchor watch.
Where is it chafed?"

"About a fathom below the water, sir," answered
the young man with an unsteady voice and an angry
gleam in his dark eyes. "When I looked just now it
was tautened out, and I saw that only one strand
remained."

"Bah," said the commander with a contemptuous
laugh; "and you have the audacity to attempt to
screen your carelessness by telling me it has chafed—
a couple of fathoms down from the hawse-pipe and in
fifteen fathoms of water! The fact is, some of the
natives have been off in a canoe and cut it under your
nose. You ought to have prevented it. Were you
asleep on your watch, Mr. Young? Answer me
quickly."

"I was not, sir," answered the young man quietly,
steadying his voice; "and I will swear that no canoe
has come near the ship since I took charge of the deck.
I believe she brought up to her anchor so suddenly

during the squall that the jerk caused the cable to part."

"That will do. I will see to this matter myself. You are all alike—every one of you. There is not an officer in the ship that I can trust. Order my boat away."

The angry, red flush in the commander's pale cheeks and the steady glitter in his light blue eyes boded ill to the young officer, whose own dark features were dyed deep with repressed passion; but by a powerful effort he overcame the desire to hurl back his superior officer's taunts, and saluting the captain with a hand which trembled with rage, he withdrew.

In a quarter of an hour Bligh stepped out of his boat on to the beach. Before he had walked a dozen paces he was met with smiles of welcome by Moana and Tinā, two of the leading chiefs, as had ever been the case during the many weeks of the *Bounty's* stay at the island.

But instead of the outstretched hand of friendship the angry officer gave them but a cold inclination of his head, and passed them by. At the entrance to the principal tent stood Fletcher Christian, who saluted as the commander approached.

"Mr. Christian," and the moment the master's mate heard the sharp, fierce ring in his captain's tones, his jaw set firmly and his eye looked steadily into Bligh's, "Mr. Christian, the cable has been cut. Most providentially, however, despite the criminal negligence of Mr. Young, the officer of the watch, one strand was not severed. That, fortunately, held the ship; otherwise she would now be lying on the reef. I am determined that the culprit shall be found and made an example of—as, by God! he shall."

"Very good, sir. Shall I send word for Tinā and the other chiefs to come to you?"

"Why so, sir? What reason have you to jump to the conclusion that this piece of villainy is the work of the natives?"

"I cannot imagine, sir, who else should be suspected."

"That is a matter of opinion. I have mine. But as you have made the suggestion I will at least put your uncalled-for suspicions to the test of investigation."

"Pardon me, sir——" began Christian, when Bligh cut him short with an imperious gesture.

"Send for Tinā."

In another minute a tall, stout, but handsome native whose speaking countenance expressed the most timid deference and respect, joined the captain and Christian.

"Tinā," said Bligh, fixing his keen eyes upon the chief's face, which already showed the deepest concern, "what does this mean? My ship's cable has been cut. Some of your people have done it. Let them be found instantly."

Like the simple child of nature that he was, the chief clasped his hands beseechingly together, and the quick tears welled up into his dark eyes ere he could speak.

"What man is there of mine, oh friend of Tuti [1] and friend of Tinā, who would do thee or thine such wrong as this?" and then with the utmost distress depicted on his face he beckoned to him a fine, handsome woman of about thirty, and hurriedly spoke a few words to her. As she quickly walked away to do his bidding, he turned to Bligh, and in pleading accents besought him to wait a little till his wife Aitia returned.

The captain of the *Bounty* nodded, seated himself upon a stool which the sentry brought to him, and waited. The chief's house was but a short distance from the tents and soon the woman returned carrying with her a framed picture of a naval officer. It was a portrait of Captain Cook, painted by Webber in 1777, which the great navigator had presented to the Tahitians, and which they treated with as much reverence as if it were a god.

"See," said the chief, taking the picture from Aitia's hand, and the accents of perfect truth rang in his voice, "see, this is Tuti," and he held it out towards the two officers; "would I, Tinā, whom he knew as Umu [2] his friend, and whose eyes love to look upon this, his face which speaketh not, would I tell thee lies? Nay, oh chief, it is my mind that none of my people have done this thing; but yet who can tell the wickedness that cometh into the hearts of men at times? And so now will I speak and seek if there be a man among my people with such an evil heart, and if there be then will I myself slay him before

[1] Cook. [2] His former name of Umu had devolved upon his son.

thee, so that the bitterness that is in my heart and thine shall die away and be forgotten."

And then, before the officer could frame a reply to the chief's impassioned speech, Aitia was at his feet, the tears streaming down her face while she repeated her husband's protestations of love and affection for all who came from the land of Peretane.

The earnest manner of the chief had its effect upon the quick, impulsive temper of Bligh—a man who could change in a moment from the violence of intemperate passion to the most winning amiability of manner.

In more gentle tones he replied that he was satisfied that Tinā would do his best to discover who had cut the cable, although if the culprit were found he hoped he would not go so far in punishing him as to take his life. Then he turned to Christian, and altering the suave tone in which he had addressed the chief, curtly ordered him to take the boat's crews and load the boats with plants.

Merely touching his hat, the master's mate repeated the order to the coxswain of the boat near by and turned away.

In an instant Bligh's pale cheek flushed angrily, and he sprang to his feet.

"What the devil do you mean by receiving my order in that manner ? Why don't you answer me when I address you ? By heavens, sir, I will teach you the respect due to your superior officer !"

Christian turned and faced him ; and Bligh, hot and furious as was his mood now, could not but notice the repressed passion in his eyes and the paleness that blanched his tanned cheeks, and realise that Fletcher Christian was not a man to drive to desperation.

For a moment the younger man did not answer, then the pallor of his countenance purpled with the sudden rush of blood to his face, the thick black eyebrows came together and his forehead showed two deep furrows as he replied—and in his voice there was no attempt to disguise the bitterness of heart within him—

"I treat you, sir, with all the respect that the rules of the Service demand; with the same courtesy"—and here his tones rang with contemptuous sarcasm—"I answer you as you show to me. Nothing, sir, shall induce me to forget that I am compelled by my *duty* to adopt that courtesy and respect. But, sir, beyond that I will take care to be no more civil to you than your treatment of me demands or justifies."

"Beware, sir; you are treading on dangerous ground—you are mutinous! I've half a mind to make a prisoner of you and keep you under arrest until we reach England. By heavens, sir, I'll stand none of your insolence and misconduct! You and every other officer of the ship shall be brought up to the mark and learn your duties."

But the master's mate made no reply, and walked quietly away after the boat's crew; and Bligh, his frame trembling with passion, went towards the house of Tinā the chief.

Aided by the willing hands of the natives, men and women, who had stood by listening with deep concern to the angry discussion between the two officers, the boats' crews soon loaded their boats, and Christian was left alone. Suddenly he felt a hand placed upon his and a voice murmured—

"Kirisiani, dost know who cut the rope?"

He started, and turned to meet the beautiful face of the girl he had talked with during the night.

"Hush, Mahina, tell me not, else must I tell his name to the captain—and that means death."

She laughed. "Thou knowest that it was I who did it. And yet tell of it if thou so desirest. What is death to me, my beloved, if thou leavest me? Listen —I will tell thee all. So that I might keep thee near me always, and my eyes look into thine, from sunrise to dark, and my hand lie in thine through the silence of the night, I swam to the ship as the wind and rain swept down from the dark valleys of Orohena, and cut the rope."

"Mahina, Mahina, 'twas well for thee that the chief of the ship is no friend of mine—even now hot words passed between us—else would I tell him 'twas thee. With us, who are servants of the King of Britain, no woman's love must count—our love to him is first of all. Forget that thou hast ever seen me."

She flung her arms round his neck and drew his face down to hers. "Thou art mine—if thou leavest in the ship then will I curse thee and die."

Ere he could say more, with an angry sob she had gone.

CHAPTER III

TWO days had passed, and now as the departure of the ship drew near the natives redoubled their kindnesses to the *Bounty's* people. Christian, with his morbid mind brooding over the scene between himself and his commander, did his duty in a dull, mechanical way and scarce spoke even to Edward Young, the one man to whom his gloomy nature sometimes relaxed. The parting, too, between Mahina and himself had had its effect upon him and he now clearly saw that, untutored savage as she was, she was yet a tender, loving woman whose heart he had cruelly tortured. " But," he reasoned with himself, "it cannot be helped. She will never see me again, poor child. She will soon cast me out of her memory."

A mile or two away from where the *Bounty* rode at anchor, at a little village called Torea, Mahina and Nuia, the handsome sister of Tinā the chief, sat together with their arms clasped round each other's waists. Mahina's eyes were wet with tears, but yet

22

there was shining through them the light of radiant happiness.

"See, Nuia, how I have wronged thee! Always, always was my heart wrung by the idle words of those who said that Kirisiani wavered in his love between thee and me."

Nuia laughed, and her bright, starlike eyes looked honestly into those of her friend.

"It is false. True, I once coveted him; but soon I saw it was for thee alone that he cared. And then it was that Steua[1] told me he loved me, and 'tis he alone that I care for now; and gladly will I help thee to keep thy lover, even as do I desire to keep mine. And listen now, while I tell thee how this shall be done."

Then Nuia told her friend how some of the seamen with whom the women had tender relations had declared for days their intention of deserting to the mountains and there remaining until the *Bounty* sailed. The women had promised to assist them, even though they knew Tinā would resent the act bitterly. They trusted, however, that after Bligh was gone, the chief's love for his sister would procure their pardon. Only the previous day Nuia and Alrema and two other girls named Ohuna and Ahi, who were devoted to two seamen named Millward and Churchill, had arranged to steal the ship's cutter during the night, land some miles down the coast where they would be met by Nuia and her companions, and make their way over the mountains to Taravao—the peninsula that con-

[1] George Stewart, midshipman.

nects the district of Taiarapu with Tahiti. Here they were to conceal themselves till "the wrath of Tinā had ceased."

"To-night, oh friend of my heart," said Nuia, placing her cheek against the bare bosom of her friend and embracing her lovingly, "this shall be done. Alrema's lover, Etuāti, who hateth the chief of the ship as bitterly as does thy Kirisiani, to-night again keepeth the watch. He hath taken the hands of these men in his and sworn to turn away his face when they steal the boat; and to-night, perhaps, will my Steua escape from the ship and come to me. Then, one by one, all those of the white men that hate to leave this land of ours will hide away, and the Arii Pirai[1] will trouble not, for in Taravao it will be hard for him to seek them?"

A fierce light shone in Mahina's eyes. "True, how could he? And yet it would please me better could I see Pirai dead. For ever is he saying bitter words to the man I love."

Nuia looked at her companion for a moment, then rose, and, going to a corner of the house, reached her hand up to the thatch; then she took down a pistol and gave it to her friend.

"See, this is the little gun that Pirai the captain gave to my brother Tinā. To-night Alrema gives it to her lover, who hath sworn to kill Pirai some day for the foul words he ever gives him, even as he speaks foul words to thy lover."

Then the two girls separated—Nuia to give the

[1] Captain Bligh.

pistol into Alrema's hand for Young, and Mahina to watch for her lover, should Christian come ashore in the evening.

At one o'clock next morning Edward Young was again keeping anchor watch. It was dark and rainy and no one else was to be seen on deck but the sentry —John Millward. Presently Young felt a hand on his shoulder, and heard the voice of Churchill, the ship's corporal—" Mr. Young ! "

" For heaven's sake be careful, Churchill ! Are you all ready ? "

" Yes, we've got the second cutter alongside. Muspratt is in her. We've eight muskets and six bags of powder and ball. Five of the muskets and some ammunition will be hidden by Alrema, who will be watching for you to escape. Why don't you come now, sir ? There are half a dozen others ready to do so ! "

" No, no, not now. I must get away alone. Alrema will let you know when."

" Goodbye, sir," whispered Churchill.

The midshipman pressed his hand, and the corporal stepped softly along the deck, till he reached the spot where Millward the sentry stood, peering anxiously out into the gloom which enveloped the ship. A quick gesture from Churchill, and the two figures dropped quietly over the side and were gone.

For some minutes Young looked for the boat through the darkness, as those in her pulled with muffled oars towards the shore.

" That's satisfactory," muttered the young man to

himself; "that's something for our amiable and worthy commander to think over at breakfast."

Lieutenant Bligh did think over it at breakfast; and soon Young was in irons and awaiting a promised flogging for "being asleep on his watch and allowing the damned scoundrels to desert," as his commander forcibly expressed it.

Four days afterwards, as Christian made his rounds of the ship he came upon Young, still in leg irons, waiting, with deadly hatred in his heart, for Bligh to visit him.

In the bosom of his shirt lay Tinā's pistol, and as the figures of Christian and a seaman darkened the entrance to the stuffy cabin his fingers clutched the weapon savagely.

"They are all taken, Young," muttered his superior officer; "they gave themselves up to Bligh this morning, and are now on board. I wish with all my heart I could set you free, for Bligh swears he will flog you."

"And I swear, Christian, that he shall die if he attempts it. My God! are we Englishmen or slaves?"

Christian shook his head gloomily, and with a pitying look at the young man, went on deck, passing on his way the manacled figures of the three captured men. They lay together in the sail locker, their backs raw and bleeding from the four dozen lashes which they had each received in the morning.

Their dreams of and dash for liberty had been brief. Landing at the spot agreed upon, Nuia and her two friends, Ohuna and Ahi, met them with the warmest demonstrations of affection and loyalty; then they learned with alarm that Oripah and Tamiri, two of Tinā's subsidiary chiefs, had forbidden the people in any way to aid or shelter them ; and that Tinā himself had bitterly reproached his sister Nuia for her share in the conspiracy—for by some means the whole plan of escape had been made known to him. Then after a hurried discussion the three deserters, accompanied by Ahi and another girl named Tahinia, set out again for Tetuaroa, a group of low-lying coral islands twenty-eight miles from where the *Bounty* lay. There they hoped to be free from interference ; for the chief of the islands, Miti, was related to Tahinia.

But when half-way across a furious squall drove them back to the mainland. Landing at a village called Tetaha the deserters remained hidden till they were surprised by Bligh and a boat's crew ; and although they were prepared to fight to the last, the girls, to their surprise, begged them to surrender.

" Milwa," said Nuia to Millward, the moment they saw Bligh approaching, accompanied by his boat's crew and Tinā, " waste neither these men's blood nor thine. Yield—and I, Nuia, swear that the ship shall not take thee away."

Relying on the repeated assurances of the girls, who wept in the earnestness of their beseechings, the three deserters came out of the house and stood before Bligh and his party.

" Surrender, you villains ! " he cried.

" Aye, aye, sir, we surrender," answered Churchill ; and under his breath he said to his companions—" to be free again before long."

When the men were brought on board, Bligh, whose face was livid with passion, turned to Fletcher Christian.

"Muster the hands, Mr. Christian. I'll show you and the others like you whether I will tolerate this spirit of mutiny and disregard of my orders."

Then in sullen silence the ship's company were mustered on the main deck to witness the flogging of the deserters.

As the bleeding form of Muspratt, the last to be punished, and the greatest sufferer, was led away from the gratings, one of the boatswain's mates named Morrison said to the midshipman Stewart in a low voice : "I'm glad, sir, I wasn't picked on to flog poor Bill Muspratt. My God, sir, how long is this to go on ? The men are bordering on mutiny. Last night the captain took away every present of food given to us by the natives and said that it was his, and that every one on the ship, from the master down, was a damned thief."

Stewart gave him a warning glance as he answered in a whisper : "Don't talk to me, Morrison ; if the captain sees you it means the cat."

Ten minutes later, as Christian was employed in hoisting in the cutter, Bligh's imperious tones were heard asking for him.

"Mr. Christian," said the captain, walking up to where the master's mate stood, and his voice quivered with rage, " I find that you had the audacity to send a coconut to that scoundrel Young to drink just now. By the Lord, sir, do you want me to send you to join him ? " And then with a passionate gesture he turned on his heel and again sought his cabin.

The master's mate, with blazing eyes and face white with anger, turned and looked at the seamen who stood around him with their hands on the boat-falls. Not a word escaped his lips, but in their eyes he read their dangerous sympathy.

That night Bligh slept ashore at Tinā's house, and when all but the anchor watch were asleep a canoe glided gently alongside, and Mahina and Alrema stepped on deck and were met by their lovers. Young had secretly been released from his irons by Christian the moment Bligh had left the ship. For some hours the four conversed earnestly together, then just as the first grey streaks of dawn began to pierce the horizon the girls embraced the two men tenderly and went quietly back to their canoe.

Down below, as Christian was replacing the hand-cuffs on Young's wrists, the midshipman gripped his companion's arm.

" Christian," he said, " as God is my judge I intend to keep faith with that girl, even if it costs me my life ; and you, Christian, are you made of stone ? Can you leave Mahina—to lead such a life as we are made to live ? "

The master's mate dashed Young's arm aside. " For God's sake, man, don't ask me. My brain is on fire," and for a minute or two he walked quickly to and fro, seemingly oblivious of the other's presence. Then he stopped suddenly and faced Young with a short, bitter laugh.

"That all depends on what happens. If Bligh treats me as a man . . . I will pocket his past insults . . . and prove a cruel, heartless scoundrel to that poor girl. If he does not . . ."

He finished the sentence with a gesture of despair, and went on deck.

CHAPTER IV

THE time to say farewell had come at last, and from early dawn the beach was crowded with natives. For two days the genial, kindhearted people had entertained their white friends with their simple sports, and the crew of the *Bounty*—save for those who lay ironed and sweltering in her 'tween decks— were given liberty by their stern captain. Sometimes in the midst of the mirth and song that prevailed during the *hivas* or dancing of the natives, strange spells of silence would fall, and Tinā the chief and his stately wife would, with tears streaming from their eyes, leave the assembled throng and retire to their house. Tender-hearted, simple, and affectionate, they had conceived for Bligh, despite his occasional outbursts of passion and his severe treatment of the ship's company, a sincere and lasting respect; and that evening, when he came ashore dressed in his full uniform, with his sword by his side, smiling in that engaging manner which seemed so natural to him at times, even those few of the natives who feared and disliked him for his tyranny, demonstrated at least their respect for his rank and position in the most marked and earnest manner.

Long past midnight the singing and dancing continued, and Bligh, as he stood on the beach, grasping the hands of Tinā and Aitia in his, was content. Nearly two-thirds of his crew were ashore, and now as he stood there watching he saw them taking farewell of their native friends, who with the most extravagant demonstrations of sorrow, begged them to remain till the morning. He had no suspicion that this was assumed and that nearly half of his men had whispered to some *taio* (male friend) or pretty girl, " We will return soon."

" Good-night," he said to the chief, holding out his white hand again, " good-night, Tinā and Aitia. Remember that to-morrow, soon after daylight, we sail. Yet I shall be pleased to see you in the morning."

Then the boatswain's whistle sounded for the men to return to the boats, and amid the weeping of those of the islanders who did not know what Mahina and the other women knew, Bligh and his men called out their farewells and pulled towards the ship.

But with the first signs of dawn, those on board, looking shoreward, saw a vast concourse of natives on that part of the beach nearest the *Bounty;* and every few minutes numbers of people of both sexes were arriving through the palm-groves from inland villages, carrying gifts of fruit and native clothing, intended as parting presents for the voyagers. The waters, too, of the little bay were alive with canoes ; many of them

had come from the distant villages of Taiarapu, a
day's journey, laden to the water's edge with simple
tokens of affection for Bligh and his crew. As the
canoes passed under the *Bounty's* stern on their way to
the shore the people in them were much affected
when they noted the unmistakable signs of the ship's
departure. They had daily heard for a month past
from Bligh himself that he hoped to sail on the
following day, but the continued delays seemed to
have inspired them with hope ; the *Bounty's* people,
they believed, had become so attached to their island
friends that they could not part from them, and it was
even possible, to their simple minds, that Bligh would
abandon the mission on which he was sent by the
unknown King of England.

Sitting a little apart from the others and apparently
taking no heed of the bustle around them, the girls
Mahina and Nuia conversed with each other in low
tones. Alrema, although accused by Tinā of helping
his sister in aiding the seamen to desert, had been
forgiven, and was just then, with Aitia, conveying to
Bligh a farewell present of two handsome *parais* or
mourning dresses, which were to be given to King
George.

" Mahina," and Nuia placed her hand on her friend's
shoulder, "all will yet be well. Why look so sad ?
Dost thou doubt our lovers' promises ? See, only a
little while ago, Alrema went on board to see her
lover Etuati—he who is now bound with iron rings
on his hands and feet—and this he said to her : ' Tell
those that love us that we will return to Tahiti ere a

moon has passed.' Come, my friend, let us go to the ship for the last time."

By this time the *Bounty* was surrounded by hundreds of canoes, and her decks were thronged with natives who, each man singling out his particular *taio*, or white friend, pressed upon his acceptance some farewell gift. Bligh, standing on the quarter deck, was conversing with Aitia and her husband, and behind him stood a boatswain's mate holding in his arms two muskets and two pistols, with bags of powder and ball. These were a gift from the commander to Aitia, whose skill as a markswoman rendered the gift specially pleasing and valuable.

Raising his hat, and addressing her as if she were some great English lady, the captain of the *Bounty* said that the gifts were in token of his own personal liking for her and her husband, and as a proof of the friendship of the king of Great Britain. Then, while a respectful silence fell upon every one on board, the stately Aitia touched her forehead with the weapons one after another, and flinging herself at Bligh's feet clasped them in her hands and wept.

Gently disengaging her hands the commander straightened his slender figure, and his sharp tones rang out : " Clear the decks, Mr. Christian ; and you, Tinā, ask your people to get into their canoes. Aitia, goodbye ; Tinā, goodbye."

Christian, who had just bidden a hurried, passionate farewell to Mahina, sprang to the ship's forecastle and then some of the seamen manned the little capstan ; the fiddler took his seat upon its head and scraped a

dismal tune, every now and then breaking off in the
middle of a bar to wave his bow to some Tahitian
friend whom he knew, as he or she went over the side
to a canoe. The ship was already hove short ; and a
few fathoms of the great hemp cable flaked upon the
deck soon brought the anchor to the cathead. The
topsails bellied out as the wind filled them ; the men
sprang aloft to man the yards at the word of command
from Bligh, who had explained to Tinā that with this
ceremony and the firing of guns the ships of King
George saluted the sovereigns of other nations ; but as
the gun-firing might injure the breadfruit plants on
board it would be omitted. The sailors aloft gave a
last cheer, the water began to ripple and bubble under
the bluff bows of the *Bounty* and from the crowd of
sorrowing people burst a cry of " *Ioarana no ti atua
ti* " ("May the gods protect thee for ever and
ever ").

A puff rippled across the bay, the ship lay over to it
and sped quickly towards the passage between the roaring lines of surf which leapt and seethed upon the
shelving ledges of coral reef. In another five minutes
the vessel's bows rose and fell to the sweep of the ocean
swell, and the *Bounty* stood out into the open sea.

Then those who watched from the shore saw her
square her yards and head to the south, for Bligh
intended to call at the Friendly Islands before proceed-
ing to the West Indies. Hour after hour, and still the
people watched the lessening canvas of the ship sink
below the horizon. Towards noon the breeze failed,
and not till the green shadows of the mountains turned

into a soft purple under the rays of the setting sun was the white speck lost to sight.

Then Mahina and Nuia, who were the last to go, turned sadly away and went home to their dwellings of thatch to wait and hope.

CHAPTER V

FOR thirteen days the *Bounty* had sailed westward over a placid sea, the light south-east trades which filled her canvas scarce causing more than a noiseless ripple under her forefoot. On the morning of the fourteenth day she sailed through a cluster of low-lying, richly-verdured islands—the Namuka Group, and dropped her anchor in ten fathoms, in the clear, motionless waters of a reef-enclosed spot off the main island. The day was beautifully fine but intensely hot, and the dying wind gave the ship scarcely way enough to bring her to an anchor.

In a very short time Bligh had opened communication with the natives of Namuka—a fierce, muscular race, who, however, professed friendship, agreeing to let him procure such supplies as he wanted from the island, and promising their assistance in wooding and watering the ship. The calm and dignified manner of the commander seemed to impress the savage, intractable, and treacherous Tongans as it had the gentle and kindly-natured Tahitians; and Bligh again showed those peculiar phases of his character which made him treat even the most dangerous natives with humanity and forbearance, and yet toward his officers and crew behave with undeserved, terrible severity.

As soon as the captain returned on board, in sharp, fretful tones he ordered the boats away; one under the command of Mr. Nelson, the botanist, and another with Christian in charge, to wood and water the ship.

For some hours the work went on without interference, till the natives, all of whom were armed with spears, clubs, and slings, began to surround the white men and steal everything they could lay their hands upon. Some of them actually took the casks of water from Christian's men and rolled them away into the coconut groves. Every moment their demeanour became more threatening and their insulting gestures and language were so unmistakable that Christian got his men together in order to cover the boats, and then paused irresolutely as to his next course of action. For Bligh had given orders that no matter how the natives behaved they were not to be molested, and on no excuse were they to be fired upon.

In a few minutes their numbers had so increased that they began to show signs of making a rush upon Christian's scanty force, evidently mistaking his forbearance for fear; and soon some hundreds of them attempted to cut him off from the boats. It was only at this juncture that he gave orders to fire a volley over the heads of the now advancing and yelling body

of savages.   To this they responded with derisive
jeers, shaking their spears and clubs and calling out
" *Maté! maté!* " (" Kill ! kill ! ").

With great difficulty Christian got his men back
into the boats without injury being inflicted on either
side, and reported himself to Bligh, who severely
reprimanded him.

Wiping the beads of perspiration from his face, the
young man replied to his commander's censure : " It
is impossible, sir, to carry on the duty unless some
steps are taken to prevent the landing party from
being cut off by the natives."

" You are a damned cowardly lot of fellows ! "
sneered Bligh ; " and is it possible that you, Mr.
Christian, an officer in the King's Service, are afraid of
a troop of savages while you and your men have firearms ? "

Christian's face paled and his limbs shook as if in a
fit of ague : " Our arms are of no avail, sir, while you
forbid their use."

" Carry on the work and don't attempt to argue
with me," was the contemptuous answer.

So with wrath eating his heart out Christian went
back to his task, and by almost superhuman endurance
and forbearance managed to complete the wooding
and watering of the ship.

At last the work was finished, and the *Bounty* once
more at sea, and on the afternoon of the 26th of April
she lay becalmed between Namuka and the island of
Tofoa, whose sharp-pointed volcanic cone could be
seen thirty miles away, with thin blue curls of smoke

ascending from its hidden fires into the windless atmosphere, while the sea was of glassy calmness and the ship drifted steadily to the eastward.

Pacing to and fro upon the quarter deck, with the red fury spot showing upon his pale cheeks, the captain presently said, in his quick, angry way, as his eye glanced along the deck—

"Morrison, send Mr. Christian here."

It was Fletcher Christian's watch on deck, and he at once responded.

"Mr. Christian, what has become of the pile of drinking coconuts which was stowed between the guns? Some scoundrel has taken them. I demand to know who was the person!"

"I cannot tell you, sir, what has become of them."

"You mean you will not. By heavens, sir, you shall! I have no doubt that whoever took them did so with the sanction of the officers."

A lump rose in Christian's throat and his voice sounded hoarsely.

"I think, sir, that you are mistaken."

"We shall see! Pass the word for all the officers to come on deck."

In a few minutes they were all assembled, and Bligh, now in a fever heat of unreasoning passion, attacked them in the same manner. For some seconds no one answered; then Fryer the master, and Christian and Young assured him each in turn that they had not seen any of the men take the coconuts.

"Then," said Bligh, and his thin, clean-cut lips curled contemptuously, "you have taken them your-

selves! Mr. Elphinstone," turning to the junior
master's mate, "bring every coconut in the ship on
deck."

"Now," went on Bligh, as four or five seamen
came on the poop carrying bunches of coconuts,
which they placed in heaps on the deck, "please tell
me, each of you, which of these heaps you individually
claim."

The officers spoke in turn, and then but one heap of
coconuts remained—that belonging to Christian.

"Is this yours, Mr. Christian?" said Bligh, in a
voice trembling with passion.

"I really do not know, sir. It is difficult to tell
one pile of coconuts from another; but I hope you
don't think me mean enough to steal yours."

"By God, sir, I do! You must have stolen these
from me or you could give a better account of them!
You infernal rascals! You are all thieves alike and
combine with the men to rob me. I will flog you all
and make some of you jump overboard before we reach
Endeavour Straits."

Calling Samuel his clerk, Bligh ordered all the grog
to be stopped, and only half a pound of yams to be
served to each officer's mess in the future—and a
quarter of a pound only if a single yam was missed.
And then, his handsome features distorted with rage,
and muttering curses, he turned upon his heel and
went below.

The officers stood and eyed each other with anger
and amazement, and began to complain audibly; but
Christian, with a strange look in his dark eyes, ordered

them in a hoarse and broken voice, some to their duty, others to their watch below.

When eight bells struck he was relieved by the master and went to his cabin.

And Edward Young, as he watched Fletcher Christian pass him, with his hands clenched and his face blanched to a deathly white, smiled to himself and said, "It is the last straw."

CHAPTER VI

THE RUBICON

W HEN Christian reached his cabin he threw himself upon his sea-chest—almost the only article of furniture that the place contained—and cursed aloud his wretched existence. He thought of the long voyage before him, each day wearisome enough even if spent in agreeable companionship with his fellows, but a very purgatory with such a man as Bligh to goad him every hour with foul language and petty insults.

His gloomy reflections were broken in upon by a voice asking permission for the speaker to enter.

"What do you want?" he asked angrily.

A seaman drew aside the canvas screen.

"The captain sends his compliments, sir, and requests the pleasure of your company to supper."

Christian sprang to his feet, his face flaming with passion. "Tell him to go to the devil and take his supper in the only company he is fit for."

Alexander Smith, the sailor who had brought the message, for a moment stared in astonishment, yet

waited in respectful silence. This was the first time
during all the long voyage that an officer had so far
forgotten himself as to express his feelings about the
commander before a common seaman. With the
seamen themselves such outbursts were frequent
enough, but here was an officer—the senior master's
mate, the third man in rank in the ship—ordering a
common sailor to tell his commander to go to the
devil, the only fit company for him !

Smith was a young man of twenty-two, the son of
a Thames lighterman ; but he had been born with
brains, and had taught himself to read and write,
while his mother had brought him up to do his duty
and respect his superiors in that old fashion which is
good. This was his first voyage in a King's ship,
but he knew what was due from Christian to his
commander.

So, instead of smiling, either openly or covertly, at
Christian's rage, he thought for a moment, pulled
awkwardly at a lock of his hair, gave a slight cough,
and said—

" Begging your pardon, Mr. Christian, did you say
that I was to tell the captain you felt too poorly, and
kindly asked to be excused? "

Christian glanced quickly at him, and then forgot
his anger. The sailor was not much to look at, a
strongly-built fellow below the middle height, with
his face pitted deeply from the effects of small-pox,
and his naked chest disfigured with tatoo marks—a
coarse, rough seaman in dress and appearance, a
gentleman in instincts—and, above all, a *man*.

"Smith, you're a good fellow to bring me up with a round turn like that ! Give me your hand, and deliver your own message, and accept my gratitude !" And the officer grasped the sailor's hand and wrung it warmly.

"Aye, aye, sir," and Smith's honest tones trembled with pleasure, for he liked and respected the young man, and felt proud of having thus won his confidence. "A few months longer, sir, and it'll be all serene with us." Then, with a respectful salute, he was gone.

The master's mate sat down again on the chest, and leant his cheek upon his hands. The last words of Smith—"a few months longer"—had once more set his brooding mind to work.

He rose to his feet again ; the close, hot atmosphere of his stuffy quarters seemed to oppress and choke him, and his brain was dulled and aching with the misery in his heart. He stepped out, and, gaining the deck quietly, leant upon the bulwarks and looked moodily over the star-lit ocean to where the steep cone of Tofoa upreared its darkened form three thousand feet in the air. It was the first dog-watch, when on ship-board men sing and make merry ; but on this ship came no sounds of violin or choruses of seamen, for all, officers and men alike, were sullen and gloomy, and brooded over the incidents of the past few days.

The wind was very light, and the ship scarce held steerage way ; everything was still, and the grave-like silence oppressed the man. Now and then a gleam of red, smoky flame would flash in the sky to the eastward, and a strange, dulled muttering would be borne over the waters as the raging forces pent up in black Tofoa boiled and seethed within its groaning heart. The sight possessed a fascination for him, and for nearly half an hour he stood and watched the shooting dull-red flame and listened to the awful sounds which broke from the mountain in the violence of its convulsions.

Presently he changed his attitude of dejection, and his eye lightened.

"Ten miles away," he muttered, gazing at the dark shape of Tofoa, "and there are beaches on the west side where landing is easy, and a network of low islets within another six leagues. By heavens, I'll risk it! Anything is better than this—better, even, the jaws of a shark!"

He went quietly forward and collected a number of boat-oars and some hand-spikes from the racks; these he brought to a place in the after part of the ship, where he was not likely to be seen, and began to lash them together.

He was interrupted suddenly by Young. "What the h—l are you doing, Christian?"

"I am making a raft."

"A raft?"

"Yes, a raft."

"Why? What for?"

"Because, Young, I can stand this no longer. I am about to try and make Tofoa on this raft."

"Madness! You could never reach there, even

if there were no sharks. There is a fearful current setting to the westward."

"I don't care. Sharks are better company than this infernal tyrant. Why, do you know, Young, that the damned, pitiful scoundrel actually invited me to sup with him to-night, no doubt thinking to propitiate me for the insults of this afternoon."

"Oh, well, you've suffered no more than I. But still, this is sheer madness, Christian. You are not, surely, such a fool as to incur all the odium of becoming a deserter, for what ?—to be turned into shark's meat ! "

"Don't argue with me, Young," he answered fiercely. " I've made up my mind to get out of this floating hell, and I mean to leave the ship either in the first or middle watch. You know of my intention. If you think it your duty, tell the gentle Bligh."

Young laughed. "Not I, Christian. I'll not move in the matter, except to dissuade you from such folly."

"Cease, cease, my dear fellow ; it is too late. Either this, or I put an end to my life. But if your sympathies are with me, do me this favour—go to the steward and on some pretence or other get me food. Put it in a bag with some nails and hoop-iron and beads, or anything likely to take the fancy of the natives, and bring it to me."

Young at once went away, and procuring a canvas bag put in it food, some bottles of water, and a few articles for barter. But at the same time he told the boatswain's mate of Christian's watch and the officers in charge of the first and middle watches, and begged them to keep the matter secret, but on no account to give the young man an opportunity of carrying out his rash project, "for," said he earnestly, "Mr. Christian is not in a fit state to leave the ship ; the man is ill in mind and body, and not responsible for his actions."

Slowly the night passed, and more than once Christian came on deck with the intention of putting his idea of escape into practice ; but he always found some one ready to talk to him, and so no opportunity came. At half-past three he gave up all further attempts, and sick in mind, lay down in his bunk. Then eight bells struck, and he was called by Stewart to take the morning watch.

As Stewart turned to go on deck he pressed Christian's hand sympathetically, and said in a low voice, "Mr. Christian, I know your design. For God's sake, sir, try to have patience, and give up your intention. If you carry it out, it only means a dreadful death."

"I will make no further attempt to-night, at least," he answered, in a strange, husky voice ; but he gave the midshipman's hand a firm grip.

For some minutes he sat upon his sea-chest, with his face buried in his hands, thinking ; and the darkness of the night, the hoarse mutterings and muffled thunder from distant Tofoa, found a responsive echo in his maddened brain.

The signs of dawn were reddening the horizon as Christian reached the deck ; and the black pall of smoke which had hovered over Tofoa's lofty peak was vanishing before the breath of a light air which was coming over the water from the south-east but had not yet stirred the *Bounty's* canvas.

Thomas Hayward, the midshipman of the watch, had mustered his men ; the wheel had been relieved, the look-out stationed, and those of the watch who were not needed had gone forward to lay about the deck to doze or sleep.

Leaning over the forecastle rail the look-out stood watching the movement of a huge shark that swam to and fro, close to the ship's port side. Presently Young, whose attention was drawn to the monster by the seaman, leant over the waist and watched also, and shuddered as he thought of Christian and his raft ; then, knowing that Christian would not disturb him, he lay down between two guns.

Pacing to and fro on the starboard side of the little poop the master's mate was waiting for the breeze to reach the ship, to give the order to brace the yards round to meet it. Perhaps had that light, cooling air which was now sweeping away sulphurous smoke from Tofoa's black sides, reached the silent ship and sent the crew hurrying about her decks, the desperate deed that was so soon to follow would never have been done. But as Christian looked aloft, he saw the pendant topsails give a feeble flap or two and then hang limp and dead as before ; a faint breath of air touched his burning temples, and then silence, deep and oppressive, fell upon the ship again.

" A dead calm still," he muttered to himself ; " I

wish to God a squall would put us on our beam ends or founder the ship—anything but this." And then he stepped to the side and watched, with a curious sense of fascination, the sullen mass of the burning mountain.

The utter impossibility of his leaving the ship unless to die by the teeth of the sharks was now forced upon his mind, for there beneath the counter he saw swimming to and fro a brute that would have made short work of him upon the fragile raft on which he had thought to venture his life. But yet—and his hands clenched savagely—submission to his lot was not possible—better death itself than endure it longer.

Then his thoughts went back to a night on the white beach at Tahiti, the murmuring sway and rustle of pluméd palms, and the soft symphony of the throbbing surf on the distant reef, as Mahina's starlike eyes, dimmed with her farewell tears, looked past his own into the cloudless vault of heaven above them; and her passionate pleadings as she placed her trembling hands upon his arm seemed even now to be borne to him across the sea, and made the quick, hot blood of youth surge madly through his veins. Madness to think of her now! Yes, he knew that; but yet she loved him—would give her life for him, even. A savage! And he a King's officer, yet a slave to a vindictive tyrant—his life one daily round of insult and shame. . . . A savage, yet a gloriously beautiful woman, whom only his duty to his King and country made him forget.

Then his face flushed hotly. Forget her! What folly to try to deceive himself! He loved her! . . .

He struck his clenched hand on the rail, and then his brain caught fire, his breath came in short, quick gasps, and the WAY OUT flashed into his mind.

What would be his life at sea ? Bligh, even if suffered until the ship returned to England, was not the only coarse, cruel tyrant in the Service. And it would be at least seven months ere the voyage was ended—seven months of torture, shame and misery. And over there, far beyond the sea-rim lay at least happiness with one who loved him.

What did it matter after all ? Perhaps after long, long years of service he would be put aside for other and younger men who had influence and social position. But then, he thought, he was an officer, a man of good family. The insults he had received might be forgotten were he one of the rough, coarse seamen for'ard—such a man, for instance, as Quintal who, when brutally flogged by Bligh, swore he would kill his oppressor. But a seaman forgot and forgave a flogging, and an officer and a gentleman must forget and—no, not forgive—an insult from his superior.

So, as he paced to and fro on the little poop and as the dawn began to break he sought to get rid of the devil tempting him ; but he sought in vain. Again and again Mahina's soft voice and choking sobs sounded in his ears. " I will love thee for ever and ever and ever ; how canst thou leave me ? "

Then the WAY OUT came into his heart again. It was so easy of accomplishment, too. He stopped suddenly in his hurried pacing to and fro and his quick mutterings ; for the man at the wheel was regarding him curiously.

"My God!" he muttered to himself, then cried aloud "I'll do it!" He stepped to the break of the poop.

"Hayward," he called in a hoarse whisper.

Hayward jumped up from the hatch where he had been lying and came to the foot of the poop ladder.

"Did you call me, sir?"

"Yes"—and his voice seemed like the voice or another man to the speaker himself—"come up here and look after her. I want to go below and lash up my hammock."

The midshipman looked inquiringly at him. "You are ill, sir," he said; "better get into your hammock instead. Hallet is sleeping on deck. Let me call him to relieve you."

"No," and his voice had a strange, sharp ring in it; "come up here."

"You are not thinking of that raft again, Mr. Christian? There's been a shark swimming round the ship all night."

"Damn you, come up here when I tell you."

"Very well, sir," said Hayward in a changed voice, and he walked aft to the binnacle without another word.

Christian ran forward. The men of his watch lay sleeping on the fore-hatch, and among them he was quick to recognise two seamen, Quintal and McCoy, men who had been severely punished for trivial offences by Bligh. Both were good seamen, and, with Alexander Smith, had a particular liking for Christian, who had treated them with a great deal of kindness. The master's mate, now that he had determined to take the plunge, seemed to have rapidly sketched in his mind a feasible plan of action. He stooped down and awakened both of them quietly.

The men sprang to their feet and would have called the rest of the sleeping watch, but with a warning gesture Christian stopped them. Then he motioned them to follow him to the waist of the ship.

"Listen," said he, speaking quickly; "I have determined to take charge of this ship. Captain Bligh is no longer fit to command her. You two know him—*and you know me!*"

The seamen, half dazed at the suddenness of the question, hesitated a moment. "My God, men!" he said hoarsely, "answer me. Heavens! Why do you hesitate? Are you men or cowards? You, Quintal, will *you* help me?"

"Help you, sir?" and Matthew Quintal, a young man of scarce twenty-one years, seized his jumper on either side with his brawny hands and showed his broad, tattooed chest. "I don't know what you mean, sir, but I'll follow you to hell."

"Good; and now, McCoy, you?"

A grim smile flickered over McCoy's features. Like Quintal he was tattooed on both chest and arms, and was a broad-shouldered, strongly-made man, with deep-set eyes and a face denoting undaunted courage and resolution.

"I am with you, sir, and with Mat Quintal."

"Go you then, McCoy, and rouse the armourer. Tell him I want the key of the arm-chest to shoot a shark. You, Quintal, rouse up Churchill, Muspratt, and Millward, and remind them of the flogging Bligh gave them at Tahiti ; then bring them quietly to me."

The men stepped softly below to the 'tween decks to carry out their orders. As soon as their backs were turned young Smith, who, unobserved by Christian, lay awake upon the main-hatch, rose and came towards the officer.

"What are you about to do, Mr. Christian ?" he said in whispered tones. "I heard your orders. Stop them, sir, before it is too late, for God's sake !"

"Ah, Smith, is that you ? It *is* too late, too late now. Will you sail under my orders, or will you make me shoot you, as I certainly will do if you give the alarm ?"

The young seaman's face paled. "Your threat, sir, would not stop me if I had not already decided. I don't like to join in a mutiny, but it is your act, sir, and not mine ; and you will have to answer for it, not me. Captain Bligh is no friend of mine ; and I'll never desert a gentleman like you for him. You can count on me, sir."

Christian took his hand and gripped it fiercely. Then McCoy returned with the key of the arm-chest, which was kept aft ; following him up the ladder came Quintal, accompanied by a fair-haired lad named Ellison, and Millward, one of the three for whom Quintal had gone below—all in a state of suppressed excitement.

"It's all right," said Quintal ; "Muspratt and Churchill are coming. They are with us, but they are below bringing up some of the others."

For one brief moment the madness of the deed
flashed across Christian's brain as he saw the figures
of the seamen coming up from the 'tween decks ; but
the phrase "they are with us" reminded him that he
was now a mutineer, and too far on his fatal course to
draw back. He set his teeth and, in another minute,
followed by his associates in the desperate venture,
was serving out weapons to his party from the arm-
chest.

The noise made by the clank of the arms, slight as
it was, had by this time wakened all the watch on
deck ; and Hayward, sitting on the wheel grating,
was suddenly astounded to see Christian running
towards him, cutlass in hand, followed by a number of
armed seamen. The watch came tramping aft, and
Christian, with a maddening sense of triumph in his
heart, felt that the supreme moment had arrived.

Quick as lightning he spoke some hot words to
McCoy and Quintal, who repeated them to the
thronging and excited sailors ; Quintal and Ellison
then rapidly passed weapons to four or five of the
watch. These, stepping apart from the others, at
once ranged themselves with Christian and his party.

Still, despite the fierce, eager mutterings and the
clash of arms from those on deck, there had been no
great noise or confusion, and none of those who slept
below were awakened ; the mutineers, from ready
force of habit, obeying unhesitatingly the orders of
the passionate man who was once their officer and
now their ringleader.

There was a moment's pause ; a dozen armed men,

grim and determined, stood around their leader, waiting. As the sun leapt, a flaming ball of blood-red
fire, from out the sleeping sea, Christian looked into
the dark and working faces of the crew and waved his
cutlass in the air ; then, following their leader, the
desperate men made a dash for Bligh's cabin.

CHAPTER VII

A L'THOUGH it was now daylight the great cabin was still in semi-darkness when Christian, followed by Churchill, by Mills, the gunner's mate, and a seaman named Birkett, burst in upon the sleeping commander.

As a flood of sunlight poured through the widely-opened door Bligh, aroused by the rush of hurrying feet, started up in his bunk to find a musket levelled at his heart, and the livid face of Christian looking savagely into his own.

"What is this?" he said in his quick, imperious way, preparing to spring out of his berth.

"If you utter another word I'll shoot you," answered Christian, still presenting his piece; then suddenly he grounded it upon the deck with a crash and turned to his followers.

"Drag him out and lash his hands behind his back," he cried. Again the commander tried to spring from his bed, his cheek white, not with fear but with suppressed rage; and again he threw himself back as Christian, whose eyes gleamed with a deadly, awful hatred, thrust the muzzle of the musket almost into his face.

In another moment the men sprang upon Bligh, and with savage fury dragged him out of his bunk, and Mills, the instant his captain's feet touched the deck, seized his white, delicate hands and lashed them behind his back with a piece of native cinnet.

"Drag him up on deck," and Christian stood aside to let the seamen execute his orders.

The moment the struggling form of Bligh appeared on deck, young Ellison, who had taken the wheel, sprang towards them, tore a bayonet from the hands of a seaman near him, and launched himself upon the captain with an imprecation, but was thrust back by Smith.

"Stand back, boy!" said Christian fiercely; "I alone will deal with him. You, Smith, and you, McCoy, keep guard over him, and if he tries to utter a word show him no mercy—blow his brains out on the spot."

In grim and ominous silence McCoy and Smith, with loaded muskets and fixed bayonets, stepped out and stationed themselves on either side of the bound man. Christian, hitherto doubtful of the fidelity of his party, noted with a savage satisfaction that McCoy's face was working with passion, and that he at least was prepared to carry out his leader's orders, while Smith's open, ruddy countenance was now set and stern.

Meanwhile Quintal, accompanied by a seaman

named Williams, who was stripped to the waist and armed with a cutlass, had burst into the cabin of Fryer, the master and senior officer under Bligh, and ordered him on deck.

Fryer sprang up with a loud cry and reached for his pistols, which were on a rack over his head ; but Quintal was too quick for him and seized him by the wrist in a vice-like grip.

" Hold your tongue, or, by God! you are a dead man, Mr. Fryer! Keep quiet and no one will hurt you ; resist, and I'll run you through," and Williams leant across him and secured the pistols.

The dangerous look in his eyes as he pointed them at the master's heart told Fryer that resistance meant death, but folding his arms across his chest he stood defiantly facing them both.

"What are you doing ? " he asked. " Have you taken the ship ? "

" Yes, we have. Mr. Christian is our captain now."

"Where is Captain Bligh ? What have you done with him, you villains ? "

" Keep a civil tongue in your head, Mr. Fryer ; we are desperate men, and yet we don't want to kill you. I'll tell you what we intend doing with the captain," and he laughed grimly ; " we are going to put him in the small cutter and let him try living on three-quarters of a pound of yam a day."

" The small cutter ! Why, her bottom is almost out ; she's worm-eaten and full of holes."

" The boat is a lot too good for him even if she had no bottom at all," answered Quintal. " Now go on deck, Mr. Fryer, and mind this, if you make one attempt at resistance you are a dead man."

As soon as they reached the deck they saw Christian standing on the poop, giving orders to get out the boat.

"In God's name, Christian, what are you about?" and Fryer, disregarding the menacing gestures of the mutineers, placed his hand on his shipmate's arm. "Are you mad, man? Consider the consequences!"

"Not a word from you, Fryer!" and Christian dashed aside his hand fiercely. "I tell you that I have been in hell for weeks past. This dog, this infernal, malignant scoundrel, has brought all this upon himself. Stand back, I tell you—I am dangerous!"

"Christian, let me implore you. . . ."

"Silence, I tell you!"

"For God's sake, Christian, let me speak. We have always been friends, and you may trust me. Resist this mad impulse before it is too late. Let the captain go down to his cabin again and leave me to tackle the men."

With a fearful oath Christian turned upon him and pointed his cutlass at Fryer's heart. "Silence! I tell you for the last time. I don't want to murder you, Fryer, but, by the God above me, I'll run you through if you don't cease!"

Fryer's bronzed cheek paled a moment, but his eye never quailed even when the cutlass point touched his breast. "Will you not at least get out a better boat than the cutter?" he said quietly.

"No! by heavens, I will not! That boat is good enough for such a ruffian," then lowering his weapon he turned away and beckoned to Smith and McCoy to leave their prisoner and come to him, and for half a minute he conversed eagerly with them ; while Bligh managed to get near enough to the master to speak.

"Mr. Fryer," he said quickly, yet calmly, "there must be some of the officers and men who will not fail me in the hour of need. For God's sake, Fryer, try to find some of them ere this villain murders us all !"

But low as were his tones Christian heard him, and stepping up to the captain and Fryer, when within a foot or two of Bligh, he seized him by the shoulder and made as if to run him through.

"Advance one step nearer, and by the God above us this cutlass goes through your cowardly, brutal heart! All the officers and men not with me are guarded below ; you can do no good now ; your authority on this floating hell is gone for ever. Here, two of you men take Mr. Fryer back to his cabin and lock him in."

By this time the cutter was afloat ; but Christian, realising that it would be impossible to crowd all of those who were well-affected to Bligh into her, had also lowered the launch, a six-oared boat measuring twenty-three feet from stem to stern.

Two officers, Hayward and Hallet, and Elphinstone, Heywood, and Stewart (midshipmen), Ledward the surgeon, Cole the boatswain, Purcell the carpenter, and some seamen, meanwhile had been secured either below or on deck. One or two of the youngsters, among whom was Peter Heywood, a lad of fifteen, scarcely understanding what they were doing in the confusion and excitement, had been compelled to lend the mutineers a hand in getting out the launch; and Bligh's keen eye happened to fall on this boy as he was helping with the boat-falls.

This was unfortunate for Heywood, who was at once put down by his commander as one of the ring-leaders, and suffered for it later.

Suddenly Christian sprang upon the poop from the main-deck, and again held a consultation with Smith and McCoy. He turned and gazed savagely at Bligh, who met his look with unflinching calmness. For a few moments the two men regarded each other with looks of deadliest hatred, and then Fletcher Christian's voice rang out.

" Pass all but Captain Bligh over the side into the boat."

Then with oaths, struggles, and entreaties some twenty men were dragged along the deck and passed down into the boat. Bligh, who stood near the gangway, now made an appeal to the leader of the mutineers, who was on the poop watching him.

" If you will stop this even now, Mr. Christian, I will promise nothing more shall come of it," he called out.

The master's mate, flinging down the cutlass he still held, ran down the poop and faced his enemy; and the crew drew back as he spoke.

" Captain Bligh, listen to me. I could kill you as you stand before me now, but I am no murderer.

Tyrant and coward, I and those who have suffered
with me have done with you for ever."

A crimson flush dyed the commander's face from
brow to chin, and he clenched his hands together
tightly at the insulting words.

Then the boat was veered astern, and McCoy,
making the painter fast to the stern rail, turned to his
leader for further orders.

Going to the stern of the ship, Christian eyed the
condition of the boat for a minute in silence, till the
boatswain made an attempt to soften his heart.

"Mr. Christian," he cried, standing up in the boat,
"let me plead with you for myself as well as Captain
Bligh."

"No, no, Mr. Cole," Christian answered. "I
have been in hell for the past two weeks and am determined to bear it no longer. You know, Cole, that
during the whole voyage I have been treated like a
dog."

"Will you not let the master, who is an old man,
remain on board, and take some of the men out of the
boat to lighten her?" called Bligh, from where he
stood at the gangway.

"No!" was the fierce reply; "Mr. Fryer must go
with you—do you think we are fools? But some of
the men may come out of the boat."

A brief discussion among those in the boat ended in
two or three seamen asking to be taken on board.
The boat was hauled alongside under the counter and
they ascended to the deck; and the boatswain, who
was a relative of one of them, said to him, "Goodbye

and God bless you, my boy ; but for my wife and children I too would stay with the ship also."

Again Bligh spoke, and there was now no sharp, imperious ring in his voice.

" Mr. Christian," he said, " I'll pawn my honour as a King's officer—I'll give you my solemn word, with God as my witness, never to think of this if you will desist from this outrage even now. Consider my wife and family."

The mutineer laughed mockingly. " No, Captain Bligh. If you had any honour things would not have come to this pass ; and if you had any regard for your wife and family you should have thought of them before, and not have behaved like the heartless villain you are."

Then, by Christian's orders, Bligh's clothes, his commission, private journal, and pocket-book were passed down, his hands were liberated, and he was ordered into the boat, which was hauled amidships to receive him. Christian handed to him over the side a book of nautical tables and his own quadrant, saying as he did so : " That book is sufficient for every purpose, and you know my quadrant to be a good one."

Again the boat was veered astern. Bligh, standing up, raised his clenched hand and cursed the mutineers bitterly, swearing vengeance against those on the ship who would not help him to retake her. Laughs and jeers from the group on the *Bounty's* poop was the only notice taken of him. Then for the last time the mutineers heard his voice and they ceased their gibes

at the dignity of his tones as he spoke to those whom
he thought yet faithful to him on board.

"Never mind, my lads; you can't all come with
me, but I will do you justice if ever I reach England."

The boat's painter was then cast off by Quintal,
and the crew took to their oars, Bligh giving his
commands in a calm and collected manner. The
ocean was calm and only a faint breeze rippled the
surface of the placid sea.

As the departing commander and his crew dipped
their oars into the water they saw Christian leaning
on the rail over the stern, regarding them intently.
Presently he stood up and gave an order; the yards
were swung round, and a cheer came over to them
from the ship—"Hurrah for Tahiti!"

 ❊   ✻   ✻   ❊   ✻

And as the crowded boat grows smaller and smaller
to the vision of the desperate man who stands gazing
at her from the *Bounty's* stern, so let those in her go
out of this story; they have no further part in it. But
the memory of that daring boat voyage will live for
ever in our country's annals. Who has not read of
Bligh's indomitable courage and resolution, his admir-
able forethought for the eighteen suffering beings
who braved the venture with him, from the first day
when the over-crowded little craft was cast off from
the ship until it sighted Timor, forty-one days after?
His successful conduct of that terrible voyage over an
all but unknown sea, losing as he did only one of his
men, yet encountering the risk of wreck by violent

6

storms, of massacre by savage islanders, of the pangs
of hunger and the agonies of thirst, well entitled him
to the honours that his country paid him.   In that act
of his life he played his part nobly, and all else that he
did ill, when measured against such fortitude in the
face of danger and death, may well be forgotten.

CHAPTER VIII

STANDING with folded arms and gloomy face, in which all passion seemed to be dead, the leader of the mutineers watched the launch gradually increase her distance from the *Bounty*. The last words of Bligh as the boat was cast off still rang in his ears : " I will do you justice if ever I reach England."

These were ominous words, and they brought vividly before him the horrors of his situation. " If justice is done," he muttered, " what will become of me ? My God ! Why did I not put an end to my life before this madness got the better of me ? "

The wild cheer of " Hurrah for Tahiti ! " from his followers roused him to a sense of his present position. It was evident that to others besides himself a return to Tahiti was one of the inducements for the desperate deed just accomplished. And he was quick to realise, too, that for the safety of them all he must assert himself and take command of the ship. Even had Bligh not heard that defiant cry as the mutineers swung

67

round the yards, Tahiti would be the first place thought of by those who would surely come in search of them. How soon would that search begin ? That it would begin sooner or later he never doubted. The possibility of Bligh and those with him not being picked up by some ship, or not reaching some place of safety, never occurred to him. And yet every one but himself realised how small indeed was the chance that those in the frail little launch would escape death in one or other of the lingering and dreadful forms to which he had so mercilessly consigned them.

The murmuring of voices roused him from his gloomy reflections, and presently McCoy, Quintal, Smith, and others of the more active of the mutineers gathered round their leader, while the rest of the men, forming a group on the main deck, were talking in excited tones of what ought to be done for the best.

He turned to those near him and spoke, with every trace of excitement absent from his voice and manner.

"Men, remember that our future safety from death at the yard-arm depends upon the discipline of a well-ordered ship being maintained. Now that the thing is done we have to guard ourselves for the future. Therefore, as you all have to rely upon me for the navigation of the ship, and as I am the only officer left, until we have settled upon some safe island, and got rid of her, you will have to obey my orders. Are you agreed to that ? "

" Aye, aye, Mr. Christian ; you can depend upon us," they answered.

" Very well, then. I have decided to take the ship

to Tubuai.¹ It will not be safe for us to remain at Tahiti ; search will be made for the *Bounty*, and Tahiti will be the first place a ship will visit. You, Smith, McCoy, and Quintal, who were among the first to stand by me in this undertaking, can arrange with me a plan for our mutual safety.

"But we want to go back to Tahiti," cried several of the others.

"Yes," answered Christian quietly, "you want to go back because of the women you have left there. Do not fear, you shall see Tahiti again. Now listen, and I will tell you what my plan is. First, let us go to Tubuai and form a settlement there. Then, when that is finished, I propose to return to Tahiti and bring away as many people as choose to come—that is if these women still run in your minds."

There was a bitter ring in his last words, and Smith, in a low voice, asked him to humour the men more, "for remember, sir," said he, "you have given them their liberty and you will have to take care how you cross them."

The caution was needed ; most of the men by no means relished the prospect of delay in returning to the delights of Tahiti, and one of them in no uncertain manner expressed his sentiments, adding—" You know Mr. Christian, we have a couple of navigators left, if you can't hit it with us."

"What do you mean by that ? " asked Christian quickly.

---

¹ An island nearly due south of Tahiti and distant from that island about 5½ degrees.

" Why, Mr. Stewart and Mr. Heywood are both below."

" What ! " and Fletcher Christian turned fiercely to Quintal. " Why were these two—one a mere child—not sent away in the boat ? Are you such villains as not to have told me, if you knew it ? "

" It was just an idea of ours," answered the seaman who had first spoken—Williams, the Guernsey man ; " we thought it just as well to have more than one navigator on board in case anything went wrong with you."

Christian did not reply. He felt that he had no claim to their obedience other than they chose to admit, and that this was but a reasonable precaution on their parts.

" Where are these two now ? " he asked.

" Down below ; kept prisoners until all the row was over," answered Williams. " Shall I pass the word for them to be brought upon deck ? "

" Yes," replied Christian ; " bring them up."

Stewart and Heywood—the first-named an acting mate, and the second a mere, ruddy-faced boy on his first voyage to sea—were accordingly brought up, and to the surprise of every one, as they came up the ladder, they were followed by the swarthy-faced Edward Young.

" What does this mean, Mr. Christian ? " said Stewart as soon as he reached the poop-deck. " Why have we been kept prisoners ? I know that you have taken the ship and turned Captain Bligh adrift with the other officers. Why have we been detained against our wills ? "

"It is not my fault you are here," answered Christian gloomily. "I thought that you were gone in the boat."

"However that may be," replied Stewart excitedly, "because you have turned pirate that is no reason why we should do so. I would rather die than remain with you and be branded as a mutineer."

"And I too, Mr. Christian," broke in young Heywood. "I have a family at home, and no act of mine shall bring disgrace on them."

Christian smiled bitterly at the lad. "These are hard words—but God knows I cannot blame you for them. Yet I hope, my boy, that you will forgive me for the misfortune I have brought upon you ; and I promise that at the first port we reach, if it be a spot where it is likely a ship may touch, you can separate from us."

"That's fair enough," said a seaman named Thompson. "'Twas I and Williams who kept you below against your wills ; and I for one will help you to leave the ship by and by."

"And what have you to say, Mr. Young ?" asked Christian, turning to him ; "how do you come to be among us ? "

The young man laughed quietly and leant against the skylight as he answered. "I am here of my own free will. I heard what was going on on deck and quietly got out of the way until you had decided matters—and I'm damned glad you have decided 'em this way. Bligh is a good riddance, and while I didn't want to take an active part in the row I wasn't going to help him ; and so long as you have the command I am ready to serve under you."

"Well done, sir," cried several of the men at this speech, which was delivered with the utmost coolness, and evoked audible expressions of disgust and contempt from Stewart and Heywood ; and then one of the seamen made some coarse jest about Alrema and Tahiti.

A look of contempt passed over Christian's features as he glanced at his dark, saturnine-faced ally, and for the instant he forgot he was the leader of mutineers, and felt as Stewart and Heywood did towards the young man. Then he remembered the situation, and taking Young by the hand, said in mingled tones of contempt and friendliness : " Thank you, Young. I am glad that I am not the only 'infernal scoundrel' (mocking Bligh's voice) on board the *Bounty*." Then turning to the others he said—

"Well, men, are you agreed ? Shall we set a course for Tubuai ? Fortunately for us the south-east trades have not yet set in for good, and we ought to make a quick run there."

" Aye, aye, sir," cried several of the leading spirits among them. " We'll abide by you ; let it be Tubuai."

" Then keep her east-south-east," said Christian to the man at the wheel, and as the ship's head came to the wind a point or two, the yards were braced up and the little barque began to slip through the water with the now freshening breeze.

An hour later, when Tofoa was but a pale blue cone on the horizon, an agreement was arrived at that

Young, Churchill, Quintal, Smith, and McCoy should, with the new commander, at once settle a definite plan of action for the future ; and the rest of the mutineers, coming aft, shook hands with one another and swore they would faithfully adhere to whatever was decided upon.

Then, under the direction of Young, the breadfruit plants were taken out of their racks and passed to two seamen, who, standing on the cabin transoms, with many a jest at this ending of the scientific expedition, pitched them out of the stern ports into the sea.

CHAPTER IX

THE council in the now denuded cabin of the *Bounty* was conducted in a friendly enough manner. In Smith and Young—both of whom were well-liked by the crew—Fletcher Christian had two powerful allies. Young, disgusted with life at sea under such a tyrannical commander as Bligh, yet without the high spirit that had moved Christian to such a desperate deed as mutiny, was willing and indeed eager to lead the life of luxurious ease that they all anticipated in the future ; for he fully recognised that he, in joining his fortunes with those of Christian, had for ever dissevered himself from all hope of returning to England; and while he despised all those around him save Christian, he was yet perfectly agreeable to associate with them now on terms of equality.

Smith, in his strong devotion to Christian, seemed to have thrown over the teachings of his youth, and showed by his earnest manner that he was ready to stand or fall by his new leader.

McCoy and Quintal, rough seamen, from long

habits of obedience and following the lead of Young
and Smith, acquiesced in all that was proposed ; the
only doubtful supporter was Churchill, who wanted
the ship to be headed for Tahiti at once.   But
obstinate as was the latter, he had no part in the
plotting that was already going on among some of
the crew to compel Christian to abandon the idea
of Tubuai and make for Tahiti instead.

The first matter decided was that Christian should
be treated in every respect as would be a King's officer
commanding the ship, until such time as the mutineers
had found a place of refuge on some island where they
would be safe from discovery or capture.   No one of
those who sat in council in the cabin for a moment
thought of ever returning to Europe to face the
ignominious death that would certainly await them ;
and Young, in his mocking manner, took care to show
the seamen who sat with him at the cabin table that
it was better for them all to die of old age on some
island than be hanged at the yard-arm in England.

Following this, it was agreed that Young, being
well liked by the crew, should be second in command
and take charge of one watch ; while Mills, the
gunner's mate, who was the next in rank as well as
the oldest man on board, should take charge of the
other half of the ship's company.

Stewart and Heywood were to be regarded as
" prisoners at large," and this decision was at once
made known to them ; but they both refused the
privilege of the freedom of the ship if it involved any
assurance on their part of loyalty to the mutineers.

"Send for them, Mr. Christian," suggested Smith, "and see if you can't get them to join us. They'll listen to you, I am sure."

Presently the two lads were brought into the cabin, and both frankly stated to Christian their intention of endeavouring, by some means or other, to reach England and doing all in their power to bring him and those with him to justice when they got there.

A dangerous look came into Edward Young's eyes. Heywood saw it, but although his fresh, boyish face paled a moment, he returned Young's frown with a look of defiance.

"As you please," said Christian shortly; "but I tell you, foolish boys, you are treading on dangerous ground. Take my advice and keep your intentions to yourselves, else you will repent your folly. There are men on board the ship who have gone too far to——"

"To hesitate at pitching two damned young fools overboard," broke in Young savagely; but a look from Christian made him cease. And then the council came to an end.

The new commander, however, took no steps to prevent Stewart and Heywood from going among the crew, though he knew they were endeavouring to form a party for recapturing the ship. He was confident that however some of the men might attempt to frustrate his plan of first making Tubuai, none would be mad enough to risk destruction by listening to any talk about the ship being recaptured.

But Quintal, McCoy, and Smith, fortunately for

the success of the enterprise, did not share their leader's
faith, and a few days after they had returned to their
old duties as able seamen they found that the daring
midshipmen had so far succeeded in alienating some
of the crew from Christian that a plot was ripe to
retake the vessel.

One night when the ship was some two or three
miles to the southward of Savage Island—an isolated
but fertile spot about three hundred miles from Tofoa
—Quintal stood at the forward weather rail, gazing at
the high cliffs of grey coral rock against whose jagged
sides the ocean rollers dashed unceasingly and sent
showers of spray high up to the dense foliage which
grew on the verge of their summits. Presently he
was joined by Smith, who whispered—

" Heywood and Stewart, with five others, will try
to retake the ship to-morrow evening. Don't talk to
me now, but follow me aft by and by ; then we can
tell Christian. That scoundrel Coleman was the first
to join them, and has promised to serve them out arms
to-morrow night. All of them, except Coleman, are
in the gunner's watch."

A quarter of an hour later, Christian, with a grim
smile, dismissed Smith and Quintal and watched for
his chance. About eleven o'clock a furious rain squall
swept down from the south-east, and among those
who were sent aloft to take in sail by the gunner's
mate, who was in charge of the watch, were the five
men who had agreed to support Heywood and Stewart.
While these were busy aloft and Coleman was asleep
—it being his watch below—Smith, McCoy, and

Quintal and another seaman made a dash for the arm-chest and conveyed it to the cabin.

Arming all those men of whose loyalty he was absolutely assured, Christian waited till the men came down from aloft and the watch was about to be relieved. Then he called the plotters aft and addressed them. A ship's lantern, held by a seaman who stood beside him, threw a broad ray of light upon the anxious faces of the men gathered on the soaking deck ; and then for the first time they saw that the men in Young's watch were grouped aft behind Christian and his fellow officer.

Calling upon the five plotters each by name, Christian addressed them—

" I have discovered that you mean to retake the ship. Now weigh my words well : if bloodshed follows it will be your fault. Some of you who are anxious to get back to Tahiti have listened to two foolish boys, little thinking of the madness of such an attempt. The arm-chest is now in my cabin, and at the first attempt on your part to take the command of the ship from me I will shoot every man concerned in it. God knows I do not want to be your leader longer than I can help, and no one among you is less content than I, but," and here he turned to those immediately around him, "it is necessary for the general safety of us all that I, and I alone, should have charge of the ship ; and, by God ! while she remains afloat and I alive I will keep command."

A deep growl of approval came from those of his party who stood near him as he finished ; then in

gentle tones Christian addressed Heywood and
Stewart, who had now come on deck. Although he
seemed outwardly cool the lads could see that he was
labouring under strong emotion and was striving to
speak to them calmly and dispassionately. He
besought them to make no further effort to retake
the ship, but to support him in his authority—such as
it was, he said bitterly—till the ship finally reached
Tahiti, and assured them that this course was best for
all parties. "And you, Heywood," he said kindly,
placing his hand on the lad's shoulder, "answer me
this : have you, or you, Stewart, ever known me to
tell you a lie ? "

" No, Mr. Christian, never," replied the boy
emphatically, looking him directly in the face.

" Well then, my lads, I beg of you both to believe
that it would be a bitter sorrow to me to hurt either
of you. I have suffered too much myself to wreck
your future lives by any needless act of mine ; nor will
you be in bodily danger unless you drive us to stern
measures. And I swear to you that I bear you no
ill-will for what has passed . . . no, my lads,
none."

Loyal as they were to their duty, both Stewart and
Heywood saw the force of his argument and believed
in his promise to set them free as soon as possible; and
assured him they would cause no further trouble.
Then the watch was changed and the matter ended.

But from that time the arm-chest was carefully
watched by men on whom reliance could be placed,
and every night Churchill, who now kept the key,

made his bed upon the box, and slept with a brace of loaded pistols by his side.

Day after day the *Bounty* crept slowly along to the eastward, till early one morning the look-out sighted the two misty blue peaks of Tubuai rising from the sea. As the ship drew nearer to the land, the peaks united at the base and showed an island of verdant hills and bright, shining beaches of golden sand encompassed by a wide belt of surf-beaten coral reef.

The wind was light but steady, and Christian succeeded in working the ship through the passage on the north-west side without much trouble, although she was beset by a great number of canoes filled with natives who made unmistakable signs of defiance to the white men.

As soon as the ship was secured, Christian and his men sought to induce the natives to come on board, but only one or two responded to his invitation; and they, by their suspicious and haughty demeanour, showed their distrust and dislike of the white strangers. Not a woman or child was visible in the canoes, and every man was armed with a club and spear. The only dress they wore was a girdle or rather bandage round their loins, and a turban of *tappa* cloth round their heads of glossy, jet-black and curling hair. They were a far handsomer and more active race than the Tahitians, much lighter in colour, and of a daring and warlike disposition, and their open hostility to the *Bounty* party was every minute becoming more apparent.

Not anticipating such a reception as this, Christian

was in a dilemma. To have to force a landing would
be a serious matter, and after a brief consultation with
some of the men, this idea was abandoned. The
ship had been brought there by him against the wishes
of the majority, and to have to fight for a footing was,
as Williams said, " more than they had stomach for."

" I will not ask you to fight," said Christian, " for
that would only mean useless slaughter on both sides.
These people are, as you can see, brave and determined,
and it is a bitter disappointment to me to find them
so hostile. But yet I have to consider this—the
island, as you see for yourselves, is of amazing fertility
and I do not think that we could find a better place to
live in. Further, it is not likely to be visited by ships,
and would be a safe retreat for us."

" That's true enough, Mr. Christian," answered
one of the seamen. " Much as I want to get to Tahiti,
I only want to do so to get the woman I left there—
and there's a lot more like me. I, for one, think that
Tubuai is a better place for us than Tahiti."

" So do I," said Martin ; " and although I want to
go to Tahiti for the same reason as most of us, I'm
willing to come back here. To my mind this island
is far better ; but at the same time we don't want our
throats cut."

Satisfied that the crew would be willing to return,
Christian then proposed that they should make for
Tahiti, embark as many Tahitians as would come
with them, return to Tubuai, and either establish
friendly relations with the people or force a landing
and build a fort.

To this the men readily assented, for they could easily see that the island was not only very rich and fertile, but also well out of the way of discovery, and with a little trouble could be made capable of resisting the attack of even an European force.

So, with hundreds of natives still paddling about the ship in their red-ochre-painted canoes and uttering loud cries of defiance, the anchor was hove up, the ship warped out to sea again, and with a light breeze filling her canvas, headed due north for Tahiti.

The following morning Christian collected together in the main cabin all the curiosities given to Bligh and his officers by the people of Tahiti, as well as all the clothes and other property left by those who had been sent away with him. Then he mustered the crew aft and addressed them, pointing to the piles of goods on the cabin deck.

"Here, my fellow pirates, is the first batch of plunder—you see I call things by their right names. Draw lots and divide it among yourselves. Everything that is there will be of value to you for the purposes of barter with the natives."

The sneering tone in which he spoke caused many an angry look, but without another word he turned from them and went on deck.

Four days later, on the 5th of June—thirty-eight days after the mutiny—the peak of Orohena lay right ahead ; at dawn the following day the *Bounty* sailed into Matavai Bay, and as the cries of welcome were heard, for awhile all else was forgotten.

CHAPTER X

O N the same hill where nearly six weeks before she had watched the lessening sails of her lover's ship sink below the horizon, Mahina again sat looking seaward. Day after day since the *Bounty* had sailed she had laid her simple offerings of fruit upon the altar of Oro and prayed for Christian's return to her, and night after night when the rest of. the people were singing and dancing upon the broad sward in front of Tinā's house she, sometimes accompanied by Alrema, sat on the hill and the two girls thought or talked of Young and Christian. But to-day her friend was not with her; and only an hour before angry words had passed between her old, fierce-tempered mother and herself about her white lover, and the girl, after a passionate burst of tears, had stolen silently away to the hill to be alone with her thoughts.

Old Manuhūru, like the average civilised mother, had certain views for her daughter, and ever since the *Bounty* had sailed had sought to induce the girl to forget

her white lover and accept for her husband Pipiri the
Areoi [1] priest. And of all the men of Tahiti who had
sought her love Mahina hated most the tall, handsome
young Areoi, for he was steeped to the lips in bloodshed. Only a few years before the *Bounty* came
to Tahiti, Pipiri had with his own hands slain his
two children, according to the rites of the horrible
fraternity, which demanded that a candidate entering
upon his novitiate should publicly kill his children and
put his wife aside, unless she too should become an
Areoi. Mahina had seen the awful deed, had heard
the wail of agony from the mother of the children
when their ruthless father had plunged his knife into
their bosoms ; and had fled the scene with terror in
her heart, for Pipiri had long sought her love, and she
knew he had only become an Areoi that he might
force her to marry him.

The girl, by every device she could contrive, avoided
meeting the young priest, and to her great joy, since
she had shown her open preference for Christian, Pipiri

[1] The Areois were an extraordinary fraternity, followers of the gods
Orotetefa and Urutetefa, and Mr. Ellis gives a full description of them
in his " Polynesian Researches." They were, he says, not only priests,
and so regarded by the people as allied to the gods themselves, but
strolling players and privileged libertines. The association was composed
of seven classes. A candidate's admission to the first class was
signalised by the slaughter of his children, as a proof of his devotion to
the principle of infanticide. Their power and influence was beyond
comprehension to the civilised mind ; and their rites and ceremonies
were of so bloody and revolting a nature, so utterly monstrous and
degrading that they "appeared to have placed their invention on the
rack to discover the most hideous crimes of which it was possible for
man to be guilty." Yet for all this the natives of the Society Islands,
especially the chiefs, looked upon them with feelings akin to veneration.

had not molested her further, although she had frequently seen him talking earnestly with her mother. Only once since Christian had sailed had she met him. She was returning with Alrema from her look-out on the hill, when the Areoi sprang upon the girls as they passed along the narrow, palm-shaded path. His face was stained scarlet with the juice of the *mati* berry, his long black hair hung loosely down over his copper-coloured shoulders, and his gleaming savage eyes struck terror into her heart; but Alrema faced him dauntlessly.

"Ho, Mahina, daughter of Manuhuru, and Alrema the saucy-tongued," he cried mockingly, "whence come ye? Are ye still waiting for the white men who will never return? Dost think that thy eyes can draw back the great outriggerless canoe?" [1]

"What is that to thee, Pipiri the slaughterer?" asked Alrema, tearing away her hand from his grasp; "and seek not to frighten us. Think not that because thou hast become an Areoi *I* fear thee!"

"Nay, I know that thou fearest no one," replied the priest fiercely; "but 'tis not thee for whom I waited here. Thou art but a chattering fool, whose tongue I may yet cut off at the roots; but it is thee, Mahina, who hast eaten into my heart—so now I ask thee once more, Why dost thou wait for this white lover of thine? He will never return, I tell thee. Heed not the talk of this fool Alrema and those like her—who have listened to their white lover's lies. Fifty and two days have gone since the ship sailed,

---

[1] The Tahitians called the first ships they saw outriggerless canoes.

and I tell thee thou wilt never see thy white man
again."

Mahina took courage from Alrema, whose rounded
bosom panted with rage at the mocking words of the
Areoi, and she sought to soften Pipiri's savage
nature.

"Why should I alone be the one woman for whom
thou carest, Pipiri? There are many others better
than I. So pray thee let me be as I am. Yet it
Kirisiani comes not back in three moons from now,
then I will be thy wife."

The Areoi laughed. "Nay, in less time than that.
Only just now thy mother swore to me that I might
take thee in one moon; for in me, too, is the same
blood that flows in thy veins—the blood of the race of
Afitā, and for that alone thou shouldst come to me."
Then without further words he stood aside and let
the girls pass on to their homes.

That was ten days ago, and Mahina, as she sat with
her face leaning upon her hands and gazed seaward,
felt the tears well up into her eyes. Her mother had
indeed promised her in marriage to the blood-stained
Areoi, whom the old woman regarded as a superior
man even to the highest chief in the land on account
of the blood-tie between them, and because of the
bitter, undying hatred he showed to the white men.
This she was always ready to stimulate, telling him
scornfully that he knew not how to dispose of a rival
or he would have enticed Christian from the village
and killed him.

Away to the westward the blue, sailless ocean

sparkled and shimmered in the rays of the sun; and nearer in, though far below where she sat, the long rollers of pale emerald swept in serried lines upon the shelving reef of the little bay, and wavering clouds of misty spume drifted slowly before the wind as the rollers curled over and burst upon the rocky barrier on their passage to the shore.

For nearly an hour Mahina sat thus, hearing no sound save the soft crooning note of some resting pigeon in the silent forest around her, or the faint murmur of voices from a party of men in fishing canoes who had landed on the white beach far below; then, with despair in her heart, she rose to return to the village. And there, with his back against the bole of a great *tamanu* tree, again stood Pipiri the Areoi, looking at her intently.

"Why dost thou watch me?" she asked, trying to pass him, but he stayed her gently with his hand.

"Because, oh foolish one, I love thee, I love thee; and I hate to see thy cheeks, that were once so round and soft, grow thin and drawn with the folly that is consuming thee. See," and he pointed with his bronzed and brawny arm to the ocean, "see how evenly the sky touches the water, as the half-shell of a coconut would stand upon my hand. No white sail will break through the sky-rim, and no white man shall come between thee and me."

"If Oro so wills it. But the time that my mother has given me to wait is not yet gone; why dost thou for ever trouble me?"

" Because Orotetefa¹ hath spoken to me from his
altar and told me to wait no longer, for thy white
lover will never return.   And to-morrow shall our
marriage feast be." ;

He ceased suddenly, for there was borne to them
through the silence of the surrounding forest a cry
that sent the blood dancing through the veins of the
girl before him with a maddening joy—" A ship !
a ship ! "

She sprang away from him to the verge of the hill
and there—not a far distant speck on the horizon, but
rounding the northern point—was a ship, standing in
before the breeze and furling her sails as she approached
the anchorage.

A quick mist filled the girl's dark eyes, and she
staggered for a moment upon her feet.   Then she
turned and looked into the rage-distorted face of the
Areoi priest.

" Thou hast lied to me, Pipiri the Areoi."

In another moment, evading the savage grasp with
which he sought to stay her, she was flying down the
hillside to the beach.

---

¹ One of the guardian deities of the Areois. He was believed sometimes to speak to any especially favoured worshipper.

CHAPTER XI

BEFORE the panting girl reached the beach the
Bounty was at anchor and her deck crowded
with natives, who greeted Christian and the ship's
company with the most extravagant manifestations of
joy. For him personally they had always shown the
liveliest regard ; not only was he one of Tuti's people,
but his uniform kindness to them had won their hearts,
and, indeed, Bligh himself was the only one of the
Bounty's company whom they feared more than they
loved.

Tinā himself was among the first to board the ship,
and his frank, ingenuous countenance betrayed his
astonishment at the return of his friends, while his
wondering, inquiring glance as his eye roved over the
group of officers on the poop-deck showed that he was
quick to discover the absence of Bligh.

"*Ia oro na oe, Kirisiani,*" [1] he said with a smile,
advancing to Christian, "and where is the chief
Pirai ? And why hath the ship come back so soon ?

[1] " May you live, Christian," the Tahitian form of greeting.

Hast thou already been to Peretane and returned in three moons ? "

Fletcher Christian was quick with his answer. "Nay, Tinā, friend of my heart, we have been fortunate. See, when we neared the island that is called Tonga [1] we there met the great chief, he whom you call Tuti.[2] He took on board his ship our chief Pirai and many others of our people and all the presents of breadfruit trees for our king. And then said he to me, ' Go thou back, Kirisiani, to the country of Tinā, my friend, and say these words to him, " I, Tuti, his friend, need yams and pigs and other food ; my people are many and I cannot feed them all, for the sea is wide between here and Britain.' And for these things have I returned to Tahiti, while Tuti awaits me at Tonga. And for a gift he hath sent thee by me much iron, for he knoweth that iron is needed by thy people."

Tinā smiled pleasantly and expressed his earnest desire to serve both Cook and Bligh ; and he and many minor chiefs who had flocked on board greeted every one of the mutineers as old and dear friends.

For some minutes great excitement and confusion prevailed, and in the midst of the pleasant clamour a small canoe, paddled by two young women, ran

---

[1] Tofoa would be unknown to Tinā, who would, however, have been acquainted with the name of Tonga, in which group it is situated.

[2] Bligh, and his people on the *Bounty*, considered it advisable to carefully conceal the fact of Cook's death from the Tahitians. This deception was practised on account of the intense veneration the natives had for him, and Bligh feared that the disclosure of his death would have a bad effect on his mission.

alongside the ship, and Mahina sprang up the ladder on deck, and with a soft, joyous cry threw herself into Christian's arms.

"Thou hast returned, my own," she murmured. "Oro hath heard my prayers, and thy heart is still mine."

An angry flush for a moment suffused Christian's cheek at this demonstration before the whole ship's company, and drawing her aside he rebuked her.

"Mahina," he said severely, "in my country it is only the base and lower sort who show their hearts in this way before all men."

The girl trembled, but quickly recovered herself, and her dark eyes flashed. Drawing back from her lover she spoke in such tones of wounded pride that Christian felt his cheeks burn with shame.

"Truly, I had forgotten that the blood of the white man is cold," then placing her hands on her eyes, she walked away, and the hot tears trickled through her fingers.

Few as were her words, they touched him. He remembered that since he had parted from this girl two months before the whole of his life had been changed. Her passionate devotion to him during the five months the *Bounty* first remained at Tahiti was the one bright spot which then had made life endurable, and now, her faithful heart bursting with love for him, he had met her tender embraces with what to her was cold brutality. "She alone is the only soul on earth who will love me to the end," he thought bitterly; "she alone will not shrink from contact with me, in the time to come." He followed and took her hand.

" Mahina," he whispered, "forgive me, for thou knowest that for thy sake I have thrown away for ever my country and kindred. Thou art the one woman dear to me in the world, and thy life is my life."

She flung her arms round his neck and, caring not for those who stood about on the *Bounty's* deck, kissed him again and again in all the abandonment of her fondness.

Whispering that she might wait for him in the cabin, he gently disengaged her arms, and turned away to look for Tinā.

That night every one of the mutineers, except their chief and Smith, went ashore to their native friends ; and as the sound of their singing and dancing floated across the bay to the ship, Mahina, in the cabin of the *Bounty*, lifted her eyes to Christian's and contentedly laid her head upon his breast.

*   *   *   *   *

The *Bounty* was once more ready for sea. Great numbers of hogs, goats, and fowls were cheerfully given by the islanders to Christian and his companions, and, for a small parcel of some red feathers— which were highly prized by the natives — Tinā presented them with a cow and bull which had been left on the island by Captain Cook. Water, wood, *mahi* (baked fermented breadfruit), yams, coconuts and breadfruit were also put on board in profusion.

After making a careful survey of the ship and listening to various suggestions made by the crew for her repair, the leader of the mutineers went ashore for the last time before his marriage, which was to take place on the following day.

Accompanied by Smith, the young man, after landing and pushing through the crowd of natives who had gathered on the beach and sought to detain him in friendly converse, made his way to a native house of considerable size and handsome construction.

Here Heywood and Stewart were living. The latter had renewed his former tender relations with Nuia, who, the moment Christian entered, met him with a bright smile of welcome.

Then she went for Stewart and Heywood, who were lying on the village lawn under the shade of a breadfruit tree. Christian had permitted the two young officers to leave the ship on the day after her arrival, principally because of the passionate entreaties of Nuia, who imagined he was her lover's enemy and would kill him for some neglect of duty, and secondly because he had induced both not to reveal the true cause of his return to the islanders, so long as the *Bounty* remained at Tahiti. As for the natives themselves, although they had begun to suspect that all things were not quite as the mutineers repre-sented them, yet they believed that Cook had good reasons for sending the ship back to Tahiti ; and that he *had* done so they never for a moment doubted. So Tina and his people were pleased enough when

Christian proposed that some of them should sail away in the *Bounty* and visit Peretane and King George. To further the deception, Christian stated that he had no objection to some of his own men, who had allied themselves to native women, remaining behind at Tahiti. This proposal was made to account for the fact that besides Heywood and Stewart several of the crew had determined to sever themselves from the ship's company; not for the same reasons which animated the two midshipmen, but because the women with whom they were living did not care to venture to sea in the "great outriggerless canoe."

In a few minutes Heywood and Stewart entered the house.

Both of them looked cheerful and well, and Christian could not help feeling pleased at the friendly manner in which they returned his greeting.

"I have come to see you, perhaps for the last time," he said, "and to thank you for the manner in which you have kept your promise to a broken and disgraced man. Heaven knows, my lads, that I would gladly assist you to return to England if it were in my power. But have no fear; that a ship will be sent out here is an absolute certainty."

Heywood ventured to question him as to when he intended sailing.

"Do not ask me," he replied hurriedly, while the hot blood mounted to his forehead; "it may be soon, it may not be for a week, but I cannot come and see you again . . . and I want you to shake hands with me before I go."

After a momentary hesitation Stewart held out his hand, but young Heywood, whose eyes were filled with tears, with boyish impulsiveness sprang forward before his companion.

" Goodbye, sir ; I will never forget how good you have always been to me on the *Bounty*."

Christian took their hands in his and wrung them. " Goodbye, my lads. God bless you both, and forgive me all the harm I may have done you."

Then he turned away, and with Smith closely following him, was soon lost to sight.

Soon after dawn the village was astir with the preparations for Christian's marriage.

Troops of natives carrying presents of food and other articles kept constantly arriving from all parts of the coast, and the first to welcome them and instruct them where to place their gifts was old Manuhuru, Mahina's mother. She was quick to recognise, as soon as Christian returned the possessor of so many riches, the advisability of withdrawing all further opposition to her daughter's marriage with the young Englishman ; for with all her hatred of the white men she was very avaricious.

Only that morning she had bidden Pipiri give up all hope of her child now that Christian had returned ; and the young warrior-priest, with savage hatred in his heart, had cursed her and sworn yet to possess her daughter if fifty white men stood in his way.

As Mahina was connected through her parents with the reigning family of Tahiti, the marriage ceremony was to be performed in the *marae* or temple of Oro instead of in the family *marae*, and thither went all the people to witness the event.

Mahina, sitting on a mat, was surrounded by a number of young girls who had arrayed her in her wedding garments ; at a sign from the officiating priest of Oro she rose and advanced to meet her white lover, who, attended by Alexander Smith and a number of young natives of strikingly handsome appearance, was now walking across the grassy sward towards her, his plain uniform contrasting strangely with the wild, yet picturesque, garb of his island friends, most of whom had their hair profusely decorated with wreaths of white and scarlet blossoms. Round each man's waist was a girdle composed of scarlet leaves of the *ti* plant, and bright yellow strips of the plantain leaf. Upon each wrist and ankle were circlets of pieces of pearl shell fitted into an embroidered net work of red and black cinnet ; the islanders' light brown skins shone with the scented oil with which they had anointed themselves, and the beautiful curved lines or deep blue tattooing with which their bodies were so freely covered stood out with such startling distinctness that even Smith, the most tattooed man of all the *Bounty's* crew, could not help uttering a cry or admiration.

When about fifty reet distant from each other, the two parties stopped, and a pretty little maiden, carrying in her hand a ripe plantain and a young drinking coconut, advanced out from among the women surrounding Mahina, and addressed the young native chief who led Christian's party—

"Who are ye that come here so gaily clad, and why do ye come?"

"I, Kirisiani, come to the altar of Oro so that I may take for my wife Mahina, daughter of Manuhuru," replied the mutineer, taking the plantain and coconut from her and giving her a piece of stained native cloth in return.

The child returned to her party, who began to chant some verses in praise of the beauty of Mahina; then the ranks opened out, and Christian, prompted by a chief, stepped to her side.

Together they slowly walked to the *marae*, where they seated themselves upon mats, Christian at one end of the temple, Mahina at the other, while the people disposed themselves round the sacred edifice in silence.

The leafy screen in front of one of the sacred dormitories opened; Harere, the priest, clothed in the vestments of his sacred office, stepped forward, and, spreading a small square of white tappa cloth in the centre of the temple, bade Mahina and the white man seat themselves upon it. Then, standing directly in front of Christian, he said, in a loud voice, " *Kirisiani, taata Peretane, eita anei oe e faa 'rue i ta oe vahine?* " ("Christian, the Englishman, wilt thou not cast away this woman?") to which the mutineer replied " *Eita* " ("No"). The same question was put to Mahina, and the girl, with a happy smile lighting up her lovely face, and her little hand pressing her lover's, quickly gave the same answer.

" Fortunate then may your lives be if thus ye

8

remain true one to another," said Harere. Then
stepping back from them and facing the sacred altar
of Oro, the priest prayed to the god that the Englishman and his wife might live together in affection,
that male children might be given to them in the
earlier years of their married life, that they might not
"hunger nor thirst, nor see blood shed within their
house."

Then old Manuhuru stepped into the sacred enclosure, bearing in her hands a heavy piece of *ahu
vavau*, or tappa cloth, which she spread out upon
the stone floor of the temple ; and Harere the priest
bade the lovers sit upon it and hold each other by the
hand while he again addressed them.

"Hearken, Englishman. It is the custom of this
land for the man and the woman who marry before
Oro and sit as thou and this woman sit now, to place
before them the skulls of their ancestors, whose
spirits, entering into the dead bones, will hear the
vows that ye have made one to the other. But thou,
Kirisiani, art from a far-off country, and it is not the
custom of thy people to carry about with them on the
sea the skulls of their forefathers. And the mother of
thy wife, though now as we are, Tahitian, is, like
thee, of strange blood—her mother's people came
from a distant land which sprang from out the sea,
and neither hath she a skull to place before thee.
And for this does Manuhuru now make a sacrifice
before Oro."

He handed to Mahina's mother a large shark's tooth
with the base embedded in a piece of polished wood.

Advancing to Christian, the old woman seized his
right arm and made a small cut with the sharp point
of the tooth upon the palm of his hand, then did the
same upon the hand of her daughter. As the blood
flowed and dripped down she caught it upon a piece
of cloth with her left hand, and with her right she
thrust the keen-edged tooth into her own breast, brow,
and left shoulder, over and over again.

"See, white man," she croaked. "Once I hated
thee and all white men, but now thy blood and mine
and my daughter's have mixed. And if thy blood is
as good as mine—for I am of Afitā—then does this
mingling of it with mine render thee equal to Mahina;
and, moreover, the mixing of blood shall bind thee
closer to thy wife."

Scarcely able to conceal his disgust at the frightful
spectacle the old woman presented, with her face and
shoulders streaming with blood, Christian was glad to
submit to the concluding part of the ceremony, which
was the brief suspension over the heads of the married
pair of a large piece of cloth called *te tapoi*.

Leaving the temple Christian and his bride were
escorted to a new house specially prepared for them in
which to receive their presents, and the young man
could not but be touched at the people's expression of
their kindly feeling towards him, and the overwhelm-
ing display of their generosity.

The rest of the day was spent in the wildest enjoy-
ment and sumptuous feasting ; then when darkness
descended upon the scene the women and girls sang
and danced, and a band of Areois delighted the people

by their wild pantomimic exhibitions far into the night.

But in the midst of the merry clamour Mahina, without bidding her aged mother farewell, stole quietly away to the ship to await her husband, who had gone to take leave of Tinā. As she paddled off alone in a tiny canoe, the tall, stalwart figure of Pipiri the Areoi appeared on the beach. For a few seconds he watched her as she disappeared in the darkness. Then he plunged into the water and swam noiselessly in the same direction.

Long before daylight next morning Mahina awoke and found that her husband was gone from her side. A wild look of fear for a moment blanched her olive cheek ; then a smile parted her lips as she heard his voice on deck.

" Man the capstan, lads."

She ran on deck and found the ship crowded with natives, among whom were Tinā and his noble wife, who wept when Christian bade them farewell. To King George the chief sent many messages, for he firmly believed that the *Bounty* was on her way to England.

Amid the sounds of weeping and the sighing of tender farewells the anchor came in sight, the ship's head swung round, and the *Bounty* was again under way.

Once outside the white line of foaming surge which thundered on the reef, Edward Young, who had been securing the anchor, came quietly aft and stood beside his wife Alrema, who, with Mahina and other women, was on the poop. Presently, as Christian passed, Young caught him by the arm.

"I didn't like to disturb you last night, and so acted on my own responsibility. Stewart and Heywood came on board and announced their determination to sail with us if you would permit them."

Fletcher Christian's face darkened. "Stewart and Heywood! What does this mean?"

"Treachery," answered Young, "and I determined to meet treachery with deceit. I told them that I was certain you would never consent to their coming on board again, but that if they liked to stow themselves away till we got out to sea I would not say anything about it, but let them discuss the matter with you afterwards."

"Are you mad, Young, to do this?"

The sallow-faced midshipman laughed. "Not a bit of it. They might do us more harm by remaining at Tahiti than they would by coming with us. Stewart has Nuia with him, and although she is as true as steel to the chicken-hearted dog, she has let it out to Alrema that he persuaded Heywood to come on board with him last night."

"What do you think is his intention?" asked Christian moodily.

"To recapture the ship, and try to sail her to England and get a commission—while we dangle from a yard-arm at Portsmouth."

"Then why let them come on board?"

"To prevent their giving us trouble in the future.

'There are lots of islands where no ships are ever likely to touch, and we can put them ashore before we reach Tubuai—and be damned to them."

" To let them perhaps die, with their fate unknown ! But there, Young, forgive me. You have done wisely. Let them come on deck, and I will watch them closely till a fitting time arrives for us to rid ourselves of them."

On board the *Bounty* were several native women, the wives of Smith, Quintal, and McCoy, and two Tahitian men, brothers of Smith's and Quintal's wives, who had determined to accompany the white men. These Christian was glad to see, as he thought they would prove useful as interpreters.

But an hour later, after his talk with Young, and when the land was twenty miles astern, it was found that many more natives had hidden themselves on board, and that altogether the *Bounty's* complement had been increased by twelve women, eight boys, and nine men.

CHAPTER XII

SEVEN days later the ship was once more at Tubuai, but the passage had been so rough that most of the live stock were washed overboard, and the natives had to help work the ship. To add to the troubles of the voyage, Mahina and the other women suffered so much from sickness that they were in the last stage of exhaustion when Tubuai was sighted. And Christian, who, from the hour he had plunged into the mutiny had repented it, grew morose and miserable with the bitterness of unavailing regret and the anxieties of his position as leader.

Well it was for him that at this time and in the black days to come, the example of Smith and Young kept alive in the rest of the crew a respect for him ; for these two men, by their undeviating loyalty to their leader and their influence for good with their fellow-mutineers, preserved the spirit of obedience to their chief, and thus averted the worst danger that could threaten such a company.

As the ship entered the passage, the Tubuaians,

instead of attacking the ship as it was feared they would, came off in their canoes in great numbers, and seeing the Tahitians on board, quickly made friends with them. They clambered up the sides of the *Bounty*, seized the ropes, and helped the sailors to warp the vessel through the reef to a safe anchorage. In a very short time barter was begun ; Christian, accompanied by Mahina, went ashore, and with her aid as interpreter he soon negotiated with the chief of the island for a strip of land on which to erect a fort.

But the Tubuaians were less friendly when they found that the white men intended to live among them, and they sought to withdraw from the treaty they had just made.

"We like not the white strangers," said one of them to Mahina. "How comes it that if, as thou sayest, the white chief is thy husband he remained not with thee in the Big Land ?[1] Why comes he here to seek a home ? "

" Foolish man," answered the wily Mahina haughtily. "Little dost thou know of the customs of these clever white men. They are as wise as the gods, and like not the ways of the people of Tahiti. And the men of Peretane are more like those of Tubuai—they eat and drink and live alike—and for this reason do they desire to remain on Tubuai."

This compliment, and the gift of a quantity of iron, induced the Tubuaians to offer no further opposition. The ground was to the eastward of the entrance at a place called Avamoa ; and here, in

---

[1] Tahiti.

spite of shoal water and the numberless coral boulders which studded the lagoon, it was determined to bring the *Bounty*.

The ship was lightened as much as possible—no easy task, for there was but one boat—and after much labour she was brought close up to the site of the proposed fort and moored in six fathoms of water. For two days the work of lightening the ship proceeded steadily, and Christian took part with the others in the task. The Tubuaians lent some assistance; but their habits of pilfering at last brought such an explosion of wrath from the leader of the mutineers that they desisted, and matters again went on smoothly for a time.

It was the custom of Mahina, Alrema, Nuia, and the other Tahitian women to sit about the poop and watch the labours of their white husbands, and listen to the loud, excited cries of the half-naked, fierce-looking Tubuaians as they swarmed about the main deck, examining with intense curiosity the strange fittings of the ship, and arguing vociferously among themselves as to their use.

Late one afternoon, just after the last boat load had left for the site of the fort, and the wild islanders had gone ashore in their canoes, Mahina was standing alone at the stern. Gazing down into the transparent depths of the lagoon and watching the many-hued fish that swam in and out among the branches of the coral forest which covered the bottom, she was startled by a touch upon the shoulder, and turning, she met the face of Pipiri the Areoi, looking at her with intense hatred gleaming from his

eyes. So changed was he by his sickness on the
voyage that she could not recognise him, and, in
addition to this (perhaps for the purpose of disguise),
he had shaved his head completely, and his once carefully trimmed beard had disappeared.

She uttered a cry of alarm, and in an instant Christian was beside her.

"What is the matter?" he asked.

With terror in her face she pointed to Pipiri and
murmured: "'Tis Pipiri the Areoi; he hath frightened
me."

Christian looked at the Tahitian and gradually
recognised his features, and remembered that the
people at Pare and Matavai had told him that if he
had not returned the Areoi would have married
Mahina.

"How do you come here?" he asked.

"I was hidden in the bowels of the ship," answered
the man, defiantly. He staggered as he spoke, and
Christian correctly surmised that some of the seamen
had given him rum to drink.

"But why? What good can come of this?"

"That I might be with Mahina—she of whom
thou hast robbed me," he replied savagely.

"Poor fool," muttered the mutineer in English,
adding in Tahitian, "Truly I pity thee, but yet thou
art a fool to have hidden thyself in the ship; for now
will I make thee work and thou shalt be a bond slave
to thy countrymen."

"Not so," answered the Areoi proudly. "Have
not others of my countrymen come with thee; why,

then, should I not live in Tubuai as an Areoi and an Aito ? " (a warrior).

"I will answer thee, Pipiri the slaughterer, thou cruel and bloody-handed man "—and Mahina faced him. "Thou hast come for no good purpose ; and truly we should be foolish to trust thee, save as a slave may be trusted. Do I not know that thou hast sworn to be revenged because I would have none of thee ? " Turning to her husband she coutinued, "Send this man away. Let him go live among the Tubuaians, and suffer him not to come near the ship nor our people. I know his bad and cruel heart."

The Tahitian laughed hoarsely. "Truly, Mahina, thou art a clever woman. I indeed will go and live with the people of Tubuai ; but I swear by my gods to return and take my revenge."

The next instant he sprang over the side, and Christian, in an endeavour to soothe his wife's fears and at her earnest entreaty, gave the order that he was not to be allowed to approach the whites in future.

Parties were now formed to fell timber, the fort was planned, and men under the direction of Edward Young began to dig a moat round the site. The *Bounty's* armament of four four-pounders and ten swivels was got on shore ; the Tahitians who had accompanied the ship took an active part in the work, principally because of the probability of their seeing the guns used in action against the Tubuaians and witnessing the destruction the weapons would accomplish.

All this labour took some weeks to perform, and during that time it daily became more evident that the people of Tubuai disliked their visitors ; indeed, during the last days of unloading the ship and digging the moat two or three skirmishes took place between them and the white men and their Tahitian allies.

Early in September, however, so far had the work of constructing the fort progressed, that most of the people left the ship and took up their quarters therein. The four-pounders and swivels were mounted in such a position as to make Christian perfectly sure that, should the Tubuaians attack the stronghold, they would suffer a disastrous defeat. But while aware that such an attack might be made, he was yet hopeful that ere long they would recognise his desire to live among them in peace. Mahina, day after day, went into the principal town, and strove to impress the head chief, Maouri, that the white men's advent would prove of advantage to his people. Still, though they received the beautiful Tahitian with the greatest courtesy and respect, they were cold and suspicious in their manner. One day, when accompanied by Alrema, she visited the village, they found the whole population assembled in the square, listening to an address by an orator. The moment the two women came in view the orator disappeared, not so quickly but that in him they had recognised Pipiri the Areoi.

"Let us go back," Mahina said to Young's wife ; " mischief is meant to us in the fort ; else why should these people gather together to listen to Pipiri, who is the enemy of us all ? "

Fearing that an attack was intended, Christian, as
soon as Mahina told him what she had seen, doubled
his sentries and kept a careful watch. For two nights
they were undisturbed, but on the third, just after
darkness had settled on the island, Talalu, a Tahitian
sentry on the western face of the fort, called them to
arms.

Scarcely had they time to snatch up their weapons
and fire a volley, when a large party of the islanders
surrounded the fort on three sides and began a determined assault. With wild cries of defiance and in
face of a continuous fire of musketry and grape from
the swivels, they jumped into the moat and scrambled
up on the other side. Scores of them were shot down
as they appeared over the bank, for many carried
torches made of the spathe of the coconut tree, with
which they intended to fire the buildings within by
throwing them over the palisade of coconut logs that
enclosed it. The light from these torches, slight as
it was, showed the assailants so clearly to Christian's
garrison, that ere they could form for their second
rush McCoy, Quintal and Smith each fired a swivel
loaded with grape into the surging mass. Dreadful
cries of agony followed, and so terrified were the
Tubuaians at the awful effects of the fire that they
wavered and were about to retreat. Instantly half a
dozen chiefs, waving their spears, sprang to the front ;
then the attacking party, beating their battle-drums
loudly, again advanced to the assault.

Suddenly, as the dark, waving line of Tubuains
swept over the undulating ground which lay between

them and the western face of the fort, a blaze of light lit up the surrounding forest, and Mahina and the other women appeared beside the white men, carrying torches which revealed not only the naked forms of the savages now trying to scale the palisade, but also the dead and wounded who had fallen from the white men's first fire, and who lay on the edge of and in the bottom of the moat. So irresistible, however, was the rush of the assailants, that fifteen or sixteen of them succeeded in clambering over the stockade and jumping down into the fort. Armed with a short stabbing spear in the left and a heavy ebony-wood club in the right hand, these daring fellows made a rush at Christian, McCoy, and Smith, who were firing through the palisade at the swarm of yelling savages outside. Loud warning cries from Mahina and Alrema made Christian turn suddenly, but too late to avoid a vicious thrust from a spear, which passed through his left arm. Then came the report of a pistol close to him— the rush of foemen bore him back to the palisade bruised, stunned, and bleeding, and there he fell exhausted.

Flinging the blazing torches into the centre of the fort, the women with knives and cutlasses in their hands, sprang down from where they stood to help their white husbands; and while some continued to fire at point-blank range into the thick mass of natives outside, the rest of the white men and Tahitians made short work of those within. Soon not one was left alive; the women, at the command of Mahina, seized all their dead bodies, save one, dragged them to the

top of the palisade and with cries of contempt hurled
them over among the assailants.

For nearly ten minutes more the Tubuaians sought
to force an entrance through the stout logs, heedless
of the fire from the seamen's muskets, which were
thrust through the spaces and discharged with deadly
effect. Seizing the musket barrels the valorous
savages by sheer strength tore them from the hands
of those who held them, then with cries of defiance
thrust their spears through the same apertures. By
this time three of the white men had received severe
wounds, and Young was just about to remove one of
the four-pounders from where it was mounted to that
part of the palisading where the assault was heaviest,
when the Tubuaians broke and fled.

"Whew!" said Young, wiping his powder-blackened
face and addressing Christian, whose arm was being
bound up by Mahina and Talalu, "that was warm
while it lasted. Not badly hurt, I trust, Christian?"

"No," answered the leader, "only a thrust from a
spear through the arm ; the rascal meant it for my
heart, though," and then he closed his eyes from
weakness. Round him stood the seamen, stripped to
their waists, with cutlasses and muskets gleaming in
the dying light of the torches which still lay burning
on the ground. With one hand leaning on her
husband's shoulder, in the other a cutlass bloody from
hilt to point, was Alrema. Like the men around her
she was bare to the waist, and her shapely arms and
bosom were as ensanguined as the weapon she carried.

"Nay, Etuati," she panted with a smile when

the light shone on her all but nude figure, and startled Young, " 'tis not my blood that thou seest ; not once did a spear touch me. Ah, these dogs of Tubuai ! Ah, my husband, thou didst not know that in our country we women go to war side by side with our husbands and our lovers."

Stern and callous as he was by nature, the young man shuddered visibly as he looked at the shocking appearance of his young wife ; stretching out his hand he unclasped hers from the cutlass, and gently led her towards the hut in which she slept.

Christian rose to his feet and was about to follow them when Mahina stayed him. "Dost thou know whose was the hand that sent the spear ? " she asked. "Come with me and I will show thee."

In the middle of the stockade lay a naked savage. By the light of the torch held by Mahina, Christian saw the tatooing on the dead man's back and legs, and knew that he was a Tahitian.

Stooping down, Mahina turned the body over, and pointed to the face.

"Pipiri ! " exclaimed Christian.

"Aye, Pipiri the Areoi ; he who swore to have thy life and mine."

"Poor devil," said Christian in English, and then to Mahina, "he hath a bullet hole through his chest. Who killed him ? "

"I," she answered, holding out Young's pistol—the pistol with which he had once sworn to kill Captain Bligh.

CHAPTER XIII

FOR a few days after the battle the white men remained undisturbed in the fort ; but instead of the elation that might have been expected from such a decisive victory, there now fell upon the mutineers a strange, brooding feeling of discontent.

Stewart and Heywood, ever bent upon retaking the ship and returning with her to England, had again succeeded in alienating some of the men from Christian, whose disregard of their wishes to remain at Tahiti had aroused their resentment.

Working upon this, Stewart, little by little, brought some of these men to believe that if they aided him in recovering the ship, they would not only be given a free pardon for any actual part taken in the mutiny, but would be rewarded for their loyalty to Heywood and himself. Tired of the hardships and discomforts of settlement on an island where the natives were so hostile, and already regretting their severance from civilisation, they were not long in promising to aid the

9   113

two midshipmen in any scheme devised to recapture the *Bounty* and sail her to England ; or, failing that, to return to Tahiti and give themselves up to the King's ship that they knew would be sent in search of them.

Morrison, the boatswain's mate, in particular, professed his readiness at any time that Stewart and Heywood might appoint to join them in either seizing the ship and making Christian and Young prisoners, or escaping from Tubuai and returning to Tahiti, and Alexander Smith, ever on the alert in his devotion to Christian, soon discovered that a second plot had been devised by Stewart, Heywood, and Morrison to steal the boat, provision her, and escape in the night. It became evident to Christian that his authority would be gone if he did not either make some concessions, or crush the malcontents at once and for ever. After discussing the matter seriously with Smith and Young, he called the people together and addressed them.

" You all seem so discontented with this place," said he, " and there are, I find, so many of you who will not hesitate to turn traitors to the rest of us, that I have determined, if you are agreed, to return to Tahiti. There, those who wish to separate from me can go, and those who wish to remain with me can do so."

This proposal was at once agreed to. It was also resolved to divide into two parts the ship's stores and fairly share them between the two parties ; then those who chose to do so could go ashore at Tahiti, and those who desired to stand by Christian could accompany him in the ship to some island afterwards to be decided upon by himself and his adherents.

And so once more the worn-out old *Bounty* was floated out to deep water, and all hands set to work to take on board her stores and armament again. That part of their labour accomplished, Christian sent parties out to collect the remainder of the live stock, which had not been seen since the attack on the fort.

But again the islanders attacked them in such force, and with such undaunted courage and fierce resolution, that the landing-party had to retreat to the ship ; and, indeed, they narrowly escaped being cut off before the boat could rescue them.

Christian, who was engaged with Mahina, Alrema, and some Tahitians in bending on the *Bounty's* after canvas, at once opened fire from the ship to cover the retreat of his men ; as soon as the boat came alongside he ordered those in her on deck for a glass of grog, and leaving the women to guard the ship, led a strong party on shore to make a second attempt.

For nearly a mile they marched through the rich tropical forest without molestation ; then there suddenly broke forth the deafening rattle of the native battle-drums, and some five hundred Tubuaians— among them many women—sprang out from their ambush and made a furious attack with clubs, spears, and slings. Fortunately the ground favoured the white men, six of whom were armed with muskets loaded with slugs, and these inflicted terrible slaughter at the first volley. Twice did the Tubuains make determined efforts to break through and separate the white men, but throwing down their muskets and keeping the Tahitians in the centre, the seamen drew their cutlasses and hewed and slashed at the naked bodies of the savages till the leafy ground was soaked and soddened into a bloody mire. But for the slaughter inflicted by the muskets of the Tahitians, however, the enemy would have borne them down by sheer force of numbers. Christian, whose great strength and skill in all muscular exercises had made him famous in Tahiti, fought with such courage and fury that he soon had a pile of dead and dying Tubuaians forming a breastwork around him ; and, leaning his weapon over their bodies, Talalu, the big Tahitian, fired into the enemy at such close range that the natives at last wavered, broke, and fled.

So exhausted, however, were Christian and his party, many of whom were badly wounded by spear-thrusts, that all further attempt to recover the stock was abandoned, and after two or three hours' rest they returned to the ship. At the landing-place they were met by a friendly chief, named Tairoa-Maina, and two of his friends, who, always having been well-disposed to Christian, took no part in the assault. They had just arrived from the principal village, where the bodies of those who fell in the attack were brought, and with grim satisfaction the mutineers learnt that fifty-six men and seven women had been killed and twice as many badly wounded, principally by cutlasses and musket slugs.

Fearing to remain on the island after the ship sailed, Tairoa-Maina besought Christian as his pledged *taio*, or friend, to take him and his two companions away with him. To this the mutineer consented.

On the following day, all being in readiness, the ship well stocked with provisions, and the wind being from the S.E. the *Bounty* once more got under weigh. Three days later she was off the island of Maitea, a high, verdure-clad spot about seven miles in extent, lying thirty miles due east from the southern point of Tahiti.

Running in close under the lee side, Christian hove-to the ship, called all hands aft, and divided everything on board into two lots in readiness for the time of separation. Then, before the lusty trade wind, the *Bounty*, not waiting for the crowd of canoes that were paddling eagerly off towards her filled with natives shouting welcome, stood away due west. At dusk Tahiti was in sight, and on the following morning the ship once more lay at anchor in Matavai Bay.

CHAPTER XIV

ONCE more were the white men welcomed with unaffected joy by the simple-hearted Tahitians, who yet wondered at their second return and made many inquiries as to its cause. Among those who thronged on board were the relatives of Pipiri the Areoi; these told enigmatically by Mahina that the priest would be long in returning, were at first angry and then suspicious; but when in answer to a direct question put to Christian, they learned that he had been killed in a fight against his countrymen and their white friends, they were seized with shame and retired with downcast faces. Later on in the day came Tinā and his beautiful wife, who welcomed Christian and his comrades with every demonstration of affection and esteem, though they too marvelled at the second return of the *Bounty;* this Christian did not attempt to explain, knowing that those Tahitians who accompanied the ship would not fail to tell their countrymen of all the events that had transpired since they sailed from Tahiti. But Tinā expressed his delight at hearing from Christian that

118

many of the *Bounty's* crew had returned for the purpose of living among his people, and readily gave
assistance to land the stores belonging to the shore
party.

For the third time the ship was now wooded and
watered and prepared for sea. When everything was
in readiness, Christian mustered the hands, and desired
all those who wished to remain on shore to go to the
larboard side of the ship, and all those who intended to
remain by him to the starboard. The first to step over
to the larboard were Stewart and Heywood, who were
at once followed by thirteen seamen. His own party
Christian found to consist of Edward Young, his next
in command; Mills, the gunner's mate; Brown, the
gardener; Martin, McCoy, Williams, Quintal, and,
of course, the faithful Alexander Smith; besides these
there stepped over to starboard Tarioa-Maina, the
young Tubuaian chief, his two friends, and three
Tahitian men with their wives, one of whom bore
in her arms a female infant. Each of Christian's
white followers had with him a native wife, and
thus the whole of his party totalled twenty-eight
persons.

For a moment or two Christian looked from one to
another of those ranged on the larboard side, then told
them in an unmoved voice to get into the boat. In a
few minutes they were gone, and the boat was being
pulled shorewards. Turning to those of the ship's
company who were still standing on the starboard side,
he informed them of his intention to sail in a day or
two, and said he would be pleased if they would not

visit the shore again. This they unhesitatingly promised.

That night—the 22nd of September—he went on shore in a canoe and, landing a short distance from the village, made his way to the house of the chief Tipa'uu, the father of Nuia, Stewart's wife.

Entering quietly he found the two youths in conversation with the old chief.

" I have come," he said, " to say goodbye again. Let us now speak together for the last time, and bury the past. I can never forget that until that morning in April we were always good friends. Shake hands then, my lads, for the last time."

" I am very sorry all this has happened, sir," said young Heywood, " and only just now Stewart admitted that you were sorely tempted," and he held out his hand.

" God knows, Christian," said Stewart, " I bear you no malice, for I cannot forget that after we gave you our promise not to interfere with your plans I induced Heywood to join me in breaking that promise. I can only plead as my excuse that I never intended to be false to that pledge; but seeing many of the men were ripe to join me in the attempt to retake the ship I felt justified in breaking it. I can only say again that although you have damned our prospects in life I freely forgive you."

" Not so, Stewart," said the mutineer, " your reputation as a loyal officer shall not suffer, nor shall this boy's. You are both innocent of participating in my crime. Be guided by me. Bligh will probably reach

England; whether he does so or not a ship will be sent out to search for us. When she arrives here, go off at once to her and give yourselves up to the commander. Tell him, as I tell you now, that this disaster was brought about entirely by me, and I alone am responsible for the act."

"I fear that we shall have difficulty in clearing ourselves," answered Stewart, moodily.

"Not if you give yourselves up at once and tell the exact truth. No one, not even my followers, not even I myself, thought of mutiny until I came on deck in the morning watch, and then the temptation suddenly came upon me. You both know what a life that damned scoundrel—God forgive me if I speak of a dead man—led us all, and how he picked me out particularly for his insults and unaccountable malice."

"That is true enough ; the wonder is that you bore with him so long. But it is too late to talk of that now," said Stewart, with a ring of sympathy in his voice ; "when do you sail, and where are you going ?"

"My dear lads," he answered mournfully, "where I am going is a question I cannot answer, and if I could it would be better unanswered, for you will be asked what has become of me. I shall leave at daylight and probably search for some uninhabited island on which to spend the remainder of my life."

"The natives say you do not intend sailing for a day or two."

"No, Stewart. I gave that out on purpose ; every one is on board and all is ready, and I hope to be clear of the bay to-morrow morning, before even a native is awake, and so by that means avoid the fuss of another leave-taking."

He was silent for a while, then turning to Heywood, earnestly besought him to see his relatives in England and tell them the truth. " Remember," said he, " when you reach England my people will have learned to hate and despise me as a mutineer. Tell them what you have seen of my sufferings and my provocation, and ask them to forgive me."

Silence fell upon them again in the darkened house, and nought was heard save the heavy breathing of the mutineer. Suddenly he rose, grasped their hands without a word, and, turning away, walked slowly down to the white line of beach whereon his canoe lay.

Old Tipa'uu awaking from his sleep a few minutes later, kindled afresh the dying fire, and as the flame leapt up and illuminated the house he saw that the faces of Stewart and Heywood were wet with tears.

An hour before daylight Fletcher Christian, who had been shut up for some hours alone in his cabin, came on deck and called the hands, and ere the mists of Orohena had begun to float away before the chilly breaths of the land breeze, the *Bounty's* anchor was up to her bow, and, with all her canvas spread, she was slipping out of the bay.

When daylight broke the natives gave a cry of astonishment, for the ship had disappeared.

* * * * *

The story of those of the mutineers who remained at Tahiti can be told in a few words. Who has not heard of the horrors of the *Pandora's* "box," the term applied to the round house built by the merciless Captain Edwards of the *Pandora* frigate on the deck of his ship as a prison for his wretched captives.

The *Pandora*, sent out to search for the mutineers, arrived at Tahiti on March 23, 1791. The sailors surrendered themselves, two seamen, Thompson and Churchill excepted, for the last-named had been murdered sometime previously by Thompson, who in turn was killed by the Tahitians, not before he richly deserved death for his atrocious crimes.

The white men had occupied their time on shore in building a schooner in which some had intended to leave the island, but they were unable to put to sea for want of sails.

Stewart's wife, Nuia, who was the daughter of the chief with whom he lived, had borne a child, and her love for her white husband has formed the theme of many a Tahitian love song. When the *Pandora* sailed the heart-rending grief of this gentle girl affected even the rough seamen whose duty it was to force her away from Stewart's side. Six weeks after she died of a broken heart.

Amid the tears and lamentations of the Tahitians, the frigate left with her prisoners on the 19th of May, the little schooner sailing with her. From the day the unhappy men surrendered until their arrival at the Cape of Good Hope, they were all treated with great brutality by Edwards—Heywood and Stewart, officers and mere youths as they were, receiving no more mercy at his hands than did the others.

Three months were spent by the *Pandora* in a vain search for the *Bounty* and those on board, and then the frigate was headed for Timor ; on August 28th, while making her way through Endeavour Strait,[1] she crashed on a reef, and on the following day was abandoned a total wreck.

The previous inhumanity of Captain Edwards towards his prisoners was, immediately after the ship struck, if possible, increased. For a long time he made no attempt to save them with the rest of the ship's company. From the box in which they were confined the only means of egress was by a scuttle on the top.

Some of them, as the *Pandora* rolled and dashed them, heavily ironed as they were, from one side to the other of their dreadful prison, bruised and bleeding, cried out that they would be drowned like rats in a hole, for already the vessel was breaking up fast, but their vindictive gaoler ordered them to be quiet or they would be fired upon. Only at the last moment did he give the order to take their irons off ; and then, if it had not been for the humanity of one of the *Pandora's* boatswain's mates, they would all have been drowned. He, brave fellow, hearing their cries, declared he would either free them or drown with them ; he dropped the keys of their irons through the scuttle, and with the greatest difficulty (for the water was up to his waist) forced off the iron bar which kept the scuttle closed.

When the survivors reached a small sand quay and

[1] Now know as Torres Straits.

Edwards mustered them it was found that thirty-one of the frigate's crew and Stewart and three of the *Bounty's* seamen were drowned.

Then began a long voyage to Coupang on the island of Timor, there being ninety-nine persons in all, divided between three boats. The story of their dreadful sufferings need not here be told ; but after a voyage of nineteen days, on September 19th, two of the boats reached Coupang, the third arriving three days later. From Coupang they were conveyed in a Dutch ship to Java, where they found the *Resolution* —the schooner built by the *Bounty's* people at Tahiti —which had early parted company with the *Pandora* and had arrived six weeks before, her crew having endured similar privations. From Batavia they were taken to the Cape of Good Hope, their numbers having been increased at a former place by the addition of more prisoners—the survivors of the Bryant party, eleven convicts who had escaped from Sydney.[1]

Embarking in the *Gorgon*, man-of-war, at the Cape, Edwards and his unfortunate prisoners at last reached England safely, and the mutineers were tried by court-martial. Bligh was not present, having sailed on a second voyage to Tahiti for another cargo of of breadfruit plants.

The trial ended in the acquittal of three seamen and the conviction of six others, among them

---

[1] PUBLISHER'S NOTE.—The story of the memorable voyage of the unfortunate convict, Will Bryant, his wife Mary, her two infant children and seven male convicts has been told by the authors of this work in a book entitled " A First Fleet Family."

Heywood. The general tenor of the evidence went
to prove Morrison and Heywood innocent. But Bligh
had left behind him statements inculpating these men.
The Admiralty, after the court-martial was over, considered the evidence and ultimately unconditionally
pardoned Heywood, Morrison, and a seaman named
Muspratt, and executed the others.

Heywood and Morrison were permitted to re-enter
the service, and both of then had honourable careers,
the first after attaining the rank of captain died full of
years and honours in 1831, and Morrison became
gunner of the *Blenheim*, in which ship, in 1807, he was
lost with all hands.

END OF PART I

PART II

CHAPTER XV

THE SEARCH FOR A RESTING-PLACE

THE *Bounty* lay becalmed within a few miles of a long, low-lying atoll densely covered with coconut trees. The wind had fallen light during the night, but though the land was then forty miles distant, the strong current set the ship steadily to the eastward, and now at ten o'clock in the morning those on her decks could see between the palm trees the pale green waters of a placid lagoon shimmering in the bright sunlight. Fifty miles north and south it stretched, and Talalu, who with others of his countrymen was gazing at the strange island from the fore-yard, his dark eyes full of expectancy, called out to Mahina and Alrema, who were on the poop deck, that he could see a great village and many people running to and fro on the beach getting ready their canoes to come out to the ship.

Sitting aft upon the skylight, with two charts spread out before him, was the leader of the mutineers.

Although but two weeks had passed since the ship left
Tahiti, the anxieties of his position had already told
upon Christian, and his face was drawn and haggard.
Mahina stood behind him, with her shapely hand
resting upon his shoulder, and looked with interest at
the pencilled line of the ship's course marked upon
one of the charts by her husband. Opposite were
Young, McCoy and his wife, and two or three others
of the mutineers, while their wives sat on the deck
and listened eagerly to what their husbands were
saying.

Turning to his comrades, Christian pointed to the
larger of the two charts.

" This island which we are now closing is called
Fakarava, and there is a good entrance into the
lagoon. If you think it advisable for us to take the
ship in, it can easily be done. But I cannot see
that any good will come from our wasting the time.
As you know, this is the seventh island we have
sighted since we left Tahiti, and every one has proved
unsuitable for our purpose."

" What's the matter with this one?" said Williams,
who had just come down from aloft. " It's big enough
for us all, isn't it?"

" Quite," answered Christian coldly, "but, as I have
pointed out to you before, while the natives of all these
islands were friendly enough, the islands themselves
were most unsuitable. They were mere sand banks
covered with coconuts, and although some of them
were of great extent, the narrow strips of land enclosing
the lagoons were barely half a mile broad. Supposing

that we had stayed on one of them, stripped and sank the ship, and lived ashore, what possible chance would there have been of concealing ourselves if a ship entered the lagoon, or what chance of defending our refuge? None. None at all. Then, the productions of such places are poor; there is literally nothing growing on them but coconuts. But, as some of you thought that in this group we should easily find an island as fertile as Tubuai, I acceded to your wishes, and we have spent ten days among them seeking a suitable spot."

"I'm sorry that I was one to persuade you, sir," said Quintal. "We ought to have stood to the south again, as you wanted to, and got among the high islands like Tubuai. As you say, it would be folly for us to leave the ship for any place that we can't live comfortably on."

"On this chart of Captain Bligh's," resumed the leader, "you will see that all these islands which we are now sailing among are marked as 'low coral lagoons.' That there are others which do not appear on the chart, and which are higher and more fertile, I have no doubt; but I believe from what Mahina and Talalu tell me, that these, which have not yet been discovered by any navigator, lie a long way to the south and east. That there is one such place I am certain. But before we listen to what my wife has to say on the matter, and before I give my own idea as to the best course, let me remind you that to-day expires the time we agreed to spend in cruising among the islands to the north and east of Tahiti."

"Aye, aye, Mr. Christian," said Smith, who with his wife had now joined the party around the skylight.

"Up to the present," resumed Christian, speaking slowly and coldly, "you have proved loyal to me, even though dissenting from my plans. I, like yourselves, am but a felon dodging the gallows, and it is better that you should bear with me a little longer, till I succeed in finding a safe resting-place for us all. Then it will be every one for himself; I shall have no further claim on your obedience, and you none of any nature on me."

An anxious look crept into Smith's eyes, but he had no time to say anything.

"Remember," continued the leader, "by leaving Tahiti with me you have cut yourself off from the last chance you might have had of saving your necks if captured by a King's ship; that being the case, we are all in the same plight, and your interests are also mine."

"Mr. Christian, you have acted towards us like a man. I don't regret what has happened, and I am going to obey you as captain of this ship till the end; and I am very much mistaken if you won't find every man on board of her of my way of thinking."

It was Smith who spoke, and when he had finished he looked at the others for approval. Every one of them answered heartily, "Aye, aye, go ahead, Mr. Christian; we'll see it through under you."

A faint smile of satisfaction for a moment lit up Christian's countenance, but the habitual melancholy, which had now settled upon him, returned the next instant, and he continued his remarks in cold, indifferent tones.

"Before we left Matavai Bay I had practically made up my mind that this island"—and he placed his hand upon the smaller chart—"was the most suitable place for us to reach. This book "—taking it from Mahina, "was written by Captain Carteret, and this chart was made by him when he discovered the island, thirty years ago. This is what he says," and opening the book, he read :—

"On the morning of July 2, 1767, a young gentleman named Pitcairn, being on the look-out at the mast head, observed a spot on the horizon, which on approaching it next day appeared to rise like a great pyramid out of the sea. It proved to be an island, one and a half miles in length and four and a half in circumference, its summit attaining a height of 1,008 feet, itself surrounded by a coral reef and covered with trees. The coast was formed for the most part of rocky projections, off which lay numerous fragments of stone, while a small stream of fresh water trickled down at one end of the island. The surf, which broke upon the shore with great violence, rendered landing impossible, but there should be no great difficulty in fine weather in doing so. The place seems to be uninhabited, a great number of sea-birds hovered around, and the waters almost swarm with fish."

"That's the place for us, lads," said Quintal, with an inquiring look at the others.

"You will see," continued Christian, "that in the big chart the island is not shown at all, but in this rough sketch of it, drawn by Captain Carteret, the position is given as lat. 20° 2′ south ; long. 133° 21′ west."

"Why, it's more than four hundred leagues from Tahiti," began Williams, when Christian checked him by a look.

"It is more than that, as you say, and whether Captain Carteret's position is correct or not, I cannot

tell; I think not; for it is known that the instru-
ments he had on board the *Swallow* were very indifferent. But in another reference to the island he says
that it was visible at fifteen leagues. I think, therefore, we could scarcely miss it, unless we ran by it in
the night."

"That's true, sir," cried McCoy and Smith.

"Well, as far as I know, no one but Carteret has
ever seen this place, and its isolated position will be a
safeguard to us. Furthermore, although my wife and
I have talked of the island often enough, I was careful
in leaving Tahiti to give neither Heywood nor Stewart
a hint of our future movements. Now listen to what
my wife has told me, and then decide quickly whether
you will agree to our standing to the south-east and
looking for this Pitcairn."

Again the rest of the mutineers answered that they
trusted him, and would follow his advice.

"Very well, then. My wife, as Talalu and your
own wives will tell you, is not of Tahitian blood. Her
ancestors were blown away to sea from an island far
away from Tahiti, which they only reached after spend-
ing many months among these islands through which
we have been cruising for the past ten days. Their
home lay, according to them, many weeks' fast sailing
to the south-east of Tahiti. Mahina, though she
knows but little of the origin of her people, yet knows
that the place they came from was called Afitā, and
Carteret's description of Pitcairn, as far as I have been
able to make her understand it, tallies in the main with
the description she has heard her mother give of Afitā.

Remember that we have with us many Tahitians, and Tairoa-Maina and the other Tubuaians, and it would be well to take them into our confidence and tell them where we are going. We cannot afford to deceive them."

He ceased speaking ; then, as no one demurred to his suggestion, he asked Young to muster all the natives aft. As soon as they had grouped behind the white men, Christian said to his white comrades—

"My wife is, I think, a favourite with all these men. Let her talk to them and tell them that we are about to look for the home of her forefathers, and they will be well content."

The seamen consented, and Christian explained to Mahina what was wanted of her. She, readily understanding, at once complied ; and it was easy to see, by the flush of pleasure upon her cheeks and her bright smile, that the task was a pleasing one.

Placing her hand on Carteret's chart, and giving a swift glance of intelligence and affection at Christian, she spoke.

"See, men of Tahiti and Tubuai, my husband desireth me to tell thee of the home of my people, so that ye may know why it is the ship stayeth so long out upon the sea. It is because that of all the lands we have seen since we sailed we have seen none so fair to look upon as Tahiti and Tubuai ; and it is in my husband's heart to find a land that shall be both fair to look at and good to live upon. But naught have we yet seen but such places as this," and she pointed to the low-lying island on the larboard side ; " and so, because I have told him of the rich land from whence my fathers came, it is in his mind that we go there and live. And I have heard Manuhuru, my mother, speak of this land, for there was her mother born and there she lived, until there came a time when, with many others, she was blown out to sea and returned no more, for their canoe was swept away by a strong south wind for many, many days till they reached strange islands. Some were killed by the people of these places, but my mother's mother, and four others with her, one day stole a sailing canoe from the people of the island called Marutea and set out again to seek their own home."

"Here's the place she speaks of," said Christian, pointing to Marutea on the large chart, "a good eight hundred miles to the north-west of Pitcairn Island."

Whites and natives crowded round the chart and looked at the spot indicated by Christian.

"But again the winds and the gods were against them, and so they sailed towards the setting sun, and on the tenth day saw the shadow of Orohena stand out against the sea-rim, and at night they landed at Tiarapu [1] and dwelt there in peace among the people, who were kind to them. But yet were their hearts always towards their own land, which, though it be but a small place, yet is green as Tahiti, and is a land good to live in ; and sometimes when the sun sank below the sky-rim and they watched the top of Orohena become wrapped in the white mists of the valleys, they would look at one another and sigh and

---

[1] A district in Tahiti.

say : 'Ah, that is like our land of Afitā rising from the sea.'"

A cry broke from Tairoa-Maina, the Tubuaian chief : "Afitā ! Truly, Kirisiani, thy wife and I are of one blood ; for I, too, know of this land which riseth from the sea, and is far away, towards the edge of the world. My father came from Afitā, and there are many others in Tubuai whose fathers came from there, long, long ago, in seven canoes. This did they because Afitā, though so rich, was too small for so many to live upon. And because of the strange blood in my veins it was that the men of Tubuai liked me not, and I desired to come away with thee. Let us, oh Kirisiani, go seek the land of Afitā, which is far towards the rising sun from Tubuai. For it is indeed, as thy wife sayeth, a land good to look upon, and rich in woods, and water and fish, and yams and bread-fruit."

For some minutes there was an excited buzzing of voices among the natives, and the men eagerly besought Christian to lead them to the home of his wife's people ; while Edward Young and the rest of the ship's company seemed equally interested and as anxious to learn more. Presently Talalu, who generally acted as spokesman for his countrymen, stepped out from the others and addressed the leader of the white men. This man, who was the tallest and strongest of all the Tahitians on board, had, like Smith, conceived a great admiration for Fletcher Christian, and had evinced it in many ways since the *Bounty* left Tahiti ; and being a man of chiefly rank, his influence over the rest of the natives on board was great.

"Kirisiani," he said simply, " I, Talalu, the son of Poahanehane, will follow thee wherever thou goest, and work and fight for thee. And as I do, so will my countrymen with thee on the ship do. This we swear by our gods, and by the blood in our veins."

And then one by one the simple brown people crowded round Christian and touched his hands and feet in token of their fealty to him ; and the dull, brooding shadow for a little time left his face as he shook hands with them all in the English fashion, his example being followed by Young and the rest of the white men.

Then Tairoa-Maina pressed forward, and the handsome chief, his black eyes gleaming with excitement at the prospect of seeing his father's island home, knelt at Mahina's feet and touched the deck with his forehead.

"And I too," he said, " will go with thy husband, Mahina, and be a true man to him ; for is he not a man of a good heart ? And together shall we search for and find the land of Afitā, thy land and mine. For now, Mahina, when I hear thy voice, do I hear the voice of my father that is dead ; and it may be that thou and I are of one blood. And for that alone would my heart be for ever towards Kirisiani, thy husband."

Christian smiled again. Despite his own morbid nature, he had grown to like the handsome Tubuaian, and the chief's devotion to Mahina pleased him greatly.

A little behind were the rest of Mahina's country-women, who, not comprehending the discussion, had now surrounded her with soft murmurs of excitement, and presently Christian, noting this, turned to his wife with a laugh—the first for many months.

" This is well, Mahina, that thy countrymen are so with thee and me ; but what say all these women to this search for the land of Afitā ? "

She turned her lustrous eyes, beaming with affection, on the mutineer. "It is not the part of a woman, unless she be a great ruler, to say aye or nay to her master's will ; and surely thou didst not think to ask these women their thoughts on this matter.   That would be folly."

" 'Tis a good doctrine, Mahina," answered Christian; " there will be no man-and-wife quarrels to break our peace on Afitā."   Then, pressing her hand, he turned away to attend to the ship.

" Here comes a fleet of canoes," called out Quintal to Young, and almost at the same moment the glassy surface of the water stirred and rippled to the breeze as it came darkening along from the north-east to fill the *Bounty's* sails.

" Never mind the canoes," answered Young, flinging down the mainbraces ; " get the head-sheets over ; and here, away to the main deck, all you women !—out of the way and give us a pull on the braces ! "

So with many a bubbling laugh and merry jest the Tahitian women tripped down and seized the ropes in their soft little hands ; and as the ship leaned gently over and the froth began to bubble under her bluff old bows, Christian put the helm hard up, wore her round, and set her head to the south-east.

Mahina, standing beside him, gazed intently into her husband's eyes as he looked at the compass; then as he steadied the ship she watched him inquiringly; and he nodded and smiled at her in return.

"Aye, Mahina, that is where we must go to seek for Afitā; may we find it soon." He gave over the wheel to Williams, walked quietly away, picked up the charts and books, and went below.

But on the main-deck, as the long, palm-clad line of Fakarava, with its white gleam of sandy beach, sank slowly below the horizon, the white seamen and their native wives and the rest of the ship's company sang and laughed and chattered; and as the *Bounty* slipped over the long ocean rollers she spread on either side white sheets of snowy foam, and surged along before the lusty breath of the ever-freshening breeze.

So began the search for the land of Afitā.

CHAPTER XVI

O N further careful study of Carteret's book and chart, the mind of Fletcher Christian was greatly disturbed, for he knew that there was much to fear if the position of Pitcairn had been wrongly laid down. The currents, too, in this part of the world were but little understood by those few navigators who had sailed among the islands; indeed, the natives themselves were far better informed of both the winds and currents of Eastern Polynesia than were the few European voyagers among the various groups since the days of Carteret and Cook.

Carteret had laid down the centre of Pitcairn in lat. 20° 2' south, and long. 133° 21'' west; but although Christian was fairly confident of sighting the island by keeping a careful look-out and heaving-to at night when he got near it, he felt that his limited knowledge of the winds and currents might lead to prolonged and tedious search.

For twenty-one days after leaving Fakarava the *Bounty* sailed south-easterly. Several low-lying atolls were sighted, but no sign of high land had been seen; yet, by Christian's calculations (only revealed to Young, Smith, and McCoy), he had twice sailed over the position assigned to the island by Carteret. His misgivings that a strong current had set him too far to the eastward were daily growing stronger. His only chronometer, through an accident, had been rendered useless, and besides this the weather latterly was gloomy and the sun seldom visible. The last land had been sighted eighteen days after leaving Fakarava, and Talalu and Tairoa-Maina, who from the break of day were continuously aloft on the look-out, assured him on that day that no land lay further to the south-east but Afitā and a little sandy island called Oeno, about half a day's sail to the northward. Small as this island was, they declared that the clamour of the sea-birds, whose resting-place it was, would reveal its presence even on the darkest night; and this alone somewhat reassured him in the hope that he had not drifted past it or Pitcairn in the darkness. A day's sail further to the eastward was another island which they said was called Fenua-manu;[1] this, too, was the home of millions of sea-birds, whose voices stilled the beating of the surf upon the reefs, so great were their numbers.

With his chin upon his hands, Fletcher Christian gazed moodily at the chart before him. Mahina, who by the cabin door was watching him with tender interest, heard him sigh wearily. Stepping up to him,

---

Ducie Island, about ninety miles east of Pitcairn. It is uninhabited now. The old name, Fenua-manu, meant "The Island of Birds.'

she pressed her cool hand to his forehead, and leant her cheek against his in loving sympathy.

In the great cabin no sound broke the stillness save the swish and swirl of the ship's wake as she slipped through the water; and presently Christian, drawing the girl's slender figure to a seat beside him, pointed to the chart.

"Mahina," he said, "you and three of my white comrades alone know that the ship hath twice sailed over the place where this island of Afitā should have been; and no sign have we yet seen, not even a drifting coconut or a piece of wood."

The girl's eyes filled with tears; for a few moments her bosom heaved, and she tried to speak without showing her emotion; and Christian, moody and pre-occupied as he was, knew by her voice that she felt for and sympathised with him.

"Kirisiani, I too have looked and looked and prayed to Oro and Tane to guide the ship to Afitā, but now I begin to fear that the gods have turned aside from me."

He pressed her hand in silence, and was about to bid her come with him on deck when the murmuring of voices at the door of the great cabin broke in upon them, and presently Talalu, Tairoa-Maina, and two other natives asked leave to speak with him.

"Let them wait awhile," he said sullenly, although knowing that in the Tubuaian chief and his Tahitian comrade he had two firm friends, who with Smith, Young, and McCoy would stand by him to the last. For nearly half an hour he remained communing with

himself and endeavouring to think out some other
course for the future, should his search be still un-
rewarded on the following day.

Already the long voyage had had a bad effect upon
most of the mutineers, and only that morning he had
noticed the gloomy faces and sullen manner of the
men when changing the ship's course another point to
the southward. Some of the Tahitians were suffering
from the effects of the strange food which, for weeks,
they had been forced to live upon, and the confinement
told seriously on their health and spirits. Yet, despite
this, their regard for Mahina, and their faith in, and
respect for Christian were unbroken, and they would
have endured the most prolonged hardships rather than
let either imagine that they were repining. With some
of the white seamen, however, these feelings were
wanting. Although there was no open expression of
discontent, more than one murmured at the delay,
declaring that Christian and Young, either through
ignorance or design, were not doing their duty to their
associates.

It was no wonder, therefore, that Christian himself
grew day by day more anxious and less confident of
finding this island of Carteret's. True, the place was
small and solitary, and, unless his reckoning was
very exact, might easily be missed. Twice had he
sailed across Carteret's position, and nothing had
rewarded his search ; and now he felt that another
day's fruitless quest would assure him either that his
observations had been incorrect or that the island had
disappeared by some convulsion of nature. Worn out

with anxiety, with constant watching, and his own sad emotions, nothing but the devotion and tender love of Mahina had kept him from ending it all with a loaded pistol which he always carried in his pocket.

He pushed the chart away wearily, and was about to go on deck when Mahina, who had remained, touched his arm, and with a timid, beseeching look asked him to let Tairoa-Maina and the other natives have speech with him.

"Come in, friends," he said, in kindly tones.

The Tubuaian chief, who, with Talalu and two other natives, had been patiently waiting at the cabin door, came in, sat silently down, and waited permission to speak.

"Speak, my brother," said Mahina to Tairoa-Maina. "My husband is wearied, and would go out upon the deck to breathe the cool wind of the night."

Pleased at the relationship assigned to him by Christian's wife, the handsome young Tubuaian looked at them with affectionate regard, and said he and those with him desired to speak of something in their minds, at which they prayed him not to be angered, "for," he added, with a grave smile, "we men of brown skin are but fools on the great ocean when the sky is dull and there is neither sun nor moon nor stars to guide us. But with the clever white men it is different; they are full of wisdom to guide a ship, even if there be neither sun by day nor stars by night. Yet in some little things we have wisdom, and that is why we now ask that thou, Kirisiani, will listen to us—who are thy friends."

"That I well know," said the mutineer, placing his hand on Tairoa's shoulder. "Speak, my brother."

"Thou knowest, Kirisiani, that for many days I have climbed the masts and watched, so that I might be the first to see the land of Afitā ; and when it grew dark I have waited upon the deck and listened to hear if the sound of beating surf came over the sea. Last night, as Talalu and I lay on the deck, and the ship rose and fell and made no sound, we saw first one and then another of the birds called *kanápu*[1] fly swiftly over the ship towards the westward. As we watched there came another, and then another, and then a flock of twenty or more, and these too all flew swiftly westwards, for we saw their shadows darken the bright strip of water that shot out from the dying moon. Then, as we lay down again, there came to our minds that on Oeno, the little sandy islet but a day's sail from Afitā, there do the *kanápu* breed in the thick *puka* scrub which groweth in the sand."

"True," said Mahina quickly ; "I have heard my mother say that on Oeno the cries of the *kanápu* when they come home to roost at night drown the noise of the breaking surf."

"Aye," said the Tubuaian, "and so have I been told. Yet only at night ; for in the daytime they fly to the lagoon of Fenua-manu, where they find many fish. We talked of this as we lay on the deck, and I desired to come and tell thee, Kirisiani, of the flight of the birds, but feared that thou wouldst chide me

[1] The Equatorial booby, whose swift flight is only surpassed by that of the frigate bird.

for doubting thy skill to guide the ship. But I have heard some of those with us say some little things."

Christian smiled bitterly. "They speak truly, my friend ; I cannot find this land of Afitā."

Leaning over towards him and placing his hand on Christian's, the Tubuaian continued : " But this morning, when the lower half of the sun was still buried in the sea, we saw many, many *kanápu* and *katafa* [1] flying swiftly towards it, and Afitā lieth between Oeno and Fenua-manu."

Christian's eyes sparkled. "Thanks, my good friend. I see now thy meaning. For two days have I thought that the ship hath come too far towards the rising sun, and that the place we seek lieth westward."

" Even so think we," answered Talalu, "for the current runneth strong towards the rising sun, and the *kanápu* and the *katafa* went westward to rest."

For a little while Christian considered. Oeno, the sandy island which both Mahina and Tairoa asserted was but a day's sail north and west from Afitā, was not marked in any of the two or three charts he possessed, but Ducie Island, the " Fenua-manu," or Island of Birds, of the natives, was, and lay due east of Oeno. And he knew the natives relied much upon simple indications to find their position when making long voyages at sea. He soon made up his mind.

" We will turn the ship to follow the *kanápu*," he said.

The natives sprang to their feet, and with animated countenances waited for him to precede them on deck.

---

[1] Frigate birds.

The *Bounty*, with the gentle trade-wind filling her sails, was steering an E.N.E. course, when Christian, with Mahina and the others, came on deck. Sitting near the wheel was Young, who had charge of the watch.

"Young," said Christian, "I am convinced that if this island is in existence it is to the west of us."

"So Alrema says," nonchalantly replied the young man ; "but I didn't think it worth while mentioning it."

"What do you say ? Shall we keep her away ? "

"Certainly—why not ? As we cannot find it ourselves by the chart let us go west by all means."

"Hands to the braces, men !" called out Christian after a moment's hesitation. "We are going to run down to the westward."

In a few minutes the yards were hauled round, and the *Bounty* was heading west by north. Telling Talalu and Tairoa to go aloft, Christian turned to Young and Smith and related the incident of the previous night.

About four o'clock in the afternoon, just as Christian was about to lie down for an hour, there burst from Talalu on the fore top-gallant yard a cry that sent a thrill through the hearts of every one on board—

"*Te fenua no Afitā !*" ("The land of Afitā ! ").

There was a sudden rush aloft, Christian himself ascending the main rigging slightly in advance of McCoy, Quintal, and Young.

"There it is, sir, !" said Quintal excitedly, pointing almost right ahead.

Then as the others saw the faint blue outline of a pyramidal peak rising from the sea, a cheer broke from them, and the people on the deck took it up and repeated it again and again.

"Thank God!" said Christian to Edward Young. Instinctively their hands met, and in silence they all gazed intently at the little spot, which at that far distance no eye but that of a seaman or a native could distinguish from a cone-shaped cloud.

CHAPTER XVII

TOWARDS sunset, when the *Bounty* was still some thirty miles distant from the land, the trade-wind as usual died away, and by eight in the evening the new moon shone over a sea as calm as a mountain lake. Fearing that the easterly current would set the ship back in the night during the continuance of the calm, Christian and Young had carefully taken the ship's bearings just as the pale blue of the distant island was changing to a shade of purple under the rays of the setting sun.

The knowledge that their long search was ended at last inspirited every one on board. After supper the men gathered on the main deck, and with their wives and their brown-skinned shipmates forgot the weary days which had tried their tempers and forbearance so severely. Alrema, who had an influence upon her countrymen almost equal to that of Mahina, was in high spirits, and Young, despite his usual seeming indifference to her vivacity and beauty, was yet secretly pleased to see the respect with which she

was treated by the others. Her conduct during the
attack on the fort at Tubuai had shown her to be
possessed of a fiery, undaunted courage ; indeed, had
the murmurers known that this beautiful Tahitian girl
with the dark, languorous eyes, and soft red lips had
advised Young to induce Christian to shoot them,
they would have remembered the incident of the
bloody cutlass, and been more careful of their speech
in her hearing. Yet now she seemed but a merry-
hearted, mirth-loving girl, and as she raised her sweet
voice in some old Tahitian love-song, while her eyes
sought those of Edward Young, the men were struck
with her bright and animated beauty.

Tired of singing and talking with the group assembled on the main-deck, she presently ascended to the
poop, where her husband sat with Christian and
Mahina discussing their plans for the future.

She seated herself beside Young, and listened till
they ceased talking—then said, clasping Mahina's
hand in her own, " Tell us, oh friend of my heart,
the story of this land of Afitā."

" Nay," replied Mahina, smiling and stroking
Alrema's dark hair, " 'tis but little I know, and that
little did I learn from my mother ; but call hither
Tairoa-Maina, and let him tell the story, for he hath
more knowledge of Afitā than I."

Christian's consent having been gained, the Tubuaian chief was called upon the poop, and sat in front
of the little group with his two faithful attendants
behind him ; his swart, handsome features lit up with
pleasure when he was told what was wanted of him.

"Kirisiani," said Mahina, caressing her husband's cheek with her soft, brown hand, "but for this dear friend, Tairoa-Maina, still might we have been searching for this land of his and my father's."

"True," answered Christian frankly, "but for him we might perhaps have never found it. Thou seest, Mahina, that in some things the white men have not the knowledge nor judgment of thy people."

"Even so," she answered gravely, "we have no such things as those *tuhi*[1] of thine which are full of wisdom. And it is strange to us that by looking at some little black marks thou couldst tell us of the sea chief who saw the land of Afitā thirty years ago. Yet, though we have no wise men among us like thee and the great Tuti and Pirai, we have memories and songs and tales which have come down from father to son; and all that is told is remembered by the children, and they, when they grow up, tell it to their children, so that all may know the beginning of things since Taaroa the father of the gods and his two sons Oro and Tane made the world."

Acquainted as he was in some degree with the wild and fabulous nature of almost every Polynesian tradition bearing upon the ancestry of the people, Christian was convinced by the many long conversations he had held with Mahina about her descent that much of what she told him had a basis of fact. The Tahitian custom of deifying their ancestors would naturally result in confusing historical facts and rendering them absurd, but his keen observation and quickly acquired

---

[1] Books, handwriting and maps.

knowledge of the Tahitian tongue enabled him to
sift out in a great measure the real from the fabulous
and visionary. He therefore, while listening to
Tairoa-Maina's story of Afitā, quickly divested it of
all that was mythological and fictitious, and accepted
the substance of it as fact.

To his mind much of what Mahina told him of
Afitā had appeared no more than the vague traditions
of native legend, but as he listened to the Tubuaian
chief's story he found a remarkable resemblance between the two accounts.

Sitting in the light of the moon, which fell upon
his symmetrical head and shoulders and revealed the
curious and delicate tracery of the tattooing upon his
polished skin, the young chief related the Tubuaian
story about the land and the people whence he came.

"Long, long ago, Kirisiani, Taaroa the Sky-Pro-
ducer, and Oro and Tane his sons, between them
created new lands by dipping their hands to the
bottom of the deep sea and dragging them up above
the surface, so that the trees might grow and men
live upon them. In those days there dwelt upon
Huahine a *taata paari* (wise man) named Poiata,
who had himself been created by the gods, and his
wife Mahinihini. In the same house lived Rumia
and his wife Motupapa; only these four were on
Huahine. At the end of two years neither of the
women had borne a child to their husbands, and Poiata
and Rumia, assailing them with bitter words and
blows, drove them away to the sea-shore, and bade
them go swim out into the ocean and drown.

"'Nay,' cried Mahinihini, 'give us a canoe, so that at least we may seek some other land and hide the shame of our childlessness.'"

"But Poiata and Rumia laughed and jeered at them, and pointing to a great shark that lay upon the water outside the reef, mockingly bade them hold on to its fin and begone.

"Now this shark was Tahua;[1] and the two women, who wept as they swam, approached him silently, and clambering upon his great back, held on to his fin while Tahua sped away with them.

"For many days he swam southward and eastward, till Mahinihini and Motupapa saw, rising out of the sea, what seemed the fin of another great shark ; so high was it that it pierced the clouds, even as does the peak of Orohena. But when they drew near they saw that it was land rising up steeply from the deep sea, and on the high cliffs there stood strange men with yellowish faces and circlets of red and green parrots' feathers round their foreheads. As the two women gazed in fear and trembling, Tahua the shark sank from beneath them, and they struck out and swam to the shore. The strange men ran down the cliffs and helped them to land, and gave them food to eat and coconuts to drink. Seven men were they, and they said they came from a great country to the east where the mountain-tops were for ever covered with white clouds."

"How came they there?" asked Christian.

Tairoa-Maina shook his head. "No man knoweth.

[1] One of the gods of Tahitian mythology.

But they were pleased to see Motupapa and Mahinihini, for there were no women with them on the
island, which they had named Afitā—'the land shot
up by fire from the bottom of the sea.' So these two
women became wives to the seven men, and they bore
seven children to each man. By and by, as the years
passed on, there came more of the strange people from
the great eastern land ; and they were pleased with
the beauty of Afitā and the great richness of the land,
and dwelt with Mahinihini and Motupapa and their
husbands. Very joyously they lived together, until
the people grew so in number that breadfruit and
taro and yams and plantains began to be scarce
because of the many mouths of children who cried
with hunger. And when the land would no longer
hold them and famine came, twenty-and-two score men
and women sailed far away in canoes to seek another
home. Westward they sailed for ten days till a storm
separated them, and four of the canoes came to the
land of Tubuai, and four to the land of Rapa.[1] Of
those that reached the land of Rapa I know nought,
save that the chief was named Teata-rua ; but of
those that came to Tubuai my father was one."

"And did he ever tell thee how appeared this Afitā,
this lonely island that springeth up from the sea like
the fin of a shark that swimmeth on the surface ? "
asked Mahina.

"I have heard my father say," answered the chief,
"that so steep are its mountains that they shut in from

[1] Rapa is situated in 27° 30′ S ; 144° 30′ W. and would easily be
made by sailing W. from Pitcairn.

the winds the rich soil of the belly of the land ; and down the sides of the hills run many streams of water sweet to drink. And save in one place no reef ran out from the shore."

"That does not agree with Carteret," said Young to Christian.

"And the great ocean rollers," added Mahina, "for ever dashed up against the face of the cliffs so that no strangers could land in their canoes, else would they be broken to pieces in the angry surf."

"But still there is one little spot on the north and north-west," continued the Tubuaian chief, "so small that only those who have lived in Afitā can find it, where the sea is not always rough. And on the eastern side there is a small bay, where, when the wind is from the west and south, the sea is quiet, and a deeply-laden canoe can land with safety."

"Is the water deep?" asked Christian.

"Aye, so deep is it, that five fathoms from the shore the water is as blue as the deep ocean ; and close to the high cliffs swim great fish that we in Tubuai catch only with lines a hundred fathoms in length. Ah, Kirisiani, to-morrow wilt thou see if Mahina and I have told thee aught but the truth."

As the pleasant tones of the chief's voice ceased there came a gentle puff of air, which filled the ship's upper canvas, and Christian and Young sprang to their feet, quickly followed by the natives, and trimmed the sails for the coming breeze.

For three or four hours the *Bounty* slid softly over a moonlit sea ; then as dawn broke and the red sun sprang from the horizon, Fletcher Christian and his comrades saw the island for which they had so long sought lying before them bright and shining green upon the sunlit sea.

An hour later the ship was hove-to as close to the land as her safety permitted, and Christian, in her one boat with Taiaro-Maina and some white seamen, was searching for the only little bay where it was thought a landing might be effected.

CHAPTER XVIII

WITHIN twenty minutes of leaving the ship
Christian and his boat's crew were close under
the cliffs of the island ; and rowing carefully, just
outside the curl of the breaking surf, they sought the
landing-place described by the Tubuaian chief as being
on the south and east side. As the strong arms of
the natives urged the boat along, Christian looked
at the grim, precipitous cliffs which rose sheer from
the thundering surf at their base, and a strange sense
of loneliness almost akin to fear came over him.
The outlines of the solitary island were savage, and the
terror of its forbidding exterior was increased by the
tumult of the waves which hurled themselves with
astounding fury against its grey coral walls. Sometimes, as a huge, swelling sea swept in like a moving
wall towards them, the natives would give a warning
cry ; and Christian, bringing the boat's head round to
meet it, would watch the mighty volume of water
fling itself, with a hoarse roar, high upwards against the
solid face of stone, to fall back in drenching sheets of

foam upon the swirling cauldron which leapt and eddied and boiled beneath. Here and there deep and narrow chasms split up the vertical mass of rock, and into these gaps, many of them terminating in caverns black as night, the sea rushed with such irresistible force that misty spray and spume shot upward over the very summits of the cliffs, like the belching smoke from the crater of a volcano in the throes of a violent convulsion. Right to the verge there drooped down in places thick clusters of a light-green coloured creeper, whose pendants, turned yellow by the salty spray, swayed wildly to and fro like banners waved by mysterious, invisible hands, so fierce were the air blasts caused by the terrific inrush of water.

Scarcely speaking above a whisper, the natives rowed quickly along, their dark eyes shining with pleasure when they saw the feathery tufts of coco-palms showing above the dense thicket scrub, where the cliffs were less precipitous and revealed a slight glimpse of the interior of the island. And now, as the boat drew near the south-western point where a high, cathedral-like rock stood, blackly-grim, amid the white seethe of boiling surge, there came a strange wild clamour, a savage symphony of crashing, thundering surf and hoarse guttural croaks and shrill pipings, and from every crag and rock and jagged pinnacle along the shore, there soared aloft a vast swarm of sea-birds, which whirled and circled above the boat with out-stretched wing and frightened eye. Then, as if satisfied with their quick scrutiny of the strange intruders, they rose higher in air and vanished behind the towering cliffs.

Keeping well clear of three or four sharp-peaked rocks which raised their black heads from the water as the receding billows uncovered them to view, the boat at last rounded the point and Christian headed her along the shore to the north-west; and almost at the same moment Tairoa-Maina drew in his oar, and sprang to his feet with an exultant shout.

"See, Kirisiani! the beach! the beach! And see, too, the leaping torrent above. 'Tis indeed the land of Afitā."

Christian, himself too excited to speak, now gave his attention to effecting a landing; the crew took in their oars and, picking up canoe paddles in their place, waited for the word to run the boat ashore during a lull in the surf, which even on the sheltered beach broke heavily. For some five or ten minutes they lay rising and falling upon the rollers; then, seeing his opportunity, Christian gave the order, the natives plunged their paddles into the water with swift, strong strokes, and sent the boat spinning shoreward on the crest of a curling wave. Twenty feet from the beach they leapt out, in another minute the boat had touched the shingle, and the crew had hauled it out of danger.

Directly in front of them was a winding path, long unused, which led to a plateau beyond; Christian and Tairoa led the way up the ascent, and they quickly gained the edge. And then even Christian could not repress a cry of excited admiration at the marvellous beauty of the scene. Back from the white beach, which like a strip of ivory lay below amid the emerald green of a belt of encircling coco-palms, there stood revealed an amphitheatre of the loveliest verdure and most enchanting appearance, surrounded on three sides by wild and densely wooded mountains. Westward, about a mile away across the plateau, a lofty peak raised itself high above its less conspicuous fellows, whose bold and romantic-looking semicircle, diversified by noble, jutting crags and tapering peaks, encompassed the softer beauties of the smiling valley. Scarcely more than a mile in width from east to west, the extraordinary fertility and variety of verdure was such that Christian and his companions gazed upon their surroundings with feelings little short of rapture. Overhead, the lofty plumes of the stately palms swayed and rustled to the flower-scented breath of the trade-wind as it stirred the rich green foliage of the breadfruit trees. Along the seaward-facing edge of the plateau clusters of pandanus palms, with their ripe, red fruit, waved their feathery banners to the breeze. Beyond the crowns of the murmuring palms, and the wide outspreading branches of the *tamanu* and breadfruit and pandanus trees, lay the blue, heaving bosom of the Pacific.

For some little time they remained spellbound, drinking in the beauty of land and sea and sky around them, and listening to the music of the mountain torrent as it wound downward through its rocky bed to the bright valley, to mingle its pure waters with the ocean. Then with a sigh of satisfaction the leader bade his men follow him back to the boat. A mile off he could see the *Bounty*, which had just gone about, and was now standing in again, her white canvas shining in the dazzling sunlight.

Before launching the boat, the crew threw into her a hundred or more of young drinking coconuts, which they had hastily gathered from the nearest trees, for the use of the women. Then, all talking together of the richness and fertility of the island, they picked up their canoe paddles and quickly sent the boat in safety through the breaking surf.

Christian was soon on deck and described the appearance and capabilities of the island to the foremost of his comrades, who were all well pleased at his account, and left their future course entirely in his hands. He was not long, therefore, in coming to a decision.

The wind was now from the south-east and blew gently but steadily into the little bay, so it was agreed that the ship should work round the south-west point and be headed directly for the beach. The deep water which ran close to the foot of the mountains all round the island, except where a narrow strip of beach separated land and sea, would enable them to get everything out of the *Bounty* likely in the future to be useful; and the destruction of the ship, Christian knew, would prevent his companions from yielding to any sudden impulse and risking his and their safety by an attempt to leave the long-sought place of refuge.

In order that Young and Brown (the gardener) might take a look at their future home, Christian sent the boat away a second time; for the wind being light it would be some time before he could effect the purpose he had in view. Two hours later, when she was within a quarter of a mile of the southern point of the little bay, the boat was seen coming out again, and soon gained the ship. Young was greatly pleased with the beauty of the place, and reported that he had searched for a suitable anchorage and had found a spot where the ship would be safe enough during the continuance of such calm weather, for the sea on that side of the island was but moderate.

But at the word "anchorage" Christian shook his head, and Young therefore pursued the subject no further. Brown, who had a considerable knowledge of botany, said that he had found many plants upon the island which were edible and would prove of value; and his and Young's remarks confirmed Christian and the others in their opinion that the island would, when the ship's stores were exhausted, yield them ample provisions in all respects save that of animal food. The varied fruits and vegetables also would be enough to support them till the ship's stock of goats, pigs, and fowls had so increased that they might begin to kill them with safety.

The boat being passed astern, Christian hove the ship to, called all hands together and told them his intentions.

"I have decided to run the ship ashore, and then burn her," he said.

Without hesitation every one agreed to abide by his decision. Then the sails of the *Bounty* were filled for the last time, and in a few minutes she was heading straight for the beach.

Every heart on board beat more quickly as the old ship neared the end of her life.

Christian, his eyes fixed upon a small rock which marked the centre of the little bay, stood at the helm. The act of severing this last link with the past almost unnerved him, and every moment of the ship's progress towards the breakers seemed like an hour. Whole years of time in the life that was now for ever gone raced swiftly in the current of his thoughts. But this, the end for him of all his past, so lingered in its fulfilment, that time after time he was on the point of throwing the ship aback, saving her from destruction before it was too late and giving him, felon as he was, a last chance to end his days, even though a fugitive, in a foreign land ; or he could return to England, and then—a disgraceful death. With the means of escape cut off perpetual exile faced him, and disseverance from all which was once dear.

A slight touch upon his arm, and Mahina stood looking into his face and reading his mind as clearly as if he had spoken aloud. With the gentle pressure of her hand, the look of unutterable love from the dark, tender eyes, his indecision was gone.

" Mahina," he said, " thou art right ; I was wavering. To all men this moment comes sometimes in their lives, and they often decide wrongly ; but between thee and what lieth beyond I should indeed be a fool to hesitate.

Her lips quivered ; bending her head over the wheel she kissed his hand, and her warm tears of silent sympathy nerved him anew.

A few seconds more, and with a voice as firm as though he were about to anchor the ship, Christian gave the word to let go the halliards and sheets, and, while the hissing of the boiling surf breaking across the entrance of the bay drowned the rattle of blocks and the flapping of canvas, the *Bounty* ploughed through the seas towards the shore. Wave after wave swept roaring past her on either side, their snowy summits running level with the tops of her bulwarks ; with slowness tormenting to her expectant crew, she gradually lost her way, struck the beach gently, ground a few feet of furrow in the glistening pebbles and sand, and then settled into her last resting-place with scarcely a quiver of her timbers.

CHAPTER XIX

WITH shouts of joy the Tahitians and Tubuaians, men and women alike, clambered from the bows of the ship to the beach ; the white men caught their enthusiasm, and they too, all but Christian, who remained with Mahina, jumped ashore, and for a while everything was forgotten but the one delightful truth that the weary quest for a resting-place was ended at last.

Christian, however, soon recalled them to the need for work. Before abandoning their old home it was necessary to build a new one. So the ship was made as secure as possible where she lay, and while the white men went to work to dismantle her, the brown people, with Christian and Mahina, set about selecting a site for their dwellings.

For the first few days after landing they lived in tents and such rough shelters as could be built with canvas and planks from the ship, and during this time a survey was made of the island. It was then by mutual consent divided into nine parts—one portion to each Englishman. As for the islanders, none of the white men, except Christian and Smith, seemed to think of them as having equal shares and rights in the undertaking; even Mahina seemed surprised that her husband should regard them as anything but servants and tillers of the soil. Finding that all the other seamen except Smith were determined against giving their brown associates any land whatever, Christian, after a few words of expostulation, withdrew all further opposition and let matters take their course, and the Tahitians and Tubuaians began to build houses and prepare land for planting.

But just as axes and hoes had been served out to the natives by McCoy and Young, and while the rest of Christian's comrades were present, the Tubuaian chief stepped out from among the natives, and fixing his eyes on the man Williams, who had especially resented the idea that land should be given them, he addressed Christian. He spoke very slowly and clearly, and even those of the mutineers whose knowledge of the Tubuaian language was limited, could grasp the meaning of his words.

"I, Tairoa-Maina, am a chief. In my own land of Tubuai, for me, a warrior and a man of good blood, to labour for others would be shameful and degrading. But I and Talalu, who is my friend, and of as good blood as myself, have no thoughts such as this now; our hearts are eaten up with love for Kirisiani and his wife Mahina, and for they alone do I and Talalu go forth to labour like slaves. Like myself, Kirisiani is a chief in his own land, that I well know.

And I know, oh men of Peretane, that there are some among you who have evil in your hearts."

"Cease, cease, my brother," said Mahina, taking the chief's hand. "Well do my husband and myself know that thou and Talalu are indeed friends to us ; but, I pray thee, make no bad blood between him and the other white men."

"You've always had too much to say," said Williams, advancing to Tairoa savagely with his hand upon his knife. Christian sprang upon him and gripped him by the wrist.

"Stand back, Williams. Raise your hand to that man and I'll choke you. Do you want to begin our new life by bloodshed ? Listen to me, and weigh well my words. I have long seen how you have tried to harass and thwart me in my endeavours for our common good ; of that which is passed I will think no more ; but, by the living God, do not attempt it again ! And do not seek to injure this man Tairoa-Maina, who has been a good friend to us all, and should in common justice have equal rights with ourselves."

With a look of bitter hatred, Williams sullenly turned away, and calling his wife Faito to follow him, left the others and took no further part in their discussions.

During the following week the *Bounty* was stripped of everything below and aloft, inside and outside ; even her planks were removed from her sides, and the copper, nails, bolts, and such useful articles carefully stored on shore, and nothing of her being left out of the water but the frame, she was set on fire. What remained of her charred hull was floated and sunk in the bay, which from that day the white men called Bounty Bay, and the Tubuaians *Te Moega te Pahi*—the resting-place of the ship.

Although Christian relinquished the command of his fellow adventurers as soon as they had landed, he was still tacitly recognised as their leader, and his advice sought and taken upon many matters. For some days the people lived in tents, and all, brown and white alike, worked at clearing the nine portions of land, and building thereon houses, the roofs of which were skilfully and quickly thatched by the women. For this they used the stiff leaves of the pandanus or screw-palm, which grew on the island in profusion, and yielded, in addition to its strong, useful timber and leaves, quantities of rich yellow fruit.

Mahina, always a favourite with the Tahitians, had now gained very great influence over them all, and Alrema, who was possessed of undaunted courage and iron resolution, was equally well-liked, and was a fitting mate for her husband, who, reckless as he was by nature, ifelt and yielded to the influence of his young and beautiful wife, whose easy manners and soft ways veiled, as he knew, a capacity for heroic deeds where her love for him was concerned or her jealousy or hatred was aroused. Unknown to Christian she had been, from the very day of their return to Tahiti, a silent force working both in his and her husband's interests to maintain their supremacy over the rest of the white men. Nothing escaped her keen observation ; danger to Christian, she knew, meant danger to Young, and she was quick to note and take heed of the slightest murmuring of disaffection, and to nullify it by inducing Christian, either through Mahina or Young, to make some concession.

Of Quintal and Williams she was especially distrustful. The former, once an ardent supporter of Christian, had of late begun to associate much with Williams, who was of a dangerous and savage disposition. Faito, his wife, was a tender, delicate girl, scarcely more than fifteen years of age ; but at a period when even the roughest and coarsest of men might have been expected to have shown her some tenderness and consideration, she received nothing but curses for her weakness and incapacity to attend fully to his wants.

" Perhaps," she one day said weepingly to Alrema and Mahina, as the three were plaiting thatch for the roof of a house, " perhaps he will again be the same to me when my child is born and I become strong again. But to-day he cursed me because, being wearied, I lay down for a little while, and he said that he was a fool to take such a weak thing as I to wife."

Alrema's eye flashed and her white teeth showed through her parted lips. " Aye, I heard the dog—and I heard more ; what said he of Malama, the wife of Kawintali (Quintal) ? "

Faito covered her face with her hands ; in an instant Mahina's arms were round her waist and her head pillowed upon Mahina's bosom.

"Nay, heed him not, Faito; Malama fears him, and never wilt thou be wronged by her."

The girl tried to smile through her tears. "It may be so; but to-day he said that 'twas Malama who should have been wife to him, for she is well and strong."

"Not so strong but that my knife shall eat into her heart if she comes between thy husband and thee," said Alrema fiercely. "Her husband is but a dull head where women are concerned; but thy husband is as cunning as a rat. And I know that they both are evilly disposed to Kirisiani and to my husband; they say this land of Afitā is too small for so many. By and by they shall have but a very small piece—so small indeed that a child may step across it."

With these ominous words Alrema went away; and so began to germinate the seeds of discontent and distrust, which later ripened to a deadly feud.

But for some little time matters went on well enough; even those who were secretly resentful of Christian's influence over their brown-skinned associates yet worked willingly enough for the common good, and performed the daily task allotted to them without murmuring.

Within three weeks, nine houses—one for each of the mutineers—were completed, and Christian one day announced that the next joint work would be to provide four similar dwellings, three for the Tahitians and their wives, and one for the three Tubuaians—who, being single men, would live together.

For some moments no one spoke—then Williams, who was sitting beside Quintal upon the bole of a large *toa* tree which had been felled for house-building, laid down his pipe, stood up, and confronted Christian.

"You don't expect us to build houses for these natives, do you, Mr. Christian?" he said, and Alrema, who stood near, noted the glance that passed between him and Quintal.

"Why should we not? Are not these people as good as ourselves? Have they not done thrice as much as we have in building our own dwellings?"

He spoke quietly, but there was a dangerous tone in his voice, and Young, Mahina, and Alrema, who knew now his slightest mood, looked with anxiety for what was to follow.

"I, for one, will be damned if I work for savages," said Quintal, rising and standing beside Williams.

"We didn't come here to work, Mr. Christian," joined in Mills, the gunner's mate, gloomily; "I think these fellows ought to work for us, and not we for them."

"You are all pretty much of this opinion?" asked Christian slowly, with an inquiring glance, and in a savagely contemptuous tone of voice.

A quick and angry murmur of assent came from all but Young and Smith, who quietly walked apart from the others and stood beside Christian.

Then Smith, after a whispered word with Alrema and his own wife, Terere, stepped out in front.

"I, for one, sir, will lend a hand right willingly. Give your orders, Mr. Christian, and I'll obey them."

This brought no remark from the rest, and Young drawing his comrade aside, said quietly, "My dear Christian, what is the use of sneering at the men in this fashion. It is scarcely likely that British seamen —damned lazy dogs they are, too—could be induced to work side by side with island savages ; and your manner of asking them invited their refusal."

Pushing aside Young's restraining hand, Fletcher Christian turned to the group of seamen, and, with flashing eyes and voice trembling with rage and contempt, said—

"Have your own way ; I have done with the lot of you, and am glad to be clear of you. For your own sakes I have, so far, kept control. If I led you into mutiny I stood by you and brought you to a place of safety. I can die or live here —I care nothing which way it is. But understand this : I will be no party to making slaves of men whom I look upon as equal to myself—and superior to such damned soldiers as you. Go to hell, the whole lot of you, in your own way !" Then he walked rapidly away, followed by the trembling Mahina, and the unmoved, undaunted Alrema.

As soon as he had disappeared among the palm-groves, Talalu, who understood enough English to comprehend the nature of the discussion that had taken place, turned to Young, and said in Tahitian—

"Do not quarrel about this matter, Etuati. There are plenty of us to build houses. Our hands are strong and our hearts are not made sore because these our friends think we alone should work on Afitā. Come, my countrymen, let us to work. Never must angry words come between us and the white men."

A cheerful assent was the response; the natives shouldered their axes and, followed by Tairoa and the others, walked off in single file towards a clump of *toa* trees.

"Why, damn it all," said Mills, with a coarse laugh, "those fellows have more sense than Christian! *They* know well enough that we ain't the sort to work for them. Why, it's agin' nature."

For a few days after this nothing occurred to widen the breach. The Tahitians worked with a will, lightening their labours with many a song and merry jest; for they were by nature an amiable and kindly-hearted people, full to overflowing of the most generous instincts and noble impulses, and their devotion to Christian and his beautiful wife was sufficient reason for them to toil unrepiningly for the rest of the white men; to their simple minds, those who sought to oppress them were of Christian's race and, as such, had a claim upon them. But underneath all their present content there was yet a hidden current of dissatisfaction which only the quick mind of Alrema had fathomed, and she was a woman who meant to make use of it when the time came. So, while the white seamen lay in their houses and ate and drank and were waited upon by their obedient Tahitian wives, the brown men let the white slowly but surely assume

the rights of masters over them, and uncomplainingly
became hewers of wood and drawers of water.

At night when the fires were blazing and the
rude lamps brought from the ship were lighted, the
islanders would assemble in front of the white men's
houses ; and with the wives of the mutineers (except
Alrema and Mahina) sing old Tahitian songs such as
the *Bounty's* people had heard in the days when their
ship floated on the placid waters of Matavai Bay.
Sometimes, when the sea was smooth, men and women
together would go down to the ledges of the cliffs
and fish in the deep waters at their base, returning
home laden with many a weighty basket. Tairoa-
Maina and his two countrymen had already made a
canoe, and the marvellous ingenuity with which it
was constructed with such rough tools—for they had
but axes and knives and a few chisels— aroused the
admiration even of the lazy Englishmen. The houses
of the white men, too, were monuments of the untiring
patience and skill of the Tahitians. Built of the
timber of breadfruit and *toa*, and thatched beautifully
with the russet-coloured leaves of the pandanus palm,
oblong in shape, they bore an almost exact resemblance, inside and out, to the dwellings in Tahiti
and Tubuai. Their furniture was nearly all of native
pattern, and consisted in each house of the owner's
share of the spoils from the *Bounty*, with rough
wooden stools and benches made from the wood of
the breadfruit, *toa* or *tamanu* tree. The floors were
first of all laid out with about a foot of smooth, sea-
worn pebbles, brought by the women in baskets from

the little beach where the ship was run ashore, and then covered over with coarse mats of coconut leaf. Over this was spread finer matting made from the pandanus leaf, and over this again squares of canvas cut from the *Bounty's* sails. Upon this a thick layer of still finer mats, brought from Tahiti, was placed, and this formed the beds of the occupants.

The long months spent at sea upon the ship had greatly changed the habits and customs of the Tahitians, until in some things there was but little difference between them and their white associates—or rather masters. But now that they were both once more on land the Englishmen were glad to adopt, in their turn, many of the ways of the natives, and so the two races gradually acquired from each other such new habits and modes of life as were best suited to their altered state.

To their white husbands the Tahitian women were always considerate and dutiful ; they ministered to the men's wants so skilfully that the rough sailors found their days slip by in the greatest ease and comfort, and had some sort of selfish affection for their wives. It was contrary to the custom of Tahiti for the women to eat with the men, or even to drink out of the same utensils as their husbands, or partake of food which had been either handled or prepared by the superior sex; and in this respect the laws of custom proved too strong to be broken, even though their husbands good-humouredly urged them to do so, they were quite content to wait upon their lords and masters and eat by themselves afterwards. But

Christian, Young, and Smith, who regarded their
wives as something better than mere chattels or
objects of selfish passion, tried hard to combat this
custom, and in some degree succeeded ; so that
Mahina, Alrema, and Terere all abandoned the
Tahitian habit of one regular meal on rising, and
taking food and drink at infrequent intervals during
the remainder of the day, and prepared and ate meals
in the English fashion.

Although no longer on more than terms of ordi-
nary civility with the rest of the white men, other
than Young and Smith, Christian would come in the
evenings sometimes from his house to exchange a few
words with them as they sat outside upon the grassy
sward before their dwellings listening to the Tahitians
as they sang and chanted or played music upon their
reed *vivos*.[1] When they were tired of singing, the
happy monotony of the long nights would be relieved
by the brown women, who, like all Polynesians, were
born story-tellers, with tales of their early childhood,
the old traditions and legends of their island homes,
and about the marvellous origin and great deeds of
their ancestors. Fabulous and absurd as was much
even of their history—for it was so interwoven with
their wild mythology that the seamen merely heard
it with a good-natured smile of contempt—there was
yet enough of truth in it to interest Christian and
Young ; and their attention pleased the wives of the
seamen greatly, and indeed helped to sow the seeds
of indifference towards their husbands, who they now

[1] Flutes of three notes.

began to perceive were men in intelligence far below the one-time officers of the *Bounty*.

But even the rough seamen could not fail to be amused at some of the early Tahitian notions of England. For instance, they had somehow acquired the idea—perhaps from travellers' tales of early voyages—that England was once a large island, the centre of which was made of iron; but continuous wars with other nations had resulted in all the outside soil being shot away with cannon balls till there was nothing left but a solid mass of iron. It was also believed that there were ships in England forty leagues long with masts so high that they pierced beyond the clouds, and that a young man in full health and strength going to the masthead grew grey before he reached the deck again; while on the great round tops of the lower masts were rich gardens of fruit, in which men lived.

Another story told how the captain of an English ship of war, which carried so many cannons that it took one man a year to count them, was incensed at the conduct of the people of a certain island; so that hooking one of the ship's anchors to a mountain, he set sail, tore the island from its foundations, and towed it away to the region of cold, where the people perished. But although these tales were believed by their narrators, they would not accept the white men's stories of stone houses many feet high and of rivers crossed by bridges of stone with no support underneath.

As time wore on, some of the women began to

adopt the semi-European style of clothing ; and this while it did not become them so well as their own native dress, yet pleased their husbands and showed the women's desire to render themselves attractive in the white men's eyes.

CHAPTER XX

GLOOMY and melancholy as ever, since the day of the mutiny Christian had gradually allowed his bitter thoughts so utterly to overcome him that even towards Mahina he showed cruel indifference. For days a word would not escape his lips, save when his wife put some direct question to him concerning his movements or intentions ; and both Young and Smith, attached to him as they were, now ceased their evening visits entirely. Sometimes, when the fires were lit after sunset, Mahina—her dark eyes filled with tears—would watch her husband go to the door of their little dwelling, stand there for a minute or two lost in thought, and walk silently away along the edge of the cliffs. Often when she would have accompanied him, he quietly, but yet firmly, pushed her hand aside, and with an impatient exclamation quickened his steps so as to be away from her the sooner. Hour after hour would pass while Mahina, weeping softly to herself, sat outside awaiting her husband's return. Sometimes her solitude would be broken by the gigantic Talalu,

whose dog-like devotion to Christian led him to
leave his own house and join her in her saddened
watch.

Early one morning Mahina, accompanied by Alrema
and Talalu, set out for a day's ramble in the wild,
mountainous interior of the island ; Christian, scarcely
noting her absence, left the house a few hours later for
his solitary haunts on the high cliffs. About sunset he
returned, and the moment his figure appeared over the
ridge behind which the little house was situated,
Mahina ran to meet him with outstretched hands, her
face radiant with childish joy. Placing her hand on
her husband's arm she told him in excited tones that
she and Talalu had found traces of her ancestors in
many places on the southern portion of the island.

Flinging down his musket, Christian seated himself
on the low, rough seat erected by the side of his
dwelling, and for some moments seemed quite
oblivious of Mahina's presence. At last, however,
in answer to her continued exclamations of delight,
he replied bitterly—

" Trouble me not with such things, Mahina. What
care I who lived here in the past ? The misery of
living in the present is enough for me," and so
saying he buried his face in his hands.

The savage energy in his voice made her tremble at
first, but the indifferent manner in which he treated
the news of her discovery touched her to the quick,
and she blazed out in hot anger—

" Thou cruel Kirisiani ! What have we who love
thee done that thou shouldst cease to care for us ?

What have I, thy wife, done that thou shouldst so answer when I speak to thee ? Were I a slave thou couldst not insult me more than thou hast done."

Christian merely shrugged his shoulders, rose and walked back towards the cliffs, although food had been prepared for him by his disheartened wife.

Brushing away the tears that would still come, Mahina entered the silent house, put out the lamp, and seated herself before the dimly-burning fire, wondering what it was that had so changed her husband's manner towards her and, indeed, to every one else. That he was engaged in working alone on one of the highest spots on the island she knew, for he had taken tools with him from time to time ; but where the spot was and what was the nature of his toil she could not even guess. He had sternly forbidden her to follow him, and even Talalu dared not attempt to discover his retreat.

So for many days Talalu and Mahina contented themselves with talking over their discoveries with Tairoa-Maina, who himself a descendant of the now extinct people of Afitā, of course took a keen interest in all that related to his ancestors.

Taking some food with them, the three one day set out to make further explorations. On the eastern side of the island some rocks were discovered among a dense, scrubby thicket, through which they had to cut their way with seamen's cutlasses brought for the purpose ; on the faces of these rocks were rude drawings of birds, fishes, turtle, and of the sun, moon and stars, besides what Tairoa-Maina said was

a chart of the islands in the surrounding ocean, showing the track to be taken by a canoe in voyaging
among them.   At another spot, not far from the high
cathedral-shaped rock on the south-east point, they
found in a cave numbers of stone spear and arrow-
heads.   Many of these were unused implements, and
the cave in which they were found had evidently been
a storehouse for food as well as an armoury ; for in its
earthen floor were a number of pits which had once
been silos for the storage of breadfruit, yams, and other
food.   Almost in the centre of the island, Tairoa one
day came across the very burial-places of his and
Mahina's forefathers.   Round this cemetery were
a number of rude images of human figures, and huge
squared blocks of stone lay about in profusion.

At evening they returned home, full of the im-
portant discoveries they had made, and would again
have spoken to Christian on the subject, but that his
distant manner forbade them.

As the days passed this moroseness so grew upon
him that there was little doubt his mind had become
diseased, and about a week after Mahina's discoveries
in the mountains he began to absent himself from her
for two or three days together.

Unknown even to his tender and devoted wife,
he had furnished a roomy cave situated in a mountain
recess on the opposite side of the island.   It was his
intention, he afterwards told Mahina, to hide in this
cavern should a ship of war by any chance arrive.   He
had stocked it with provisions and water, and arms and
ammunition, so that he might defend himself to the

last in case of discovery, for he swore that he would never be taken alive.

The completion of his hiding-place seemed to please him somewhat, and he now at times was more sociable with the other white men when by chance he passed their dwellings or met any of them in his lonely walks; and sometimes, to their great joy, he would join Talalu and the other natives in a fishing excursion. Then, as she saw him ascending the cliffs towards their home, Mahina's face would brighten, and she and her girl friends would eagerly welcome him, and instantly prepare to cook the fish he brought.

For some little time matters went on without change in Christian's home till towards the close of the year an event occurred which temporarily roused him from his lethargy. This was the birth of his first child—a boy.

To Mahina's great happiness, her husband consented that the customs of her race should be observed, and at her request he went away to his cave to remain there till the child was born.

In the meantime, under the direction of Quintal's wife, the oldest Tahitian woman present, the others prepared in the centre of the great room a sort of bower of leaves and fine matting. Upon its floor was placed a heap of heated stones, which were constantly replaced by others as they cooled. Upon the stones were thrown great bunches of such sweet-smelling herbs and flowers as the island afforded, and these were from time to time sprinkled with water, so that the house was kept filled with the perfume of the herbs.

In this bower Mahina remained till the birth of her
infant ; and then Christian was waited upon by the
other women and asked what *amua* (gifts) he had
ready for the child.

Having been previously instructed by Quintal's
wife, he replied—

" This is all that I, Kirisiani of Peretane, have for
mine and Mahina's infant, for it is all that this land of
Afitā yields," and he placed in their hands small quantities of breadfruit, *taro*, and such other fruits as grew
on Pitcairn. This was all that was expected of him,
and the women went away pleased that he had allowed
them to follow their native customs so far. In Tahiti
it was the practice for a woman to live some weeks
with her new-born infant in the sacred grounds of the
maraes or temples of Oro and Tane, in order that
the favour of the gods might be assured for the child's
future. But under the influence of their white husbands the women of Pitcairn had abandoned much of
their religious ceremonies, and so this one was not
observed by Mahina, on the plea that, although they
had found a *marae* on the island, there was nothing to
show that it had been built by worshippers of Oro and
Tane, but really because she knew that Christian
disliked her clinging to Tahitian customs.

After Christian had presented his gifts, he was
followed by all the others, each person bringing an
amua either of food, live stock, clothing or matting.
These were deposited at the mother's feet, and the
ceremonies were concluded.

To Mahina's delight Christian remained constantly

with her for some weeks after this event ; his manner
to her and the infant was gentle and kind, and she now
began to hope that her husband's former affection for
her had not entirely died away.   Poor girl, she was
soon undeceived.

One evening she and her friends were at one end of
the room silently toying with the infant ; Young,
Smith, and Christian were sitting smoking on the
bench outside.   The evening was wonderfully clear
and still and, but for the ceaseless throbbing of the
surf upon the cliffs below, no sound disturbed the
silence.

Presently she heard Young's voice addressing her
husband, and (for she now spoke English fairly well
and understood it still better) listened to hear what
they were saying.

"What do you intend to call the boy ?" asked
Young.   "Will you name him after yourself ? "

" No," answered Christian, with intense contempt ;
" do you think that I will let the little savage per-
petuate his father's name and shame ?   She can call the
brat by any name she pleases, except mine."

Both Young and Smith were silent, and the latter
looked troubled.   Attached as he was to Christian, he
felt that Mahina's steady devotion had deserved better
of her husband.

" You are a strange man, Christian," said Young,
presently ; and calling Alrema he took her by the
hand and led her away, giving Christian only a curt
" good-night."   He was soon followed by Terere and
her husband ; Christian remained alone outside, lost

in thought, and heard nothing of a soft sobbing within.

Midnight was long past when he rose and went inside. He thought Mahina was asleep, but just as he laid his head upon the pillow he felt her hand upon his forehead.

" Kirisiani, I heard thee speak to-night. Not all did I understand ; only this—that thou dost despise thy child, and wilt not give him thy name."

" Call it by some Tahitian name, Mahina ; 'tis not an English child."

" True," she answered brokenly ; " but yet 'tis thy child, and his eyes are thy eyes; and when I look into his face I see thy eyes looking into mine, as they did when thy heart was warm with love for me, its mother. And for this do I desire to call it by a name of thy tongue and by no other."

" Very well," he answered, after a moment's thought, " have your own way—stay, I have a name for it. It was born upon a Thursday in October. Call it Thursday October, for "—and his voice grew hard and sneering—"'tis the way they name negro children in the West Indies. It is only fitting that this little savage should have some such name."

And Mahina, not understanding the full meaning of his words, called her first-born by the name given it by her husband.

CHAPTER XXI

ALL day long, from the red blush of sunrise till the mantle of the quick, tropic night enshrouded the lonely island, thousands upon thousands of sea-birds circled round the high mountain peaks and vine-covered crags of Afitā, and filled the air with their wild clamour. At one place, where the grim cliffs started sheer upward from the crashing surf, they had made their rookeries upon a series of narrow ledges which traversed the face of the rock in undulating lines from the summit. The highest of these ledges was perhaps fifty feet from the scrub-covered edge of the precipice; the lowest just out of the reach of the drenching spray that in stormy weather sprang upward in misty showers from the wild commotion of the waves beneath.

Here, with faces turned seaward, the great black frigate birds and the blue-billed *kanápu*, with many other species of ocean rangers, sat upon their eggs and hatched their young, and the weird cries of the fledglings mingled with the hoarse, croaking notes of the parent birds all through the night, and were borne

in strange, mournful cadences and mysterious quaver-
ings through the darkened forest to the dwellings of
the mutineers and their brown-skinned associates.

The eggs of these birds were much relished by
the white men, and it was one of the duties of their
patient wives to hazard their lives along the line of cliffs
in collecting them. Sure-footed and agile, the women
would sometimes be lowered by their companions
above to the perilous ledges full fifty feet down, fill
their baskets with eggs, and be hauled up again in
safety, thinking nothing of the dreadful death that
awaited them if the rope parted or they became over-
whelmed with giddiness. The topmost ledge, where
the fierce-eyed frigate birds had made their rookery,
could be reached by clambering down the cliff and
along its jagged face.

For two or three days great numbers of these sea-
birds had been seen flying swiftly towards the island
from the eastward, and the Tahitians understood that
the breeding season drew near, and that very shortly
the female birds would be sitting.

Early one morning Faito, the gentle, delicate-featured
wife of the coarse and brutal Williams, set out along
the edge of the cliffs to see if the frigate birds had
begun to lay. She was alone. Heart-broken as she
was at her husband's cruel conduct, her loving nature
impelled her to venture her life upon the cliffs, so that
she might be the first to bring the much-coveted eggs
to her savage master.

Presently, as she walked along, softly singing to herself some chant of her Tahitian childhood, a pretty

black and white kid—the progeny of one of the goats brought to the island in the *Bounty*—sprang out from the dense thicket scrub which bordered the mountain path, and darted along the edge of the precipice.

The cry of delight that escaped from Faito at the prospect of catching the animal reached the ears of Talalu, who was some few hundred yards away, cutting down a *toa* tree.

"Take care, take care, Faito," he cried, as the girl sped swiftly along, her black hair streaming behind her, her dark eyes glowing, and her bare bosom panting in the excitement of pursuit—for she knew that the capture of the kid would at least bring a pleasant word from Williams; then, ere Talalu could shout another warning, her flying feet caught in a creeper, and without a cry she pitched headlong over the cliffs, with the sound of happy laughter yet upon her lips.

Dashing through the thick scrub, Talalu reached the edge of the precipice and looked over; there, on a little pebbly beach, hollowed out in the face of a chasm in the cliffs, he saw the dead and bleeding body of Faito lying upon the stones.

This was the prologue to a bloody tragedy yet to be enacted on Pitcairn.

Clambering down to the bottom of the cliffs by a devious and dangerous route, Talalu at last gained the spot where the body of the dead girl lay. He took it tenderly in his arms and pressed his face to hers, with streaming eyes and sobs of pity, then slowly and laboriously began the perilous ascent.

It was noon when he reached the settlement.

Williams and Quintal were sitting together in front of the former's house when the Tahitian drew near with his burden.

"What the hell's the matter now?" asked the dead woman's husband roughly, when he saw his wife's figure lying in Talalu's brawny arms; then, brute though he was, his dark features paled when her countryman turned Faito's dead face towards him.

"Thy wife is dead, oh worker of iron. She sought to catch a kid, thinking to please thee. She tripped and fell—and died."

Gently laying the body down upon the couch or mats, he walked away without a word.

The tidings of Faito's death soon brought the rest of the white men's wives to Williams' house, sobbing as they ran. The first to fling herself weeping upon the cold bosom of the dead girl was Nahi, the wife of Talalu. She was a tall, slenderly built woman, with big, passionate eyes, although she had the gentle, timid manner of a child. Seating herself by the body of the girl, Nahi first pressed her lips to the cold face of her friend, and then in whispered tones directed the others in their ministrations to the dead. Towards sunset, as they moved to and fro in the great room of the house, a figure darkened the doorway and Williams' harsh voice broke in upon the silence.

"Hallo, Nahi," he said in English, without even glancing at the shrouded figure upon the floor, "how are you? It's not often I catch a sight of you—and, by God! you're too pretty a woman not to see often."

Slowly Nahi rose to her feet. She understood every

word that was said to her, yet curbed her anger, and
with downcast eyes and trembling hands answered him
in Tahitian.

"We come, Iron-worker, to mourn for Faito, thy
wife."

Something in her voice, and in her trembling, yet
indignant attitude, made the callous-hearted man turn
away without a further word. He stepped to the
door, stood there irresolutely for a moment, and then
disappeared into the darkness.

All through the night the mourning watchers sat
beside the dead girl; at dawn the brown men dug her
grave in the garden, some distance from the back of
Williams' dwelling. Just as the sun became level with
the summit of the cliffs and shot its bright darts
through the leafy forest aisles, the little funeral pro-
cession gathered round the grave, and Faito's body,
lying upon a bier covered with garlands and wreaths of
flowers and leaves, was placed beside it. Then, one by
one, each of the men and women brought offerings of
food and young drinking coconuts and placed them by
the bier, for to them the girl's soul was hovering near,
and her body would need refreshment on its long
journey to the world beyond. Nahi (who was not
only a devoted friend of Faito, but a distant blood-
relation as well), seated herself beside the grave, and in
her soft Tahitian tongue, chanted stories of the dead
girl's life; she sang of her innocent childhood, of her
deep affection for her parents; of her loving, gentle
nature; of her soft, tender beauty; of her love for
the white iron-worker, and her voyage with him in

the *Bounty*. And then the singer's soul seemed to quicken, and her voice quivered and broke as she told the story of Faito's death; and from those who sat around came quick, responsive sobs of grief.

When she ceased the women took keen-edged sharks' teeth, and thrust them into their arms and shoulders till the blood poured forth, while the men covered their faces with their hands, and bent their heads to the ground.

For nearly an hour they sat thus, then in silence the men rose and walked quietly away, leaving the women to mourn by themselves, in accordance with Tahitian custom, for two days beside the grave.

That night Mahina, who was alone in the house with her child, sought out Christian in his cave, where he had been for the past two ·days, and told him of Faito's death.

"Her troubles are over," was his moody answer. "Would that I had the courage to leap over the cliffs and so end mine. But why come and tell me this? It concerns me not."

"She was ever my friend," answered Mahina, gently, "my friend and thine. I pray thee come mourn with me at her burial, else will shame fall upon me if thou art absent."

He raised his dark face to hers, and an angry gleam shone in his eyes. "I tell thee, Mahina, thou dost but pester me. The woman is dead. Would I were in her place."

"Thou cruel man," she said, and the tears fell quickly from her eyes as she pressed her child to her bosom, "thou art always in this strange mood now. Alas! what evil has happened to thee and me? What wicked spirit has turned thy heart against us? Art thou tired of thy wife? Is thy child, born to thee out of my great love, hateful to thy sight?" Then the infant awoke, and she pressed it to her aching breast to soothe its cries.

Christian sprang up from the matted couch upon which he lay, and with the light of madness in his eyes, cursed her, her child, and himself. "Go," he said at last, hoarsely, "go, leave me to my misery."

CHAPTER XXII

MAHINA went alone to the burial of her friend, and the other women, when they saw her, knew that her sorrow was not so much for the dead girl as for the dead love of Christian.

Returning from her husband's cave, she met Edward Young, who spoke so kindly that her overwrought feelings brought a flood of tears, and Young, with a strange look, had drawn her to him and bidden her be of good courage. He would always be her friend, he said, and it grieved him to see her sad. And Mahina, drying her tears, pressed his hand gratefully, and in her innocent fashion placed her cheek against his for a moment ; for was he not her husband's friend and brother, and therefore hers. And Edward Young, as she walked away, watched her with a smile on his lips, and muttered to himself—

" The man is a fool. She is a glorious creature, and I—well I don't suppose *he* cares."

On the second morning, long ere the sun had dried

14   193

the glittering diamonds of dew trembling on every leaf and blade of grass, Williams came across the greensward towards his wife's grave and addressed the mourning women.

"Come now," he said roughly. "Faito's had enough of this foolery, and so have I. Put her in the ground, and make an end of it."

Then Talalu and his countrymen stepped quietly out from beneath the shade of a great *tamanu* tree which stood near. They had brought their final offerings to the dead, and as they placed these at the foot of the grave, all the rest of the white men but Christian appeared upon the scene.

At the harsh command of Williams, the women huddled timidly together, looking fearfully at one another; and Talalu, leaving his countrymen, softly besought the man to allow them to continue their funeral customs, so that the spirit of Faito might rest in peace. Mahina, too, joined in his pleadings.

To the brown-skinned people Williams had ever been a cruel taskmaster for whom they worked without murmuring for the sake of his wife, whom they loved; and now that she was dead he seemed to care nothing, and would not even permit them to "comfort her spirit."

The remaining white men looked on in curious silence, while Talalu and Mahina begged Williams not to interrupt them. Williams had, however, acquired a certain influence over his countrymen, and they were not disposed to interfere.

Again the harsh voice of the man bade the

mourners cease. " Let this folly end," he said
angrily in Tahitian ; " begone, and get back to
work."

The words stung Talalu to the quick, and with
flashing eyes and clenched hands he faced the white
man.

" Thou dog without a heart ! " he cried fiercely,
" may thy mother's skin be made into a water-
bottle ! Not content with our service and thy wife's
devotion, thou would'st harrow the soul of the dead
with thy harsh and cruel voice. Shame on thee for
a pitiless man ! Go home and leave us with the body
and the spirit of our kinswoman. She is nothing to
thee now. Thou canst not harm her body, but her
spirit is tormented by thy very presence here."

With a furious gesture Williams advanced towards
him, cursing him for an impudent slave, in the coarse
language he always used towards the Tahitians.

But quick as lightning Mahina intercepted him.

" Stop, thou low-born sailor," she said, " and leave
us, as Talalu hath desired thee, or it will go ill with
thee ! I swear by Oro and Tane and the bones of
my father to stab thee to the heart if thou dost but
even raise thy hand to Talalu."

Callous as the white men were, they drew back
and muttered to Williams to leave her and her fellow-
mourners alone ; and Williams himself blanched before
the slight figure of Christian's wife, and with a savage
threat of vengeance against Talalu, turned away, followed by the rest of the mutineers except Young.
He, walking apart from them, seated himself on the

trunk of a fallen tree near by, called Alrema, and told
her to hasten to his house and bring his fowling-piece,
as he intended to shoot some sea-birds.

As soon as her graceful figure disappeared among
groves of breadfruit between the grassy sward and the
houses of the white men, Young walked over to where
Mahina sat, apart from the others.

"Dear friend of my heart," he said, taking her
hand, "thou knowest that I am thy friend, dost thou
not?"

"Truly," said Mahina, "always my friend—my
friend and my brother, and the friend and brother
of my husband."

A disappointed look swept over Young's face, and
he dropped her hand moodily. "Nay, not so now.
It is always in my heart that he whom I once loved
as a brother hath acted cruelly to thee. Thou art a
woman fair and sweet, and to be for ever loved. And
because he hath neglected and turned his heart away
from thee and thy love hath my friendship for him
grown smaller and smaller day by day."

"By and by, when the evil moods have left him, he
will love me again," said Mahina, looking straight
before her, and as she spoke, the falling tears belied
her hopeful words.

For many minutes they sat thus, she weeping softly
to herself, and Young watching his opportunity to
speak again. Presently he saw Alrema returning with
his fowling-piece. He rose and touched Mahina
lightly on the shoulder.

"Farewell till to-morrow," he said in a low voice.

"Remember that I am always, always thy friend—
and that I love thee—*he* no longer does."

She looked up with a low, startled cry, and hastily
rising from her seat, went over to the other women
and took her child from Terere. The tone of Young's
words had filled her with a strange feeling of misery
and fear.

CHAPTER XXIII

FOR some time nothing happened to disturb the uneventful life of the islanders. Mahina, with aching heart, saw Christian daily grow more melancholy and morose, and was heedless of all else. But as the year drew to a close her saddened face and sorrowful eyes must have touched her husband's heart, and when the birth of her second child was drawing near he left the cave and dwelt with her till the infant was born and she was strong again.

"Call him Charles," he said to her as she sat with with him one evening nursing the infant ; and the words, simple as they were, filled her still loving heart with a great joy. Twice only had she met Young since the day of Faito's burial, and though he had tried to detain her, she managed to get away from him ; for she now felt that he cared for her more than his loyalty to Alrema justified.

During the same year others of the mutineers became fathers. In addition to Mahina's two there were now three other children playing upon the

matted floors of their parents' dwellings by day, and
lulled to sleep at night by the ceaseless throbbing
of the surf that beat against the stern cliffs of their
island home.

The houses occupied by Christian and Mahina,
Young and Alrema, and Smith and Terere were a
considerable distance from those of the other white
men. That of Christian was furthest north-west of
all ; indeed, it was quite shut out of view from the rest
by a short, abrupt spur which shot eastward from the
mountains almost to the verge of the beetling cliffs.

Williams and Young lived near to each other.
Some months after the burial of Faito the former
called upon his neighbour and asked him to come
outside for a few minutes. Alrema, who had noticed
that her husband and Williams were becoming very
intimate, gave the visitor an angry glance from her
dark, long-lashed eyes, as he sat upon the bench in
front of the house.

" Let's go for a bit of a walk," said Williams presently as Young joined him ; " I want to have a talk
with you over that little matter " ; and he laughed
coarsely, and by a gesture indicated his own dwelling.

Young nodded, and Alrema saw the two men
saunter off together along the cliffs. She had always
disliked Williams, and thought he was in some way
responsible for her husband's manner to herself, which
had so altered of late. Passionately fond of, and
fiercely jealous of him, her quick perception of the
change in his conduct filled her with a vague, undefined alarm ; and although as yet she did not doubt

his loyalty, she had seen how his face brightened
visibly whenever Mahina and her child came to visit
them. Of Mahina herself she had no misgivings;
but it seemed strange that whereas in former days she
had always accompanied Young to Christian's house,
he now frequently went there alone, although she had
told him that Christian was in his cave. Mahina, too,
seemed different, and her face wore a troubled, nervous
look which her friend could not understand.

After the birth of his second child Christian remained, for a time, constantly with his beautiful
wife, whose face grew radiant with happiness. But
soon his brooding mood returned to him in all its
former force, and he resumed his lonely walks along
the cliffs and spent his nights alone in his mountain
cave. Mahina, Alrema knew, had long since resigned
herself to her husband's fits of gloom, yet now she
appeared more than ever a prey to melancholy. In
some way Williams seemed to be connected with this,
and Alrema noticed that whenever Young went to
Christian's house Williams had preceded him there.

Taking up her infant daughter in her arms, Alrema
went outside and sat down under the shade of a breadfruit tree to wait her husband's return. For nearly an
hour she amused herself playing with the child, till,
overpowered by the soft, languorous morning air, she,
pillowing her head upon a rolled-up mat, slept.

The sun was high when she was awakened by
hearing voices near. She at once recognised Williams'
harsh, and her husband's cool, quiet tones. As they
talked they were passing through the breadfruit grove

and stopped quite close to where she lay. Williams was speaking.

"Well, that's understood. You stand by me and I'll stand by you. I'm going to get the woman I want if I have to shoot every damned red-skinned savage on the island to get her."

"I'm not going in for anything like that," she heard her husband reply; "I am quite content to wait till——"

"Till that lunatic jumps over the cliffs and leaves a widow for you," said Williams, with a coarse laugh. "Well, you've got more patience than me. If I wanted her I'd make just as short a job of him as I mean to make of this Talalu. Anyway, I'm going to set you a good example by taking another wife. Man alive! what are you afraid of? She'll be willing enough before long to come to you. She ain't the kind of woman to stay by herself while her husband leaves her to live in a cave. I daresay," he added, with another rude laugh, "that Alrema would lend you a hand to talk her over. That's what I'd have made Faito do."

An angry exclamation of dissent from Young, and Alrema heard him leave his companion and go towards the house. Then, her brain reeling with dreadful suspicions of the man she loved and the friend she trusted, she took up her sleeping infant and followed him.

Williams, with a wicked look upon his evil face, strode away towards his own dwelling. He had managed to secure one of the best and most fertile portions of the nine lots into which the island was divided, and by his domineering conduct succeeded in making the islanders perform more labour in its cultivation than they expended upon any other of the mutineers' land. As he drew near his plantation he saw the gigantic figure of Talalu and the slender, graceful form of Nahi, his gentle wife, moving about in the garden. They were building a low wall of coral stones to enclose the plantation, and Williams' eyes gleamed savagely as he saw Nahi, who had just placed a stone in position, look up at her husband's face with a smile, to which Talalu responded with an endearing expression and a loving caress.

The white man stood for a while watching them. The woman's lithe, supple figure, her bared bosom and long mantle of black hair falling over her rounded shoulders fascinated and yet irritated his savage, sensuous nature. "That fellow, that cursed, great hulking brute to possess such a woman! And he only a slave!" He watched her white teeth gleam, as her lips parted in an admiring smile, when Talalu, raising a huge, jagged stone in his brawny arms, placed it lightly upon the smaller one her slender hands had lifted.

Williams sat and waited. He knew that at noontime they would cease working for an hour to rest and wait upon him while he ate his mid-day meal. And then he meant to act.

Presently, Talalu, glancing up at the sun, spoke to Nahi. They ceased their labours, and walked towards their own little dwelling of thatch. Outside stood a hollowed tree trunk filled with water. Then Williams

saw Nahi, dropping the garment of tappa-cloth which
encircled her waist, deftly replace it by a girdle of
leaves, then her husband taking a cocoanut shell,
dipped it into the water and poured it over her
shoulders again and again to wash away the dust
which stained her clear, bronzed skin. Nude to the
hips, her lissome figure glinted and shone like a
polished statue of metal in the bright morning sun, as
the water ran down over her back, bosom, and legs,
while her shapely arms were raised as she held up her
glossy mantle of hair. Her bath finished, she took
the coconut shell from her husband's hand and
motioned him to stoop ; but Talalu, with gentle,
jesting rudeness, pushed her away, and filling the
shell poured stream after stream of the cooling water
over his own body.

"That's the last time you'll ever do that for her,"
said Williams to himself, as his lustful eyes revelled in
the beauty of the girl's figure. He got up, went
inside and threw himself upon his couch. They
would be in presently, he knew, to bring him his
dinner of yams, fish, and birds' eggs.

Nahi came first. In one hand she carried a platter
of woven coconut leaves, upon which were a baked
fish and some roasted breadfruit, in the other a young
drinking coconut. Outside, Talalu, thrusting a pointed
stake into the ground, began to husk some more nuts
for the white man to drink.

"*Haeri mai*" ("Come here"), his master called.

The Tahitian's huge figure stood in the doorway,
holding a half-husked coconut in his hand.

"You needn't do any work to-day, Talalu," said Williams, with a growl of apparent good nature. "Tetihiti and Nihu are going out fishing for Kawintali (Quintal). You may go with them. Nahi can stay. Malama (Quintal's wife) will be here soon with her husband, and she can help Nahi to work upon the mat she is making for the floor."

"Good," answered the unsuspecting Tahitian, with a pleased smile; "'tis well, oh Iron-worker, that the mat be soon finished. Then will Nahi and I carry up many baskets of fine pebbles, so that the mat may rest flat and even on the ground."

"May you be lucky in your fishing," called Nahi, as her husband, a minute later, passed the door, carrying his basket of fishing tackle. Then, the white man's meal being in readiness, she took up a fan and stood by him while he ate.

For some minutes he ate his food in silence, then motioned to the woman to come nearer. She obeyed him with a timid glance, and a slight tremor quivered her bare shoulders for a moment.

Suddenly Williams pushed his stool back from the table. Fixing his eyes on Nahi's expectant face, he said to her in English—

"Nahi, my girl, I've always had a fancy for you, and I want you. You're going to be my new wife."

With a look of wild terror she shrank back, her hands covering her face. The next instant the man seized her by the wrists.

"Come, now, none of that, Nahi! I'm going to have you for my wife, so don't be a fool."

"Let me go," she pleaded in Tahitian ; "how can I be wife to thee? Am I not wife to Talalu? 'Tis but a poor jest to so frighten a weak woman."

He laughed fiercely. "'Tis no jest. Thou art my desire and I will have thee. As for thy husband——" he made a contemptuous gesture.

The woman's eyes blazed. She tore her hands from his grasp and faced him. "Thou coward! He is better than thou art. He is of chief's blood—thou but a slave in thine own land," and with a sudden spring she bounded through the open doorway and ran swiftly in the direction of the other white men's houses.

With panting bosom and gasping breath she reached Christian's house and darted inside. Mahina was seated on the matted floor crooning to her youngest child ; Christian, as usual, was away at his cave.

Shaking with fear and anger, Nahi, generally so calm and gentle, flung herself at Mahina's feet and wept.

"What is this, friend of my heart?" asked Mahina, laying her infant down and drawing the girl's head upon her lap. She listened in grave silence until Nahi had finished her story, which ended in an earnest appeal. "Kirisiani," she said, "was strong and powerful, and none of the white men dared face his anger. Surely he would not let the Iron-worker do this wrong."

"The white men, I fear, care little what becomes of us of Tahiti now," said Mahina sadly; "yet will we go to my husband and tell him thy trouble. Still do I fear that he will not heed thee ; and then indeed must thou go to the Iron-worker."

Nahi wept silently ; when she ceased Mahina sought to comfort her, telling her that if the Iron-worker succeeded in taking her away from Talalu it would not be her fault—she would but yield to circumstances.

The woman turned her tear-stained face to Mahina in open wonder.

" What ! Hast thou no other words of comfort for me than these ? Put thyself in my place. How can I do this wrong to the man I love—he who hath toiled and fought for me ? Wouldst thou so wrong *thy* husband as to listen to words of love from another man ? "

" My husband ! " — Mahina laughed bitterly. " Little does he care if other men speak words of love to me. His heart is dead, and I am but a leaf in his path."

" Nay," said Nahi gently, placing her hands on her friend's shoulder, " thy Kirisiani hath still a true heart for thee. He is not as these low-blooded dogs of sailors. He is an *arii* (a chief) of the same blood as Tuti ; and the sailors fear him. Come then, dear friend, and join thy voice with mine, so that he may save me from the Iron-worker, whom I hate and fear."

" We will go, Nahi. Yet hope for nothing. Kirisiani's love for us, which was once so strong and hot, has grown cold. For me, who would give my life for his, he cares naught. But a little while ago, when my babe was born, he was kind to me and sat by my side here when the sun sank in the sea, and let his hand rest in mine." Her soft voice trembled in mournful pathos. "But again the black thoughts came to him, and he left me to return to his cave. He careth for me no longer. Yet will we go and pray him to protect thee from this evil man."

In an hour the two women reached Christian's cave at the furthest extremity of the island. It opened from a high ridge of black, jagged, and almost inaccessible rocks. Near by was a tiny cascade, leaping noisily from ledge to ledge as it coursed towards the valley.

From its situation the cave commanded an extensive view of the horizon round the whole island, and its occupant would see a sail long before any one else on Pitcairn could discern it. Approach was so difficult that, even if a large party succeeded in crossing the dizzy, narrow ledge of rocks connecting it with the mountain spur beneath, Christian could have shot every one of them before they were within a hundred feet of his refuge.

As they passed through the little settlement on their mission, the two women called at the other houses, and told the story of Williams' design. Just as they reached the ridge they heard some one following them, and looking back saw the stalwart figure of Smith, who had come to help them in gaining Christian's assistance. Behind him came Young.

As the sound of their voices ascended to the heights, they saw Christian emerge from the cave. He was dressed in shirt and trousers only, and his long black hair hung, loose and neglected, about his shoulders. For a few moments he regarded them without speaking ; then as Mahina in a timid voice said they desired to talk to him, he descended the ridge to meet them.

"Why is this ?" he asked sullenly, with an angry look at each in turn ; "am I to have no peace, no rest ?   Can I not live alone ? "

Smith's honest, open face flushed deeply, but he said nothing; the women should speak first, he thought, then he would try.

Nahi, in a trembling voice, told her story, and sobbingly besought his help, and Mahina joined her in her earnest entreaties.

He heard them through in moody silence, and turned to Smith. " From the time of our landing here, on this cursed rock, I have avoided all interference with any of you. You have made slaves of these Tahitians, who are better than any white man on the island except yourself and Young. If they retaliate upon you, it will be your own faults. I don't say that you and Young are like the rest ; but yet you have permitted those scoundrels, McCoy, Quintal, Mills, and Williams to oppress these unfortunate people. Still, I will make one more effort for the common good, and try to dissuade this ruffian from stealing Talalu's wife."

" Well spoken, Mr. Christian," said Smith. " By God ! sir, I'll not see Talalu wronged in this fashion if you'll help me ; and I dare swear Mr. Young will join us in clapping a stopper on his game."

Accompanied by Nahi and Mahina, the three men

returned to the settlement.   As they walked, Young tried to speak to Mahina in a whisper, but with a nervous look she quickened her pace and caught up to her husband, who was in advance of them all.

CHAPTER XXIV

W HEN they reached the settlement, they found
nearly all the little community assembled
outside the large storehouse.

Williams himself was not among them, neither was
Talalu ; but Lunalio, a Raiatean girl, the wife of
Martin, whispered to Nahi that he was coming. A
look of joy overspread Nahi's face. She knew
Williams' savage disposition and feared that Talalu
had met with some treachery as he returned with his
companions from fishing. And, indeed, Williams,
with a loaded musket in his hand, had taken up his
position behind a rock on the path leading up from
the cliffs, intending to shoot the unsuspecting man as
he ascended. But it so happened that Talalu, instead
of taking the mountain track, came with his companions along the wider and more frequented path
leading directly to the storehouse ; and the white
man, hiding his musket among the rocks, had waited
till the natives were out of sight, and then followed
them. A quarter of an hour later he sauntered coolly

towards the assembled people, and the babble of excited
tongues told him that the Tahitians were discussing with the whites his intention to appropriate
Nahi.

A dead silence ensued the moment he made his
appearance. Standing in front of the storehouse
were the white men, most of them armed with
muskets and cutlasses. Whether they were for or
against him Williams could not for the moment tell,
but he had no doubt of the feelings of the islanders,
whose dark eyes blazed with hatred. A little apart
from the rest of them stood Talalu, in his hand a
keen-edged turtle-spear, and with a look of suppressed
fury upon his face.

Squaring his shoulders, and placing his hands jauntily
upon his hips, Williams bade the white men a mocking
good-day.

"Quite a little gathering, I see. Ain't I got an
invitation, or didn't you think my company good
enough? Are you talking about me?" and he shot a
fierce glance at Fletcher Christian, who regarded him
with unmoved features.

"We *are* talking about you, Williams," said
Christian quietly, stepping out from the other white
men. "What are you trying to do with this man's
wife? For the peace of our little community—for
God's sake—think before you go further."

"That's all very fine, Mr. Christian," he answered
rudely, "but 'tis hard if I can't do as I choose with
my own."

Christian looked at him contemptuously. "Your

own ! What right have you to speak of this woman Nahi as yours ? "

" Who are you to question my right ? You are not an officer of the *Bounty* now."

Christian's face paled at the insulting words, but he restrained himself.

" I do not ask you as a right, Williams, but as a favour, not to attempt this thing. I am sure every man but yourself sees that you will rue it if you do."

" That is what I told him long ago," broke in Quintal, who, rude and overbearing as he was in some respects to the Tahitians, was never tyrannical, and often tried to check Williams' brutality.

" I am glad to hear you say this, Quintal," said Christian. " Williams does not seem to know what it is he contemplates." His eye fell upon the stalwart figure of Talalu, who with gleaming eyes and clenched hands was looking at the persecutor of his wife.

" Come here, Talalu," said Christian.

The islander looked at him for a moment ; then thrusting the barbed point of his turtle-spear into the ground, he walked slowly over to the white man.

" What is it thou wouldst say to me, Kirisiani ? " he asked in deep, guttural tones, which quivered with passion.

" This," and Fletcher Christian's voice rang out loud and clear, as he pointed contemptuously to Williams—" this do I say. This Williams the Iron-worker is but a poor, uncultured slave, who knows naught that is good, and the evil in his heart hath killed all knowledge of what is right and just. I pray thee have patience with him, and we will try to teach him better."

"What the hell do you mean?" asked Wiliams savagely, who understood Tahitian sufficiently well to know what Christian had said. "What sort of talk is this? Do you mean to tell this cursed, naked savage that he is a better man than I am?"

"Better than you! By heavens, you ruffian, you are a thousand times more of a savage than he? And I, who am to blame for bringing such men as him from their homes and exposing them to the danger of contact with such sweepings of the hulks as you are, will take care you do him or his countrymen no more wrong than you have done already."

"No, no, Mr. Christian, don't talk like that," said Brown. "Williams is as good a man as any of us, and I don't see why you should aggravate him by such words."

"Damn such talk, I say," said Mills insolently, walking apart from the others and standing beside Williams, "if the man wants the woman, let him have her. He ain't got a wife, and you can't expect a white man to go without one when one can be had for the taking."

Talalu turned upon him. "I will kill him or any other man who tries to take my wife from me," he muttered with set lips.

"None of that, my fine fellow," said Brown in English. "Take care what you say about killing people. You will find that we can do some killing if we are put to it."

Williams looked at Christian with rage and hatred in his face. " What do you think of it now, Mr. Christian ? Am I to do as I like and as my ship-mates want me to, or are you going to join with these damned savages and try to stop me ? "

" I'll tell you plainly what I will do, Williams. I will protect these people at the hazard of my life ; and though I stand alone I will prevent this outrage, even if I fight the whole lot of you."

" He is mad to say this," whispered Edward Young to Mahina, as he pressed her hand, " but," and he gave her a meaning look, " for your sake, Mahina, I will stand by him." Then he stepped out and stood beside her husband, and said—

" You'll not stand alone, Mr. Christian, while I am here. While I don't altogether agree with you, I don't believe in Williams taking the woman against her will. Let us come to some arrangement about her."

" I, too, am with you, sir ! " cried Smith.

" And I ! " " And I ! " echoed Quintal and McCoy.

" Thank you, my lads," said Christian ; " I knew there were some among us with a sense of justice."

Williams looked at the four men one after another and folded his brawny arms across his tattooed chest.

" All right," he sneered ; " there's not going to be any fighting over this. But you can make certain of one thing. If you won't give me my own way in this matter you may go to hell, the whole lot of you, before I'll sweat at the *Bounty's* forge making tools for these cursed savages to till your ground. And yet, by God! I'll get my own way all the same in the end!"

Then he walked away towards his house.

"Trouble will come of this, mark my words, Mr. Christian," said Brown. "'Tis a pity you should in-interfere with the man. You'll find he'll have the woman in spite of you, never fear."

"Then his life will pay the penalty," answered Christian fiercely. "You do not seem to understand, Brown, that while a single girl may be taken by force sometimes the marriage-tie among the Tahitians is held as sacred as among civilised people. But I think Talalu will take care of his wife, and there are three or four men who will help him to do so."

Then, with a few words of farewell to the islanders who thronged around him with protestations of grati-tude, he turned quickly away with Mahina by his side.

Before they had gone a hundred yards they heard some one running after them, and Nahi, flinging her-self on the ground before Christian, clasped her arms around his knees and kissed his feet, wetting them with tears of gratitude.

That night Williams cooked and ate his supper alone, for Talalu and Nahi had taken shelter in the house of Tairoa-Maina, the Tubuaian chief.

CHAPTER XXV

F OR three days nothing happened. The people
of Pitcairn, white and brown, went about their
daily occupations as usual, but there was a suppressed
excitement and an ominous calmness that augured ill
for the future, and the rift between the two parties—
those who sided with Christian, and those who supported Williams—widened slowly but surely.

Ever since the day of the quarrel the islanders had
been sulky and suspicious in their manner to all the
white men except Christian and Smith. Young,
although openly declared as Christian's *taio* or friend,
they regarded with distrust, even though Alrema,
doubtful as she was beginning to feel of her husband's
loyalty to herself, strove to persuade them of his good-
will towards them.

To them Christian had always been a fair and just
man, refusing to recognise any distinction between
them and his white comrades. They would have
fought for and followed him to the death had occasion
arisen for the sacrifice.

Tairoa-Maina and the other Tubuaians, being un-

216

married, lived by themselves in a separate house, and thither went Talalu and his gentle wife for refuge for the time being from the savage Williams. Fearing to remain much longer near his former master, Talalu determined to build himself a new house among the mountains in a secluded little valley about half a mile lower down than Christian's cave. Every morning, axe on shoulder, accompanied by Nahi, he set out to work.

"I will live like Kirisiani," he said, when his countrymen asked him why he desired to leave them; "even as he lives so will I. These white men are bad masters; no longer will I work for them like a slave."

On the fourth morning after the quarrel, Williams rose from his bunk and began to make preparations for his breakfast. The fertility of the island was such that this gave him little labour. In his house were supplies of breadfruit, yams, and bananas, and overhead on the cross-beams hung strings of dried fish. In addition to these he had his share of the stores from the *Bounty*, such as wine, biscuit, rice, and salted pork, but his extravagance had left him but little of the meat, and he uttered a savage curse when on lifting the little two-gallon wine keg he found it empty. To procure more meant a walk to the storehouse, some distance away; and before he could get the wine he would have to ask Quintal, who, by common consent, was in charge of all the stores that remained. He had always been accustomed to drink wine with his food, and the loss of it annoyed him.

"If that cursed Talalu had been here," he thought,

" this wouldn't have happened. What right had the fellow to clear out, and take his wife with him too? And the breadfruit and yams were cold. If Nahi were here they would have been heated for him. Curse them both, the damned copper-hided savages."

As he ate he worked himself into a state of savage fury. What right had that fellow to have such a handsome woman as Nahi for his wife? If he were out of the way she wouldn't make such a fuss; would no doubt be proud to become the wife of a white man. Damn that fine-talking fellow, Christian! Only for him the thing would have been done. Brown and Mills would have stood by if Talalu made a noise about his wife being taken. By God! he'd stand it no longer. He'd bring the pair of them back to work at once.

His eye caught his musket, hanging on brackets over his bunk. He took it down, loaded it, and then walked rapidly away in the direction of the house occupied by Talalu and his wife.

With murder in his heart he reached the dwelling of Tairoa-Maina. Neither the chief nor his two countrymen were visible, but Talalu and Nahi were at work in the garden at the back. They were digging yams, and the white man watched them in sullen silence for a few minutes. Every movement of the woman's graceful figure angered him against her husband. What was he? A slave; a cursed savage. A man who had no right to possess a beautiful wife. He would not only have the woman, but make the man work for him as well.

Creeping along the wall of coral stones that enclosed the garden, he reached a spot not twenty yards
from them. Then he stood up and covered the man
with his musket.

"Come back with me, you two," he called fiercely,
in Tahitian ; "if you don't come outside at once, I'll
kill the pair of you."

Nahi, with heart full of love, threw herself before
her husband, but Talalu said something to her in
a low voice, and she turned and faced the white
man.

"Even as thou wilt, master," replied Talalu quietly,
and taking Nahi's hand he came outside the wall.

With his gun over his shoulder the white man
followed them, triumphantly smiling to himself at
this proof of his power of command.

Very quietly they walked before him, till they
reached his house, then entered it, and Nahi seated
herself upon the matted floor.

Williams stood in the doorway for a moment,
regarding them with a smile of victory. He intended
to let them feel their position at once.

"I've a damned good mind to give you a lacing,
Mister Talalu," he said in English, "but I'll put it
off for a bit and give you another chance. But I
want something to eat. You, Nahi, go to Kawintali
and ask him for some rice and wine and salted meat ;
and you, Talalu——"

He never spoke again. The Tahitian sprang upon
him like a tiger, seized his throat with both hands, and
squeezing his windpipe, forced him to the ground.

For a minute they struggled fiercely, but the white man, though strong and active, was but as a child in the giant's grasp. They swayed to and fro a little, and then Williams lay upon the ground with the brown man's knee upon his chest, making feeble efforts to free himself from the grasp of death.

Presently he ceased to struggle, and was only conscious enough to know that all hope was gone and his time was come. One glance from his bloodshot eyes into the death-dealing face of the man above him told him that.

For a little while the Tahitian relaxed his hold. Beside him, her eyes dilated with triumphant hatred, Nahi bent over the prostrate figure, all the bitterness of the past reflected in her dark face. She had watched the struggle with a sense of victory. Who in the old days at Matavai could vie with Talalu in wrestling? And when she saw the huge form of her husband bear the slighter figure of their joint oppressor to the earth, she laughed.

With the foam of the agony of death flecking his lips, and breathing in awful, fitful gasps, Williams lay before them, one hand of Talalu still gripping his throat. The musket lay upon the floor beside the men. Williams had carried it at full cock, and the priming had been spilt when he dropped it to meet the onslaught of Talalu.

Still keeping his hand upon the sailor's throat Talalu turned to his wife.

"Take thou the powder horn and prime the gun," he said.

She took the horn from the peg upon which it hung and did as he told her.

"Now put the end of the gun to this dog's temple."

She dropped upon one knee and pressed the muzzle of the gun to Williams's dark forehead.

"Now pull the little piece of iron," said Talalu, "and let his black soul depart unto the land of evil spirits."

There was a flash and the heavy musket-ball dashed out the wretched man's brains, ploughed through the matted floor, and scattered the coral pebbles in a white shower against the furthest side of the house. Then Talalu, with bloodied right hand, rose to his feet and stood regarding the body of his enemy.

Picking up the lifeless form of Williams, the Tahitian motioned to his wife to follow, and walked towards the cliffs to the same place where, a few months before, he had seen the wife of the dead man fall.

Standing on the jagged cliff edge, he looked down. Far below him lay the rough, pebbly beach upon which Faito had fallen and dyed the stones with her blood. Then he raised the white man high in his mighty arms and cast him over with a bitter curse.

"Lie there, thou who slew thy wife with cruel words, and would have stolen mine," he cried, as he dashed the body upon the stones.

He looked down a while longer at his dead enemy, and then, taking Nahi's hand in his own, turned homewards.

CHAPTER XXVI

THE report of the gun which killed Talalu's oppressor was heard by all who happened to be in their houses at the time. Each thought it was but a shot fired at some ocean bird winging its way seaward from one of the many islands rookeries, and no one imagined that it was the beginning of a fatal and bloody epoch in the history of their island home.

But Talalu, as he returned with his wife by his side, knew that his deed would bring forth great things in the near future, and set himself to prepare for whatever might happen.

Half-way between the cliffs and his own dwelling, he stopped and spoke to Nahi.

"Hasten, oh pearl of my heart, to the houses of all our countrymen and to that of Tairoa-Maina the Tubuaian, and bid them come to me. And this shalt thou say to them : 'Talalu sendeth greeting and saith that "The sun hath risen a bloody red ; and the white men will seek for revenge for what hath been done."

Talalu saith also "The hand to the club, for death cometh swiftly and suddenly to men unprepared."''

"Oh husband with the strong hand and brave heart, why should'st thou fear? The white men are just, and will not harm thee for killing the Iron-worker, that man of evil heart and cruel will. If I give this message of thine, will not they think that all the men of our race are plotting to slay them?"

The giant Tahitian placed his bloodstained hand upon his wife's shoulder. "Do as I bid thee. I tell thee the white men will not forgive me the death of the Iron-worker. And it is well that we be prepared for their wrath."

"Nay," pleaded Nahi, "surely Kirisiani and Etuati and Simeti[1] are our friends."

"It may be so," answered Talalu bitterly. "Who can tell? Hast thou not seen that they have no faith in each other? Dost thou not know that Etuati, whom I once thought the true *taio* of Kirisiani, hath spoken words of love to Mahina his wife?"

"That is but the custom of our country."[2]

Talalu interrupted—"Thou dost not know, Nahi, that this our custom of *taio* is held in abhorrence by men of chief's rank and blood in Peretane, such as Etuati and Kirisiani. Often hath Kirisiani told me, when speaking of the customs of white men, that for a man to cast the eye of desire upon the wife of his friend is counted shame."

[1] Smith.
[2] Of the privileges extended by the Tahitian female to the *taio* or sworn friend of the husband or male relative the less said the better.

She bent her head in mute obedience to her husband's will. Surely Talalu her husband, who was for ever talking to the white men of the customs of their country, knew what was right.

So she sped quickly away, first to the house of Tairoa-Maina, and there told the Tubuaians of Williams' death and gave her husband's message.

Without waiting to be questioned, she added— "And see, oh men of Tubuai, that ye bring with ye guns and powder and lead ; for even as my husband sayeth the sun hath risen a bloody red."

Then leaving the wondering and excited Tubuaians she went to the hut of the Tahitians and gave the same warning. As she passed from house to house the wives of the white men saw her and sought to question her, but she evaded them and disappeared among the boscage of the mountain forest towards the dwelling of Mahina and her husband.

Through the open doorway of the house she saw the figures of Alrema and Mahina. They were seated together preparing their morning meal, and Christian's two children played beside them.

Panting with excitement, Nahi threw herself upon the couch at the further end of the room and asked for a drink. Alrema opened a young coconut and and brought it to her.

" Why dost thou breathe so hard, my friend ? " she said with a laugh. " Drink and then come eat with us."

Nahi drank, but refused to eat. " 'Tis well that I have met thee here, Alrema."

Something in her face made them rise quickly and asked what brought her.

She laughed nervously. "Listen thou, Alrema, wife of Etuati, and thou Mahina, wife of Kirisiani the chief. My husband hath slain the Iron-worker."

Mahina, with a cry of fear, clasped her infant in her arms.

"Aye, he slew him with his own gun, because he sought to take me. And when the fire leapt from the mouth of the gun, and the lead dashed out his brains, Talalu took up his body and carried it upon his shoulders to the cliffs and cast it upon the stones where Faito died. And this message hath my husband sent to the men of Tahiti and Tubuai 'The sun hath risen a bloody red ; be prepared.'"

The two others exchanged a quick responsive glance of alarm, but Nahi, excited as she was, did not notice it.

"But thou must not tell Tahinia, nor Malama, nor Lunalio, nor any of the women who have white husbands. Even of thee, friends of my heart, was I frightened, but I remembered that thy husbands have ever been of kind hearts to us of Tahiti. Did not thine, Alrema, and thine, Mahina, and the husband of Terere seek to save me from the dog whom my husband hath slain ? And for that shall no harm come to them or to thee."

Mahina, with a terrified glance at the exultant face of Nahi, turned appealingly to Alrema. What should she do to warn Christian? He was in his cave. Perhaps in his lonely morning walk along the cliffs he might meet some of her countrymen who, never thinking of all that he had done for their welfare, might shoot or spear him.

Fearful for their husbands, Mahina and Alrema saw the lithe figure of Nahi glide away into the darkness from Christain's lonely dwelling. Despite the knowledge that Young was wavering in his loyalty to her, his wife still loved him passionately, and never felt anything but friendship for Mahina ; so, urging her to go to Christian and warn him of the impending trouble, she set out in search of Young, who had gone fishing for the night. And Mahina, leading one child by the hand and pressing the other to her bosom, walked quickly along the rocky path towards the cave.

A strange silence already seemed to deaden the clear morning air. Soon after the first rosy flush of dawn had changed the grey of the wooded mountain sides to a living green, Matthew Quintal, gun in hand, came along the path from his house towards the cliffs, wondering why he had met none of the brown men on their way to their work in the white men's gardens. He was going towards a great *toa* tree which grew in a little valley near Martin's house, where at early morning many frigate birds roosted, for he had promised Malama to shoot some for her, and wanted Isaac Martin to join him.

But ere he came in sight of the shipmate's house Martin met him. His thin, sallow face wore an anxious look, and to Quintal's surprise he carried a pistol and cutlass as well as a musket.

"I was going to look for you, Mat," he said; "there is something in the wind. One of the Tahiti men was here a little while ago telling my wife that Talalu had killed Jack Williams. Didn't you know it?"

"No!" replied Quintal with a startled exclamation and look of alarm. "What had we better do?"

"Let us go and tell the others. There's going to be fighting, I can see. Every one of those fellows thinks a lot of Talalu, and as far as I can make out only we two know that Williams is dead. We'll find them all working at Young's."

CHAPTER XXVII

YOUNG was building a new storehouse upon his ground, and thither went the two men. As soon as they emerged from the forest path upon Young's clearing they could see him with Smith and Brown at work.

None of the Tahitians had appeared to assist them, and the three men were discussing the cause of their absence. Young, who had been fishing in the *Bounty's* boat all night off the south end of the island, was in a bad temper. He had been obliged to land at an inconvenient spot through the sea rising suddenly, and on returning home just after daylight found that Alrema was away. Such an unusual occurrence mystified and irritated him ; for how could he know that the loving girl had waited at the usual landing-place in Bounty Bay till past daylight, and then returned home, unhappy and anxious at the absence of her husband ?

But as Quintal and Martin came walking quickly along towards Young and his companions, Alrema appeared on the path, far in advance of them. She was followed closely by the wives of two of the Tahitians, who were plainly watching her movements.

"Beware, Alrema," said one of them, "we know why thou hast come here. Talalu hath done no wrong, and our husbands will stand by him if it cometh to the shedding of blood."

"Aye," fiercely said the other, a short, powerful woman, whose long hair, wetted with the morning dew that had fallen on her head as she came through the narrow forest path, hung black and lustreless upon her brown, naked shoulders, "and I, Toaã, will strike this knife into thy heart if thou goest nearer to the white ₐmen," and she showed Alrema a short broad-bladed dagger.

"Ye fools," answered Alrema contemptuously, "can I not labour in my husband's garden without listening to thy silly threats? What doth it concern me that Talalu hath killed the Iron-worker? Stay me not, I tell thee. I have but come to dig yams for our morning meal."

Without further words she entered the walled enclosure, apparently taking no heed of the three white men who were now talking earnestly together. She meant to tell them of their danger, but how to do so with the two women close beside her she knew not.

"Here, you two, come and help Alrema to dig yams," called out Young angrily in English to the other women. "I'll make some of you work for me to-day."

Fearing to disobey, they silently followed Alrema, and began to assist her in her labours ; and as they worked Alrema sang. Sweet, clear, and loud her voice rang out in the morning air, and the white men looked at one another in surprise, for at the end of the first verse she added in English another line.

" Listen to my singing, white men."

The two Tahitian women near her looked up suspiciously. Unlike Alrema, who now spoke the white men's language with perfect fluency, they barely understood a dozen words of English. Still they kept close and Toaā watched Young's wife narrowly. With apparent composure she went on with her song—one of the old Tahitian love songs, half recitative but full of melody, and presently noticed that Young and the other men had drawn nearer, and were listening, though with apparent unconcern.

The second verse told how a girl of Raiatea, pursuing a phantom lover, journeyed over sea and land moon after moon, till she sank faint and dying under a grove of coconut trees on the beach of an unknown land, whither her quest had led her.

> " So she lay there faint and dying ;
> Bloodied were her cinnet sandals
> With her journey long and weary ;
> And her eyes were raised above her
> At the young nuts, thick in clusters,
> Growing close, yet far beyond her ;
> For her hands, too weak to reach them,
> Bruised and bleeding
> Lay upon her aching bosom."

With a swift glance at the white men she changed into English.

> "Listen, white men, to my singing ;
> Dead is Williams, Iron-worker ;
> He was killed at early morning,
> Know you not the man who slew him ? "

"By God ! Do you hear that ? " said Young.
"Sh ! wait a bit, she'll tell us more presently," whispered Smith ; "can't you see she's afraid of the other women ? "

Again Alrema's bird-like notes went back into Tahitian. Striking her spade into the ground as she sang—

> "And the heavens swirled about her,
> With her pain, and thirst, and hunger ;
> But her heart kept calling, calling,
> For the lover who had mocked her."

She raised the end of a yam from the rich black soil, turned round and placed it in a basket behind her ; then her voice, quivering yet strong, took up in English the thread of warning to the listening white men.

> "Do you hear me ? Understand me ?
> Go away and get your muskets ;
> All the brown men now are arming,
> Arming so that they may kill you ;
> Go away and warn the others."

"Thou art a vain fool," said the woman Toaā to her in a tone of contempt ; "dost thou think to charm the ears of our masters with thy croaking voice ? "

Alrema tried to laugh good-naturedly, and again went on with the Tahitian love-song. The women, however, she feared suspected her, and she sang the next verse quickly, while Young, Brown, and Smith with bated breath listened for her next words in English.

> " See these women working with me,
> They suspect me, they will kill me,
> If they know I give you warning.
> Go away and tell the others,
> Leave me here to follow quickly."

" By heavens, that's enough ! " whispered Young to his companions. " Let us get away as quickly as possible. My wife's warning is clear enough. We must go and tell the others."

" Here's Quintal and Martin coming down the ridge now," said Brown. " They seem to know what's up, too."

"Go and meet them," replied Young hurriedly, " and tell them to wait till Smith and I come. We must not let these women know that we have any suspicion of what is wrong; listen, do you hear that ? "

Alrema was singing again in English, and telling them she was sure the two women had been sent to get powder and ball from Williams' house.

" Off you go, Brown, but don't walk too quickly. Tell Quintal and Martin that Smith and I will be with them in a minute or two. Then slip through the breadfruit grove to Williams' house, and get all his ammunition."

Presently Alrema saw with satisfaction that Brown
was sauntering away, and as soon as he was out of
sight Young and Smith came over to where the
women were working.

"We are going to McCoy's house," said he,
addressing Alrema quietly ; "you can stay here and
cook us some yams." Then with sudden severity he
turned to Toaā and the other woman. "As for you
two, stay here and dig till we return, or 'twill be
worse for your backs."

They gave him sullen glances in reply and muttered
acquiescence. Smith and Young left the garden and
went to join Quintal and Martin, but the moment
they were out of the women's sight they ran, and
soon reached the other white men.

For some minutes the three women worked on in
silence. Alrema picked up her basket of yams, and
was moving towards the house when Toaā called her
back.

"Whither goest thou ?" she asked.

"Oh fool and dull of hearing," Alrema replied
coolly. "Didst you not hear my husband tell me to
cook these yams ? I haste to do his bidding."

"Thou liest," said Toaā fiercely ; "thou hast told
him something in thy cunning song," and she sprang
at her, knife in hand.

But Alrema, by an agile movement, escaped the
savage thrust, and, seeing that it was now too late for
concealment, leapt over the low stone wall of the
garden and fled swiftly after her husband.

With Young leading the way, the three white men

ran quickly towards the houses of the other Europeans. In a few minutes they were overtaken by Brown, who reported that Williams' house was in the possession of Talalu and his friends, and consequently he had not dared attempt to enter it. By the time they reached the summit of the rise overlooking the rest of the houses, they were joined by Alrema, who had cleverly returned unobserved to her husband's house, fearing that Young had not secured all the arms there. This, however, he had done.

"Where is Christian?" asked Young, as they gained the top of the hill and stopped to draw breath for a moment.

"In his cave," answered Martin, "but it's no use waiting for him. Alrema says that Mahina has gone to call him. He'll be with us presently. What are we to do?"

There was a hurried consultation, and it was quickly resolved that Talalu must be taken prisoner and punished.

As they talked they were joined by McCoy, Christian, and Mahina. Christian unconsciously assumed the leadership, and after deciding upon their plan of action they proceeded in a body towards Williams' house, determined at all risks to quell the revolt which was threatening their safety.

CHAPTER XXVIII

"HIS HEART'S DESIRE"

I N less than half an hour the white men reached the low stone wall enclosing Williams' house and garden, and saw that the door of his dwelling was closed ; but the two unglazed windows were opened, and from them half a dozen brown, excited faces peered out upon the Europeans. Each native held a musket at full cock, along the barrel of which his eye glanced.

Suddenly Christian stopped, and help up his hand to the white men who followed him. Then grounding his musket he spoke.

" I have come with you, because on the spur of the moment I thought it my duty to make common cause with men of my own colour against a common danger. I forgot that this man Williams deserved his fate. He was a thorough-paced scoundrel, and has met, I have no doubt, his just deserts. Therefore, I will take no part in this affair ; settle it yourselves. I leave it to you to consider, before you harm Talalu, what you may bring upon yourselves by becoming his murderers."

Walking away from his surprised and angry fellow-countrymen, he sat down quietly upon the wall and waited to see what would happen.

" Very well," said Edward Young contemptuously, " if you won't stand by us in a matter like this we must do without you. For the sake of my wife and child I will not let this fellow escape punishment. You, it is easy to see, care naught for yours," and he glanced quickly at Mahina, who stood near.

"Right, Mr. Young," said Quintal; "you lead us and we'll follow."

Telling the rest of the white men to stand back, Young advanced close to the house and called to Talalu that he wished to speak to him.

The heavy wooden door swung open, and the gigantic figure of the Tahitian faced the white man. He was stripped to the waist and held a musket in his hand, but, seeing that Young's piece lay on the ground, he put his down also.

" What is it that ye seek, Etuati ? " he asked quietly.

"We come to seek thee ; thou hast killed the Iron-worker, and we will see justice done. No one, white or brown, must slay his fellow-man and be allowed to escape," answered Young quickly.

" He sought to rob me of my wife. Am I a slave to suffer such a wrong as that ? "

" Let us shoot the beggar ! " called out Martin and Brown together, and Mills, too, urged Young to stand aside and let them end the matter at once.

But Young begged them to have patience. He wished to avoid unnecessary bloodshed.

Talalu listened quietly, his eyes fixed upon Christian, who sat with his chin upon his hand, regarding the two parties with an aspect of utter indifference.

"Listen," said the Tahitian to Young, "so that there may be peace between the white men and the brown, I swear by the god of the white men, and by the god Oro, to do in this matter as Kirisiani wills. I know that he is a just man and will do no wrong either to me or to thee."

"Be it so," answered Young, "speak to him and tell him this; for but a little time ago he told me he cared naught for any of us."

He fell back to the white men, and told them of the Tahitian's proposition. To it they all consented, feeling sure that, however much Christian kept himself aloof from them, he would never actually take sides against them with the islanders.

"Very well," said Christian coldly, when Young asked him to speak to Talalu. "As I have said, I will take no side, but if Talalu wants my opinion I will give it. Whether he acts upon it or not will not trouble me." He walked through the little gateway up the path to the door of the house, but half way he stopped; for the big Tahitian with hands outstretched advanced towards him.

"Thou art a just man, Kirisiani," he said, "as just as Tuti, and I, Talalu, son of Totaro, have no fear of thee. This do I say—mine was the hand that slew the Iron-worker ; and thou art a just man, and will not let these thy countrymen kill me because I did that which was right."

For a moment or two Christian hesitated, and then with a bitter laugh replied in a cold voice—"Thou foolish man, dost thou think my countrymen care for thy wrongs? Thou hast killed their comrade—a man who was useful to them because of his skill. Thou art but a savage; thy skin is brown, theirs is white; and in their eyes he of the brown skin hath neither rights or wrongs. Therefore, oh man with the brown skin, who hast no heart to feel, and no soul to suffer, lay down thy weapon and feel the justice of these thy masters."

The mocking bitterness and contempt which rang through his voice cut the faithful Talalu to the heart.

"Is this thy justice, Kirisiani? Thou, the husband of Mahina! Thou, for whom we of the brown skins and loving hearts would lay down our lives! Thou of whom Nahi my wife said, when I cast the Iron-worker over the cliffs, 'Kirisiani is thy friend and will stand to thee!' Hast thou no other answer for me but this?"

"Talk to me no more," Christian replied passionately; "I care neither for thee, nor for these white men, nor for myself. Do as thou wilt—it matters not to me; so that none of ye trouble me, I care not. Farewell," and with angry impatience he turned away and was soon lost to view. Mahina, with her infant in her arms, quickly followed, endeavouring to over-take him.

Then Talalu, with his hands clasped together and downcast head, returned to the house.

"Give me my gun," he said sadly,to Tairoa-Maina.

Holding the weapon up over his head, he turned to Young, who had by this time with the help of Smith succeeded in quieting the most turbulent of his comrades.

Throwing his musket at Young's feet the gigantic Tahitian spoke—

"Do with me as it seems best to thee. I swore by Oro my god that Kirisiani should decide between us. But his heart has turned to stone. Do with me as you will."

Something in the despairing accents of Talalu's voice touched even the callous heart of Young, and he could not help admiring the loyalty to his word which made the Tahitian, savage as he was, surrender so quietly.

"This is well," he said, picking up the man's musket from the sward. "Come with me ; I promise that no harm shall befall thee till this thing that thou hast done hath been well considered. But say this to thy friends in the house—if before the sun sets they do not lay down their arms and bring them to my house, I will kill thee with my own hands."

"Tell them that thyself," said the Tahitian proudly ; "how can I, a man, say this to them ? "

Advancing to the house Young gave the natives his warning, but ere one of them could reply Talalu sprang to his side with a haughty gesture.

"Heed him not, my friends. The words are his,

not mine. I, Talalu, give my life because of the oath I swore to Kirisiani, who hath deserted me. Am I a dog to buy my life from these white men because of thy friendship for me, oh men of Tahiti and Tubuai? If I die, do thou, Tairoa-Maina, friend of my heart, take Nahi for thy wife."

The door was shut again with a cry of defiance, and again the musket barrels protruded through the windows.

"Leave them alone for the present," commanded Young; and with their prisoner walking calmly before them, the white men marched away.

*   *   *   *   *

Clasping her child to her bosom, Mahina followed her husband as quickly as her strength would permit. The events of the past few days had exhausted her in mind and body, and she began to fear her husband's morbid behaviour was turning into actual madness. Thrice as she caught sight of him in the rough ascent of the rocky path had she called his name and asked him to stop, but he seemed to take no heed. At last when she gained the summit of the ridge which over-looked the valley wherein his house stood, she saw him standing, his gaunt figure silhouetted against the sky-line, with folded arms, and head sunk upon his chest. As she came near he seemed to be asleep, for he made no sign to show he knew of her presence.

Setting the sleeping child gently down upon a mossy cleft in the rock, she stepped softly to him and touched his arm.

"Kirisiani," she said, panting from the long and

hurried walk, "I pray thee, come home to thy house to-night. I fear to be alone, so far from thee."

With a savage oath, and the light of madness gleaming in his eyes, he thrust her rudely away.

With a despairing, heart-broken cry she staggered and fell upon the jagged rocks, and Christian, without even looking behind, resumed his journey to his cave.

An hour later, when Mahina awoke to the consciousness of her misery, she was alone in her husband's house with her head pillowed against Edward Young's bosom, whilst he kissed her again and again.

"Thou art my heart's desire," he said.

CHAPTER XXIX

THE TONGUE OF A WOMAN

DARKNESS fell on the lonely island, and the muffled roar of the breakers beating against the cliffs of Afitā was the only sound that disturbed the silence of the night.

In the big living-room of Edward Young's house Talalu sat moodily upon a mat in one corner, wondering what had become of Nahi. His captors, at Young's request, had not bound their prisoner, but had left Alrema on guard over him with a loaded musket and pistol.

"Where was Nahi?" he wondered. "Why was she, the faithful, loving wife, not with him now?" Alrema, by Young's direction, had given him food, but it lay beside him untasted. Young himself was absent; for soon after bringing Talalu to the house he had quietly left again. Alrema sat at the open doorway, her pale, handsome face wearing a disturbed expression. Where was her husband? Why was he so eager to get away at such a time as this, when men's minds were disturbed and the scent of blood was in the air! But for her proud and haughty nature she would have watched his movements, and would now have gone in search of him. But Mahina's soft, gentle face rose before her, with her pleading eyes, and Alrema lowered her head and wept silently. How could she kill Mahina, who had ever been her friend, and who had eyes and heart for Kirisiani alone? And yet—ah! she could think no longer. Perhaps her husband was gone elsewhere, and Mahina slept alone with her children.

The long, long hours passed slowly away till midnight; then a step crunched upon the pebbly path, and Young entered the house. His face was calm, but Alrema saw that his dark eyes burned with unusual brilliancy.

As he seated himself, Smith came in.

" Mr. Young," he said, " the others have just held a sort of meeting at Brown's house, and are now coming up to demand that we wait no longer for the Tahitians to surrender. They say their lives are in danger while the natives have arms in their possession. I have tried to persuade them to leave the matter to you, but they won't listen."

" All right," answered the other quietly ; and Alrema noticed that he spoke somewhat brokenly, as if out of breath. " I can do no more, but if they insist in pursuing this quarrel to the bitter end, I must see it through with the rest of you."

Alrema handed him a young coconut to drink. He took it from her hand, but his eyes avoided his wife's face. Then, taking his musket and putting a pistol in his belt, he spoke to Talalu.

"You must come with us," he said, not unkindly to the Tahitian, "so that your countrymen may see that no harm hath been done thee. I will try and reason with them." Then, leaving Alrema with her child, the three men stepped out into the darkness to meet the others.

*   *   *   *   *

Nahi had not deserted her husband in his extremity. While he sat a prisoner in Young's house, wondering why she had not come near him, Nahi was busy with her tongue. Since nightfall she had been in Williams' house talking to her countrymen, and with passionate eloquence stirring their hearts to the doing of a great deed; and the Tahitians and Tubuaians, as they watched her flashing eyes sparkle and glow like diamonds in the faint light and listened to her fiery appeal, shifted uneasily and muttered to one another in low tones.

"Why dost thou urge us to such a bloody deed, oh Nahi?" said Manale, a short, stout man, who, with his musket upon his knees, sat cross-legged on the floor. "'Tis not for blood we seek, but for the right to live and work for ourselves, and no longer remain slaves. Thou art but a woman, and shouldst not urge——"

"A woman!" and she clenched her hand fiercely round the hilt of the knife she held—"a woman, yes. But thou, Manale—bulky as thou art in body, thy

heart is as the heart of a tiny fish.   Will ye five
be slaves to these cruel white dogs ?   Shame on ye
all !   Is there no one among you better than a
Mahu ? " [1]

"Nay, insult us not, Nahi, with such bitter words,"
said Tairoa-Maina ; "we are *men*.   It is in our minds
that Kirisiani will help us."

She laughed bitterly.   "Kirisiani !   He whom my
husband trusted before other men—only to be betrayed !   He has turned from our people, and cares
not if his countrymen rid themselves of us.   Death
is before ye all, I tell thee.   Will ye let these white
men slay ye one by one ?   Have ye not guns in thy
hands ?   Five pieces of iron, and death lieth within
them, ready to leap out with flame and smoke.   Live
and be slaves !   Act and be men ! "

She ceased ; the lamp of *tui tui* nuts flickered,
wavered and died out, and darkness fell upon them.

"Let us talk," said Tairoa-Maina in a whisper to
the other four.

"Aye, talk," said Nahi, "talk.   And think that
even now my husband lies dead because ye have
proved cowards ! "

Five minutes passed ; then Nahi, with fierce joy,
saw them rise.

"Come thou and see us act," said Manale to her, as
he touched her arm, and they all filed out in silence.

Young and Smith, with Talalu walking between
them, had scarcely gone a hundred yards from the

[1] A class of degraded Tahitians, now happily extinct, who affected
the dress and manners of women.

house when they met Quintal and McCoy coming down the rugged path towards Young's dwelling.

"Mr. Young," said McCoy, "we have determined to clap a stopper on this mutiny at once. We can't let these fellows take charge of the island any longer, and we want you to come along with us and surprise them before daybreak."

"Very well, I'm agreeable. But at the same time" —and Young laughed ironically—"it does me good to hear you—or any of us—talk about putting down a mutiny."

"Call it by any name you like," said McCoy, roughly. "But it won't do for us to let this thing go on. We came to you because we know you won't leave us in the lurch, like Mr. Christian has."

"All right; lead on. Where are the others?" said Young.

"They've gone on ahead slowly; we'll overtake them before they reach the house."

Following Young in Indian file, the three white men and the Tahitian walked as quickly as the night would permit along the narrow path which wound gently up a hill thickly covered with hibiscus shrubs. So sinuous was their course, however, that objects even a few yards ahead could not be perceived.

No sound disturbed the silence of the island night, save for the throbbing of the ever-restless surf and the strange, plaintive cries of the young sea-birds in their rookeries on the cliffs.

Suddenly there rang out, and echoed and re-echoed in quavering reverberations in the hollows of the hills,

three musket shots in quick succession, followed by
the hoarse, weird clamour of tens of thousands of birds
as they rose and circled in wild alarm.

"By God!" cried Young, "we must run; that's
our men firing."

"This comes of too much palavering. While we've
been paying out fathoms of talk the fight has begun,"
said Quintal, angrily; and the four white men, leaving
Talalu to his own devices, took to their heels and ran
excitedly in the direction of the firing, which seemed,
however, to be nearer the white men's houses than to
that of the Tubuaians.

"Looks as if our fellows had grabbed 'em while
they were asleep, and court-martialled 'em on the
spot while we've been arguing over the thing," said
McCoy as he ran with the others.

But their surmises were entirely wrong. Before getting more than two hundred yards further Smith, who
was in advance, stumbled and fell over something in the
darkness; the hands he put out to save himself plunged
into a pool of blood which was oozing from the body
of Brown, who lay dead in the middle of the track,
with a jagged bullet-hole through his chest.

"By God, it's Brown!" cried Smith, feeling the
man's face, "and he's dead!"

"There's been a fight. Come on, men, for heaven's
sake; we may be in time to save the others"; and
Young, followed by McCoy and Quintal, rushed
along the track in search of their comrades, and in
a few seconds had left Smith many yards behind.

Stooping down again over the body of the murdered

man, Smith felt his heart to satisfy himself that he was dead. He lifted the still bleeding figure, carried it a few yards away from the path, and proceeded to grope for his own musket, which he had dropped.

As he stooped a dark form silently stepped out from the thick undergrowth lining the path. A clubbed musket was raised in the air, and Smith fell and lay unconscious close to the corpse of his fellow-countryman.

"*Aue !*" said Manale the Tubuaian to Nihu the Tahitian, who accompanied him, "'tis Simeti whom I have slain. And I would not have harmed him, for he hath ever been good to us. But this dog"—and he spurned the body of the other white man—"was our enemy, and my hand was strong with hate when I slew him."

Young and the others ran on, but only for a short distance, when again an exclamation of horror burst from them ; this time two dead men lay in their path—Mills and Martin.

Then, before they could realise what had happened, five muskets blazed out from a rocky ridge above, and several naked figures sprang from their ambush with savage yells.

None of the white men were struck, but Quintal and McCoy, terrified out of their wits, dropped their muskets and fled. The intense darkness favoured them. They succeeded in evading the rush of their opponents, and were soon clambering down the mountain side in the hope of finding better shelter in the dense scrub of the valley. Young alone stood his ground, and fired his musket at the first of the natives who sprang upon him ; but he missed his mark, and before he could club the weapon Nihu struck him a blow on the head with a musket, and laid him sense-less.

The five figures bent over him for a moment, and talked hurriedly among themselves.

"'Tis Etuati," said Tetihiti ; "he lieth as one dead. For the sake of Alrema, his wife, who is of my blood, let him live, oh friends" ; and he warded off the musket of the savage Manale, who had pressed the muzzle of the weapon to Young's heart. "But the other two, Makoi and Kawintali, must die."

So they sped away in pursuit of Quintal and McCoy.

CHAPTER XXX

FOR some minutes Edward Young lay stunned upon the rocky path, a stream of blood oozing from a severe cut in his head. Presently the cool night air brought him back to consciousness, and, as by slow degrees his senses returned he feared that he alone was left alive of all the white men on the island, and it was likely enough that even his hours were numbered. With a struggle he rose slowly and painfully, dragging his footsteps along the road until he reached his house. Fearful of again encountering the enraged islanders he proceeded with the greatest caution, stopping suddenly, when at a turn in the narrow track he saw three figures in a crouching position.

He dropped upon his hands and knees and scanned them carefully. Presently he recognised Nahi, Alrema, and Terere. The three women were supporting Smith, who was too badly hurt to stand upon his feet. As Young watched, doubtful whether to approach or not, he saw a fourth figure join them, and knew Mahina by the black mantle of hair falling down her back.

"Is *he* dead, I wonder?" he muttered to himself. "Better for him if he is. I will never surrender her again."

He rose to his feet and advanced towards them. The women gave a startled cry, and Smith fell back upon the ground with a groan of agony.

Alrema's arms were round Young's neck in an instant, and her fearful, panting bosom pressed to his lovingly. "My husband, my husband," she murmured, "thou art wounded; yet Nahi said thou wouldst be safe." She turned fiercely upon the wife of Talalu, who covered her face with her hands and wept.

"Alas! what have I done?" said Nahi, "the fire of anger in my countrymen's hearts was kindled by me, and in their wrath they knew not friend from foe."

Mahina drew near, trembling from head to foot; and Alrema, with an agonised heart, saw her husband's hand steal out to her friend's and give it a quick, warm pressure. Then Mahina sank upon her knees in the darkness and wept silently. Did Alrema know that she, her friend, had yielded, and that Edward Young no longer cared for the brave, loyal wife who had fought and bled for him in the days gone by in Tubuai?

Alrema did know. But maddened as she was by the discovery of her husband's faithlessness, she was yet true to Mahina; and all her love for Young welled up fresh and strong in her heart when she felt him swaying to and fro on his feet from weakness.

"Thou cruel Nahi," she cried bitterly, "dost thou think that thy husband is more dear to thee than mine is to me "—a sob choked her utterance—"he for whom my life is ever ready to be given? If he comes to further harm I swear I will kill thee, thou false and wicked Nahi."

Nahi sprang to her feet, and her black eyes gleamed with fire as she threw her arms wide out. "What I have done was for the love of Talalu! But let us not waste time in words; hide thy husband and the husband of Terere until the fury of our people hath spent itself."

It was now agreed that Young, who was only just able to walk, should go on ahead and conceal himself in a cave in the mountains, known only to the women, who would bring him food and water until he was safe from pursuit or further vengeance from the brown men; and, supported by Alrema and the trembling Mahina, the wounded man set out, and the three toiled slowly along. Then Young began to talk.

"Leave me by myself," he said weakly in English. "You, Alrema, return home and see to our child. Maybe she has come to harm. You, Mahina, look for your husband, he may be dead."

"What matters it to me?" burst from Mahina. "Would that I, too, were dead."

"Take thou my husband to the cave, Mahina."

It was Alrema who spoke, steadying her voice through unseen tears. "Take him to the cave whilst I seek out thy husband and bring him to thee—to thee and to his friend—his true and good friend."

The bitterness of the words, "his true and good friend," pierced the anguished heart of Christian's wife like a knife-stab.

"Nay, nay, Alrema, leave me not, I pray thee. See, thy husband needs us both. Stay with me; for the love I have always borne thee, stay with me."

But Alrema only answered her with a sob, and in another instant was gone, to fall upon her face a few yards away and weep out her shame and bitterness of heart. "For the sake of my child," she moaned, "for the sake of my child, neither his blood nor hers shall redden my hand."

Then rising to her feet she went to seek Christian.

* * * * *

Smith had fainted. His wife, as soon as he returned to consciousness, assisted him to his feet; they set out towards the cave where Young was gone, and in another hour their journey was successfully accomplished.

The wives of McCoy and Quintal—Puni the Huahine woman, and Malama—meantime sat alone in their houses, weeping at the thought of the fate which they felt sure had overtaken their husbands. Nahi, on her way to seek Talalu had called in and spoken words of encouragement which somewhat allayed their fears. She promised that she would restrain her countrymen from further attacking the white men; then still fearful as to what had become of her own husband, she quickly ran the rest of the distance to her little dwelling in Williams' enclosure. When she entered she found the gigantic Tahitian quietly seated cross-legged upon a mat, with his musket beside him, eating his supper. She embraced him tenderly and began to tell him of all that had happened.

He interrupted her in the middle of her recital. "I know all, Nahi. I was hidden in a clump of trees and saw all that took place between thee and the wounded white men. And now that thou hast returned in safety I myself will go to Manale and the others, and stay their hands from further killing. Enough blood has been shed."

Towards dawn the islanders returned from their fruitless search for McCoy and Quintal, and as they filed one by one into Williams' house they were met by Talalu, who had just missed them in the darkness.

In a few words he so worked upon their feelings that they readily agreed to do no further harm to the remaining white men, and consented to meet and discuss their future relations towards each other.

Christian, slumbering in the loneliness of his mountain cave, had heard the report of the muskets and guessed what was happening; but he was perfectly indifferent as to how the quarrel might end, and so remained where he was. About two or three hours before dawn he felt a touch upon his arm and saw a woman's figure bending over him.

"What now?" he said angrily, thinking it was Mahina who had disturbed him.

"I have come, Kirisiani, to tell thee that three

of the white men are dead, and Simeti and Etuati wounded. Didst thou not hear the guns?"

"I heard them, Alrema, but it is naught to me."

"Naught to thee? Hast thou no thought to ask if Mahina and thy children be alive or dead?"

He laughed bitterly. "None. What care I for Mahina? Dost thou think I am blind? Hast thou not seen what I have seen?"

The woman sank on her knees beside him, and, taking his hand in hers, wept passionately. "Aye, I know it now. But yet Mahina is my friend, else had I killed her. And because of that and for my great friendship for thee have I brought thy two children, so that thou mayest take them to their mother."

"Where is she?" asked Christian as he rose, and with steel and flint lit the rude lamp of coconut oil.

"She is waiting for thee in the cave with Simeti and my husband. And see, this do I swear—only because I bade her stay and help the wounded men did she remain away from thy house and children. Else would she have come, and with them sought thee here."

Christian regarded her for a moment or two in silence. He admired her intense loyalty and devotion to Mahina, which was put to such a test, and so restrained himself from sneering at her weakness.

"Where are my children?" he asked.

"They wait outside. I feared to bring them to thee till we had spoken together a little."

"Bring them in," he said, "and stay with them here till I return."

She placed her hand upon his shoulder. "Thou wilt hurt neither my husband nor Mahina?" she said beseechingly.

"No," he said in a low voice, "neither. For the sake of these, my children, I will not."

She took his hand and kissed it again. "Forgive her, Kirisiani. When thou didst cast her aside from thee on the cliffs she became in the hands of my husband, who is a cunning man, as a twig that is bent by the fingers of a child. Only for this she had remained true to thee and he true to me."

Again he laughed with bitter scorn. "All women are alike, and all men are false to their friends and their duty when a woman's face comes between. Stay here till I return."

Just as dawn broke, Christian, guided by the directions Alrema· had given him, found and entered the cave, and was greeted with an exclamation of joy from Smith; Young, who lay upon a couch of leaves, merely nodded to him and said nothing. Mahina was not visible.

"I am glad to find you both alive—*both*," he added, with a steady glance at Edward Young, whose eyes dropped before his, "although if every white man on the island had been killed it would have been but justice. How can these people trust men who, even among themselves, are guilty of the blackest treachery to each other?"

For a little while no one spoke; then came a murmur of voices outside, and Talalu stood before the three white men.

"'This is my message to ye, oh white men who were once my friends ; these are the words of Temua, Nihu, the men of Tubuai, and I, Talalu. Let there be peace between us. We sought not blood ; only when it was forced upon us did we fight and kill. Let there be peace."

"I blame neither thee nor them," said Christian quietly, "and now I tell these two men here, who were once my friends, but whom I wish to see no more, that they will do well to make peace with thee and thy countrymen."

Without a word of farewell he turned and left them with Talalu, who, as both Young and Smith saw, was unfeignedly glad at their escape ; and they in their turn were relieved to hear that McCoy and Quintal were safe.

As the sun rose they heard plaintive notes of wailing for the dead rising from the valley below, and soon after, Nahi and some of the Tahitian men came, unarmed, to tell them that their comrades' graves were being dug.

Still weak from loss of blood, Young and Smith managed to leave their retreat and, assisted by the now friendly Tahitians, reach the valley, where they saw standing round the three bodies a little group of brown people. As they drew near, Manale stepped out from the others and offered his hand to Young.

"Is it peace between us ? " he asked.

"It is peace," said Young and Smith, both taking his hands.

Presently they were joined by McCoy and Quintal ;

and the bodies of the slain men, having been wrapped in mats by the women, were placed in their graves in silence, broken only by the sobs of their wives.

Walking slowly away from the cave, Fletcher Christian, with white, despairing face, went first to his house, intending to bring away some further articles for his own use in his retreat. The door was closed, but not fastened on the inside. Pushing it open, he saw the figure of his wife upon her couch. She had been weeping, and as he entered the room trembled in every nerve ; then, ere he could restrain her, cast herself at his feet and flung back her head.

"Kill me," she cried ; "kill me, else will I die as did Faito."

He drew back from her coldly. "Thou art but a woman, and men do not kill women in my country, even though they be false to their husbands. Listen to me. So that I never see thy face again I am content. But still would I see my children sometimes. Therefore with thee they shall remain, and sometimes will I come to them."

In another moment he was gone, and Mahina looked wildly after his retreating figure. Then she swayed and fell, and an hour after Alrema, with tears of pity filling her star-like eyes, came in with the children and embraced her friend lovingly.

"He will yet love thee again," said the loyal girl—"'tis but a black cloud that will vanish. And see, I too forgive thee."

CHAPTER XXXI

"MINE THE HAND!"

A MONTH had elapsed. To Mahina it was a month of misery.

With her children she passed her days and nights in solitude, broken only by visits from Talalu and Alrema, who both knew the secret of her suffering. Once or twice only had she caught sight of Christian as he wandered about his cliffs at dusk, and had been impelled by her love to follow and speak to him; but with a cold gesture of indifference he had waved her back and walked slowly on, oblivious to her heart-wrung sobs.

And not to Mahina alone had come suspense and grief; Alrema suffered too, for her husband now neglected her for the company of McCoy and Quintal. Since the deaths of Brown, Mills, and Martin, a period of incessant watchfulness and suspicion had ensued—the white men dreaded the brown, the brown suspected the white. Edward Young, fearful of more bloodshed, had tried to persuade the islanders to give their arms up to him; but this, though they repeated their assurance of good will towards the seamen, they refused to do.

"To Kirisiani alone will we give up our guns," said one of the Tubuaians, "for in him alone have we faith. And Kirisiani himself saith that there is no faith or honour in any among ye. Thou, Etuati, who wert once his sworn *taio*, knowest if he speaketh truth."

Young winced at the native's words, but said nothing. His mad infatuation for Mahina still remained, yet he was sensible of his own degradation and treachery to Christian, and a sense of shame kept him from approaching Mahina since that fatal evening. Mahina herself, though the man had acquired a strange power over her, forcing her to believe his passionate declaration of love, trembled with fear lest she should see him again.

Talalu, ever faithful both to her and her husband, was the one man on the island with whom Christian now held converse, and the big-hearted fellow more than once sought him out in his retreat and tried to induce him at least to meet and speak to his wretched wife.

"She is but a woman, Kirisiani; and see, oh friend, her heart is eaten up for love of thee. Canst thou not take her to thee again? Thou art strong; she is weak. Are women of Peretane never unfaithful?"

But Christian, though he listened to the friendly Tahitian, would answer, "Let it be as it is—she is nought to me, nor I to her."

One night as the two sat together on the edge of the cliffs, looking over the wide expanse of star-lit ocean, the Tahitian began to talk of the condition of affairs between his countrymen and the whites, and urged Christian to destroy, if possible, the growing unrest and suspicion which disturbed both parties.

"Thy countrymen," he said, "go about in fear of us, with their muskets ever to their hands. Thou, who art a chief among them, canst still make them listen to thee ; then will they forget all that is past, for we of Tahiti and Tubuai do not seek more bloodshed."

"I can do nothing for thee, Talalu. Bitterly do I repent the misery and death that I have wrought to white men and brown ; but I can do nothing—no longer will I interfere between thy people and my countrymen."

One night all that remained of the mutineers assembled in Young's house. The last to enter was Smith, accompanied by Terere, whom he placed outside to watch. The door was carefully closed, and the men sat on the rough wooden benches which, with a table, formed the furniture of the living room. For some minutes they conversed in low tones ; then Young rose and spoke.

"We can delay no longer," he said. "The Tahitians, my wife will tell you, intend to attack us at daybreak. They firmly believe that we shall not rest until we have avenged the murder of our countrymen."

The other men looked at each other and nodded acquiescence.

"Yesterday, so Alrema says, they came to the horrible resolution of killing us all except Christian. Him they look upon as mad, and, as you know, they have a curious feeling of regard for mad people. They consider the insane as inspired and protected by the gods, and their lives are held sacred. Now, God knows, I have no wish to see more bloodshed on this island ; but," and here Young's face paled and his words came slowly, "it seems to me that my wife's advice, however dreadful it may appear, should be followed. Either they or we must die."

McCoy struck the table with his huge, heavy fist. "Speaking for myself and Mat Quintal, I think we ought to have done it long ago. Mr. Christian's damned fine ideas about the rights o' these bloody-minded savages is all very well when you haven't got to live with them. I am for settling it at once."

"I don't agree with you," said Smith, "but I suppose my opinion won't alter the matter one way or another. Since Mr. Christian won't have anything to do with us, I am willing to look to Mr. Young as our leader. If he considers it necessary for our safety to murder these people—why I've gone too far to hold back now."

"Murder is an ugly name, Smith," said Young quickly, "and I've no mind to accept your help. McCoy, Quintal, and myself can do what is to be done without you. We must either kill or be killed."

"Aye, aye, Mr. Young," said Quintal approvingly. "Smith had better go to his friend, Mr. Christian, and live in his cave. We three can settle this business. We don't want any white-livered man among us at a time like this."

With a fierce glance Smith sprang to his feet.

"Damn you, Quintal, you are too ready with your tongue. I'm no more white-livered than you are. You knew that when we took the ship off Tofoa. If Mr. Young says the word I am ready to fight, or murder, or whatever you like to call it, all the Tahitians myself. To my mind he's a King's officer still —leastways so far as my obedience to him goes. Say what is to be done, and I'll have a hand in the doing of it."

"Words, words, idle words, and nothing is done. In a little time it may be too late. While ye talk, and talk, I, Alrema, will alone do the deed. Mine shall be the hand to strike."

Alrema was sitting in a corner of the house, her dark eyes watching with intense interest each movement of the white men, and listening to every word spoken ; and her husband, as he turned towards her, saw in her eyes the look he had seen long ago on Tubuai, when she held in her hand a blood-stained cutlass.

" I alone will do it," and seizing an axe from a toolrack on the wall she waved her hand to the whites, opened the door, and was gone.

Picking up their muskets the four men hastily followed Alrema along the narrow track which led to the dwelling of her countrymen and the house of Williams.

At the doorway of Williams' house sat the huge Talalu, musket in hand, keeping watch while his countrymen slept. For some weeks they had never rested without setting a watch, for their wives warned them continually that the white men were dangerous and were plotting mischief. Nahi, who seemed animated by the bitterest feeling of hatred against all the whites save Christian, had continually declared that sooner or later the remaining Englishmen would avenge the deaths of their comrades by a sudden massacre. Her repeated warning had so worked upon the fears of her countrymen as to force them into believing its truth, and they resolved to be beforehand with the white men.

"Kill them, kill them," she urged. "Only when their blood runs shall we be safe."

So they sat together in the darkened room and agreed to make an attack next morning at daybreak. in which Nahi and the wives of the Tahitians were to take part. After arranging the details, the plotters lay down to sleep, leaving Talalu on watch. He was to call them at dawn ; and as the brown men spread their mats upon the gravelled floor, Nahi whispered in his ear, "To-morrow, my husband, those who sought thy life will be silent for ever."

But Nahi little knew that Alrema, ever on the alert, had learned from Puni the danger that overhung the white men, and had guarded against it.

Talalu, sitting dreamily on the doorstep of the house, with his musket across his knees, woke with a start. Surely a footstep rustled the dead pandanus leaves that lay along the path ? He opened his half-closed eyes and listened. Nothing broke the stillness but the murmuring hum of the surf, and the strange weird rustle of the wind as it soughed through the groves of pandanus and coco-palms. He bent his head again and dozed, then in an instant was upon his feet. Some one was approaching, for this time he heard clearly the crackling of dead leaves underfoot.

Leaning on his musket his keen eye eagerly scanned the darkness of the night. A soft footfall behind him—and it was too late. Before he could rise and face the intruder, or call an alarm, Alrema's axe had cleft his skull in halves, and the watcher's cry of warning mingled with his dying groan.

Swinging the weapon over her head, Alrema, followed by the white men, dashed into the house, and then, in the dim light of the flickering lamp, began a horrible slaughter of the sleeping men. Manale, who lay nearest the door, fell as he rose, beneath a blow from Alrema's axe, which sank deep into the broad, naked bosom ; and three shots from the white man's muskets did the rest of their bloody work.

One of the Tubuaians alone succeeded in leaping past his assailants and gaining the door ; but Young drew a pistol from his belt, sprang before him and pointed the weapon at his head.

"Shoot!" cried Alrema, "shoot ! spare none, so that we may have peace afterwards."

The savage thirst for slaughter in her voice steadied the wavering hand that but for her would have spared. For a moment he hesitated, then aimed the pistol at the Tubuaian's breast, pulled the trigger, and the last of the brown men fell upon his face on the blood-stained mats.

CHAPTER XXXII

TOO terrified to aid their husbands, and each moment expecting to share their fate, the wives of the murdered men crouched together in horror at one end of the room, nor could all the endeavours of the Englishmen soothe their fears. At last Young and his companions went away and left them with their dead. Alrema, fearless as she was, went with them, for there was in Nahi's face a look of such deadly hatred that even her iron-souled nature quailed before it.

At sunrise next morning two people alone on the island knew nothing of what had happened—Fletcher Christian and Mahina. That morning she sat beside him in the cave, fanning his flushed face and aching head, for he was ill and suffering in mind and body. Two days before, at sundown, as he wandered along the wild and rugged track leading to his mountain retreat, she had watched him unseen, and saw that he staggered as he walked and had scarce strength enough to drag his weary feet along. She waited till darkness set in and then followed, her heart beating fast in an agony of hope and fear. Peering cautiously in she saw her husband fling himself upon his couch and mats and lie there, his face turned away from her, breathing heavily and painfully. For some minutes she stood and watched him with tears of loving pity filling her eyes. Her husband! He whose love was once hers, and might yet be again! And he was ill and weak. Surely he would not curse her now?

Softly she crept in through the darkness and sat near him, longing yet fearing to speak ; but soon she knew by his low mutterings and the way in which he flung his arms about that he was ill of fever. She had surmised as much when she saw him going towards the cave, and knew how perfectly helpless even a strong man became in a few hours from the first attack.

Quickly she made her way in the darkness back to her house, filled a small basket with some ripe limes, roused her children, and, leading one and carrying the other, returned as quickly as possible.

Short as was her absence, she knew as soon as she entered the cave by the sound of Christian's breathing that he was much worse. Placing the children—of whose fretful cries her husband seemed quite unconscious—by themselves in a corner, she quickly cut some of the limes in halves and squeezed them into a coconut-shell, with a little water. Then she raised Christian's head upon her knees, and the fever-stricken man, suffering from the agonies of a burning thirst, eagerly drank the life-giving draught. All that night she sat beside him, cooling his aching head and giving him at short intervals a mouthful of lime-juice. Towards morning the violence of the fever abated. He slept, and Mahina was happy as she watched.

The dawn came, and Christian's breathing grew soft and regular. Mahina took his hand in hers, and raised it to her lips; then, overcome by weariness, she lay beside him and slept too.

As the first streaks of sunlight, piercing the mountain mists, lit up the dark and jagged rocks which hid the cave within their bosom, Christian awoke, and knew that the fever was gone. Then a cry escaped him, as he saw the sleeping figures of his wife and children; and the basket of limes and the wet bandage just fallen from his temples told him all. She had come to him when he was ill and suffering; come to him when his last words to her had been a curse. A great pity welled up in his heart as he looked at her pale, worn face, so full of pain and suffering. Her thick mantle of black hair seemed like a funeral pall to her body, now so weak and thin.

A blade of yellow sunshine shot in through the mouth of the cave; it touched her face and glorified it with a strange radiance, and Fletcher Christian's better nature came back to him once more.

Sinking quietly back upon his pillow he reached out his hand and placed it gently upon her head.

"Mahina!"

A broken cry of trembling happiness, then in an instant she was on her knees before him, with her hands clasped tightly together, and a look of unutterable yearning in her dark, sad eyes. He drew her to him and kissed her lips.

" Thou art my wife," he said.

With streaming eyes she flung her arms round his neck and sobbed out her joy to live again upon her husband's bosom.

All that morning she remained in the cave, for Christian was still weak from the fever. In the afternoon, to her great joy he told her that henceforward she and the children should remain with him there, as he had no desire to return and live in the valley. Mahina eagerly set about removing all their possessions to the new home. When she returned, the sight of Christian playing with and caressing her children filled her with a wild sense of happiness, and already her face was glowing with all the old beauty which had once fascinated the man she loved.

In her excitement about removing the contents of their old house, Mahina did not notice the absence of the people from the village. That night, however, when after so many months of misery she and her children lay beside her husband, she talked with Christian of the growing suspicion and hatred now again rending the life of the little community.

" Only thee of all the white men do my people trust," she said. " Wilt thou not yet come and decide between them and thy countrymen, ere it be too late ? Is it not better, my husband, for all men to dwell together in peace ? A hot word leadeth to a blow, and the hand toucheth the musket, and death leaps out from the hollow iron."

" True, Mahina," he answered mournfully; " I alone am to blame for the bloodshed in Afitā. But never more will I interfere."

How long they had slept they knew not, when suddenly they awoke to the report of firearms.

" What new horror is this ? " muttered Christian to himself, as he hastily rose and dressed.

" 'Tis my countrymen who have again attacked the white men," answered Mahina, trembling with fear lest her people should seek Christian's life in their mad lust for slaughter, and her newly-found happiness come to a sudden end.

" 'Tis as likely that the white men have attacked the brown," answered Christian bitterly. " Are we not all rebels and murderers ? "

Determined to shoot the first man who should attempt to enter with hostile intent, he took a stool to the mouth of the cave, and sat there musket in hand, waiting for the dawn. No further sound reached them from the valley, and they were beginning to hope that they had heard only the Tahitians discharging their pieces to frighten away "evil spirits," but as the day broke, they saw the figure of Alrema clambering up the path along the ridge.

" What has happened ? " cried Mahina to the girl.

" Alas ! Mahina, the white men are well, but all ot our countrymen and the men of Tubuai are dead ; the white men have slain them all. And their wives have now fled in fear and hidden themselves."

In a few words she told her dreadful story, and

added how, when daylight came, the wives of McCoy and Smith, going to comfort the widows of the murdered men, found nothing there but the cold bodies of the victims—the women had fled. So while the four seamen buried those whom they had slain, their wives went in search of the missing women, and Alrema had come to the cave, thinking that they might have taken refuge with Christian.

"Thou cruel murderess," said Christian sternly to Alrema, "so thine was the bloody hand which took the life of Talalu! May the gods punish thee, thou cruel and wicked woman!"

His savage words terrified her, and she shrunk back in alarm. Disdaining further speech with her, Christian turned to Mahina.

"Come, Mahina, let us seek for these poor creatures who in the madness of their despair and terror may do themselves injury."

Leaving the sleeping children, and closely followed by Alrema, Christian and Mahina began to descend the mountain by the narrow and intricate path winding to the plain. Sometimes it led through huge crevices in the rock, which shut out the light on either side, and left only a patch of blue sky overhead; sometimes it ran sharply over the dizzy summit of the broken mountain, from whence they could see the surf-beaten beach below.

Suddenly the quick seaman's eye of Christian detected moving figures on Bounty Beach, and he stopped and gazed intently down. Away from the wash of the waves the *Bounty's* boat lay bottom upwards, rapidly falling into decay from disuse; and the figures he had seen were turning it over upon its keel.

Even while he looked he saw the three women, the moment they had turned the boat over, begin to drag her towards the water; but they were not strong enough to make much progress in their efforts.

A cry of pity escaped Mahina.

"What would they do?" she said. "The boat is old and rotten, and they seek to drag it to the water! Save them, my husband, ere they die by the sharks."

"Nay, it is I who have filled them with fear, and 'tis I who will save them from death!" And Alrema bounded down the dangerous path, her long, black hair flying about her naked shoulders as she sprang from ledge to ledge, thoughtless of danger to herself in her effort to avert this last calamity.

Christian and Mahina followed closely, but when Alrema gained the beach the women had succeeded in floating the boat and, using her bottom boards as paddles, had sent her some little distance from the shore.

"Come back, come back, thou foolish Nahi!" Alrema cried frantically from the beach. "Come back; I swear by the gods that no harm shall come to thee!"

A heavy roller lifted the boat and carried her back for some distance shoreward, and the women had all they could do to keep her from broaching to; but Nahi while she paddled looked over her shoulder at Alrema and cursed her bitterly.

"Thou murderess!" she cried, "rather will we drown or go into the bellies of the sharks than live in this bloody land of Afitā with thee."

Alrema took no heed of her words, but cast off her waist-cloth of tappa and plunged into the sea. She could see that there was a brief lull in the succession of rollers tumbling in upon the beach, and that, poor as their boards were, the women would succeed in getting out to deep water unless she managed to reach the boat quickly.

"Paddle, paddle," panted Nahi to the others; "let not the red-handed woman touch the boat!" and she plunged her board into the water with all her strength—it broke in halves, and the boat broached to.

She stood up in the stern, with despair in her eyes, and looked round her. Already Alrema was within a few feet of the boat, and in imploring tones was calling to the women to return, when Nahi spoke to her two companions in a low voice. They looked inquiringly at her, and she answered their looks with an impatient gesture to cease paddling.

Panting, and now almost exhausted, Alrema at last gained the boat, put out her right hand and grasped the gunwale.

"Come," she said faintly, "come back with me, Nahi."

Looking down at her with savage hatred, the wife of Talalu smiled cruelly at the pleading face.

"Aye," she answered, "I come." And, without another word she sprang out of the boat, clasped her arms round Alrema's neck, and uttering a curse with her last breath, dragged her enemy to death with her beneath the water.

CHAPTER XXXIII

THE BREW OF DEATH

A FORTNIGHT after the last of the tragedies which had marked the life of the island dwellers, Christian withdrew himself for ever from all association with the rest of the white men, and spent his whole time in the cave, scarce speaking even to his now heart-broken wife, though her patient, winning ways won from him sometimes a mute caress.

By day she watched with the tenderest solicitude over her husband's lonely wanderings ; by night she listened to the strange mutterings which broke his sleep ; torturing her mind with dread that the end of her brief happiness was near.

The other women still lived in constant fear of some new horror, and when the white men's wives had performed their daily round of tasks for their husbands' homes, they gathered together in the dusk of the evening with the widows of the murdered men, and tremblingly asked each other what the morrow would bring forth — would it be death for all ? Nothing that the white men could say could quiet their fears ; and at last in their extremity they came to the resolution to poison all the white men who remained, lest their masters should plan some new attack upon them.

But as soon as they had come to this determination, some of them, fearful that their plans might miscarry, and their intended victims retaliate upon them with some dreadful punishment, secretly informed Young, Smith, McCoy, and Quintal of the plot. At first the white men listened incredulously, and when they did believe the story they understood that the women had been driven to this horrible device through fear alone, and not from any desire for vengeance upon their husbands' murderers. And so when one by one the plotters confessed and begged for forgiveness, Young and the others not only readily granted it, but tried hard to persuade them that their terror was groundless.

Worn with the results of a fever which, soon after the tragic end of his wife, had wasted his once great strength and muscular frame, Edward Young was now greatly changed. As he listened to the women's tale he raised his hands above his head, and swore by their gods and the Christ-God of the white men that no harm should come to them.

"Let us who are left dwell together in peace," he said.

With fresh hope kindled in their bosoms, the poor women bent their heads to the ground and kissed his feet, and swore to work for and obey him and the other white men to the end of their lives.

So the months went by in quiet and uneventful life, and although the little community at the settlement sometimes saw Mahina and her two children, her husband never came near them. Twice he and Young met, and the latter's face flushed deeply at the memory of the past, but Christian spoke to him calmly, without a sign of either anger or bitterness, and then went on his way indifferent to all around him.

Young himself had now so far succeeded in controlling his passion for Mahina as to marry the widow of one of the murdered Tahitians, and sought by his conduct to make her and the other women feel that their lives were in no danger. The terrible fate of Alrema had had a good and lasting effect upon his reckless nature, and there now seemed no likelihood of a further tragedy breaking the monotony of existence on the lonely island. Christian lived entirely in his cave, but occasionally worked with Mahina in the garden of their deserted house, and cheerfully gave part of its yield to those of the community whose lands were not so fruitful.

*   *   *   *   *

Three years passed, then there came a change. One evening McCoy walked over to Quintal's house, accompanied by Puni, his Huahine wife. Quintal and his wife Malama were rolling into a cylindrical shape a bundle of wild tobacco leaf, while their little half-blood son lay asleep.

Seating himself cross-legged on the matted floor

beside his comrade, and briefly nodding to Malama, McCoy said, " I'm sick of this damned life, Mat ; the same round day after day, night after night—no change, no pleasure. Young and Smith don't have much to say to us, and Christian is as good as a dead man, for all he has to do with us."

" I'm as tired of it as you are, Bill," answered Quintal ; " but what are we to do ? We can't leave here even if we had a good boat—we dare not."

" No, I know that well enough ; but I've an idea how we can make life a little pleasanter—for us two, at any rate."

" How ? "

" Do you remember once I was telling Brown about a ship's company that was cast away at Martinique, or some island near there, who found a plant, out of which they made barrels and barrels of good grog ? "

" Well, this isn't Martinique."

" No ; but the same plant grows here. Just before poor Will Brown was killed he told me—it's the thing the women call *ti*.[1] Why, it's growing all over the island—there's acres of it in the little valley at the back of Tautumah."

" How are we going to make it ? " said Quintal, with sudden interest. " It would be a glorious thing to have a taste of grog again."

" With the *Bounty's* copper boiler and my knowledge of the thing. I worked in a distillery in Dublin

[1] *Cordyline terminalis.*

when I was a boy, and it'll go hard if I can't make a still."

" I'm with you, my hearty. Come on, it's a fine night—let us go and get the copper out of the store house. We'll make a cradle for it, and Malama and Puni here can carry it up at once. If you can make grog out of *ti* root I'll say you're a damned clever fellow."

A week later McCoy rushed into Quintal's house, " It's done, Mat, I've got good spirit ; come and try it."

Quintal did try it, not once, but several times. An hour afterwards he and his comrade reeled up to Young's house, where Smith was seated at the table, receiving instruction in reading and writing from Young. Of late this manner of passing their evenings had become a settled thing between them. What few books were on board the *Bounty* when Christian had run her ashore had been quietly taken possession of by Smith, and from these, with the aid of Young and his own intelligence, he was rapidly improving himself.

As he and Young sat together at the table their women occupied themselves in stitching clothes made from tappa cloth, and as they worked they spoke in low tones, lest they should disturb their white husbands.

With a drunken laugh, McCoy, followed by Quintal, staggered into the dimly-lighted room, and, steadying himself with one hand on the table, addressed Young and Smith.

"Come and have a glass of grog, Mr. Young," he hiccoughed.

"Yes, come along and drink confusion to the King, and bring the women with you," cried Quintal, leering amiably at Terere and Young's wife, who had sprung to their feet in alarm ; "it's good liquor we've got—none of your *Bounty* slops, none of Old Grog's slush, but the real thing."

"Why, these fellows are drunk or mad," exclaimed Young, with a look of astonishment at Smith.

"Where could they get drink ?" answered Smith, looking first at one and then at the other. They met his expression of wonder with coarse guffaws.

"Get it ! Why, you damned fools, we made it ! I made it ! What's your book learning amount to ? It couldn't teach you to make prime liquor like it," said McCoy, who was ready to quarrel with any one.

"If you have found a way of making spirit, it is about the worst thing you could have done. You'll kill yourselves with it," said Young, who remembered that both McCoy and Quintal were several times punished while on the *Bounty* for drunkenness.

McCoy answered with a curse, Quintal made a threatening gesture, and a desperate quarrel would have ensued, but Smith interfered ; and finally, to pacify the drunken men, he and Young went across to McCoy's house to taste his brewing.

It was fortunate for both Young and Smith that each conceived a dislike for the fiery liquor at the first taste. When McCoy and Quintal, with drunken insistence, urged them to make a night of it, and kept

swallowing drink after drink, the other two surrepti-
tiously threw theirs on the ground. Promising to
return later on, they at last managed to escape, and
get back to their frightened wives.

On the following evening the drunkards, who had
slept till near noon, again appeared. This time they
were so savage in their demeanour, and threatened
such fearful villainies, that the other two men feared
bloodshed, and hid themselves with their wives in a
thicket near the house. For two days and nights the
two seamen continued their drinking bout ; each evening their drunken yells and horrid blasphemies reached
even the dwellers in Christian's cave, and made Mahina
tremblingly press her infant to her bosom.

On the morning of the third day, McCoy in his
frenzy, rushed from his house, followed by the equally
maddened Quintal, took the path along the edge of
the cliffs, and, reaching the highest peak, threw himself
headlong upon the rocks below.

A hideous laugh of approval came from Quintal as he
saw McCoy leap to death, then, with a look of insane
cunning, muttering and gibbering to himself, he returned to the settlement, and went inside his house.
There he poured out a pannikin of the fiery liquid, and
tossed it off ; then, picking up an axe and a burning
brand, set off at a run towards the other houses. His
dreadful appearance and the wild curses he shouted
upon every one sent the Tahitian women fleeing before
him to seek refuge with Smith and Young, who rushed
to the doorway and saw the demented creature destroy-
ing Williams' house with his axe. In a few minutes

he had utterly wrecked it, and then, flinging down his weapon, he advanced towards Young's house, waving the firebrand in his hand.

Apparently unconscious that his movements were watched, he sprang over the low stone wall and made straight for the house, looking at the thick drooping thatch, and grinning like a fiend.

" Stand back," cried Young, as musket in hand he pushed past Smith and the terrified women, and faced Quintal, " stand back, Quintal, and throw away that firestick, or, as God is above me, I will shoot you ! "

A mocking laugh was the wretch's answer ; he staggered past, and seizing a bunch of the light, dry thatch in his left hand thrust the firestick into its centre.

" I'm going to burn your——" He never finished, for Young, raising his musket, fired, and shot the miserable man dead.

CHAPTER XXXIV

CHRISTIAN, as soon as he heard of the death of Quintal, bitterly reproached himself as the cause; his old brooding manner returned to him in all its former intensity, and, nothing that Mahina or Smith said could soften the feeling of passionate remorse which now took possession of him."

"God knows, Mr. Christian," said Smith to the mutineer in an endeavour to rouse him from his melancholy, "you have nothing to reproach yourself with. You are not responsible for what led to the death of these men. If my musket had been loaded I would have shot Quintal myself; and I am no lover of bloodshed."

Christian made no answer, but buried his face in his hands; and presently Smith, seeing that he seemed to have become unconscious of his presence, returned to his house. Descending the ridge he met Young coming up. His face was very pale, and Smith saw that he was suffering deeply.

"You shouldn't overtax yourself like this, Mr. Young," he said. "Where are you going?"

A deep flush dyed Young's sallow face. "I am going to Christian. Do you think he will see me?"

Smith looked at him curiously for a moment, then held out his hand, "I am sure he will, sir. God knows you have done him bitter wrong, but he said to me only the other day, when he was speaking of his wife, that he had too many sins upon his own head to judge either you or her."

Edward Young's hand trembled a little as he leaned upon his stick; and without another word he turned and went towards Christian's cave.

The dead silence of the place oppressed him, and the sight of Christian's figure, as he sat with his hands to his face at the entrance to the cave, made him hesitate and shook his resolution, but only for a moment. He took a few quick steps and touched the man who had once been his friend on the shoulder. Christian raised his head and looked at him.

"I have come to you, Christian, for the last time. I am not a sentimental fool, but I feel that if you would once more give me your hand and think of me, not as the cowardly scoundrel I have proved, but as your old and trusted messmate of days gone by, I should be less miserable. I feel that I am a dying man—will you forgive and forget?"

Only the sound of Young's panting breath was heard for a few moments, and then Fletcher Christian stood up and held out his hand.

"I forgive you freely, Young. Not for the sake of

our comradeship in crime, but in the knowledge that I, too, need forgiveness in the sight of God for the bloody deeds that my mad folly and hasty temper have brought about. There is my hand."

For a little time neither of them spoke. Young, looking at the gaunt figure of his old shipmate, was filled with pity.

His memory flew back to the days at Matavai when the young officer had vanquished in friendly contest the picked wrestlers of Tahiti, and Tinā and the gentle Aitia had praised his strength and courage. And Christian, as he listened to Young's laboured breath and almost whispered tones, knew that his time was not far off, yet that for them both there was at least some hope of a brighter future, short as it might be.

Presently Young, with his hand on Christian's shoulder, broke the silence.

" Let us try, old friend, to reconcile ourselves to our lot. I have not long to live, but by God's help will try to lead a better life than I have done. I think it is Smith's teaching. . . . And so I want you to come down to the settlement and live with us again. . . . The men who were ever a disturbing influence here are dead—one by my hand. . . . You alone can inspire all that are left of us with hope for the future. What is there to keep you from us now ? "

" Remorse, Young—the misery of my thoughts— the constant dread—but there, my dear fellow, leave me to myself. You and Smith alone, of all the fated wretches who participated in my villainy, have striven to lead decent lives. If the others had been like you, our life here would have been different. It is too late now ; I cannot bear to think of it. My crime was bad enough when I saw it in all its hideousness five minutes after that morning off Tofoa, but now——"

"Christian," and Young's voice took a deep earnestness, "you suffered under Bligh as none of us suffered. I, aye, and Smith too, were equally guilty with you and the mutiny was no crime."

"No crime ! Is it no crime to have been the murderer of nineteen persons ?—nineteen of my fellow-countrymen turned adrift to die of the horrors of hunger and thirst in an open boat ! "

"They may have reached land."

A faint light came into Christian's eyes— "Young, if I could but dare to hope it ! God knows I would give my life twenty times over to know it. But, even if they did, all England knows the infamy of Fletcher Christian, the disgraced mutineer. . . . But what difference does it make ? Have I not the blood of those who landed here with me upon my soul ?"

He rose from his seat and paced to and fro in the gathering dusk, and Young could see that his emotion had for the time mastered him.

"Come," he said at last, "try to forget the past. Once more I implore you, Christian, to return to the settlement. Your wife "—and he turned his face away as he spoke as if fearful that even darkness could not hide the burning flush of shame upon his cheeks—" your wife is in no fit state to live here. The dreadful loneliness of it is killing her."

A step sounded near, and the next moment Smith joined them.

"Aye, indeed, Mr. Christian. She was never a strong woman, and her time is near. Surely you will let her come and be tended by our women ?"

The sincerity of the appeals touched him at last. "You are right, Smith. God bless you, old friends both, for making me think of her a little. Yes, we will come and dwell in the settlement till the child is born."

The next day Mahina came down from the cavern with a great joy in her heart; for the loneliness of her life, even with her husband to watch over her, robbed her of both health and strength, and she loved to hear the sound of her countrywomen's voices.

A few weeks afterwards her third child was born ; and while the other two played with the children of McCoy, Quintal, and Young, Mahina was tenderly nursed and cared for by the Tahitians till she grew strong again.

But soon, unable to conquer his aversion to the society of his fellow-men, Christain again left her to return to his cave, bidding her to follow him when she was well enough.

* * * * *

The first day of the nineteenth century came in as did most days at Pitcairn—a flush of sunlight melting the mists of the mountain tops, piercing the dark shades of the wooded valleys with broad blades of golden light, and rousing the sleeping rookeries of sea-birds into clamorous life. Long ere the glittering dews of the night that hung in beady drops from every leaf and blade of grass had quivered and fallen to the first breaths of the trade-wind, Christian awoke from his broken slumbers, and was moodily taking his accustomed walk along the eastern cliffs.

What had happened in the world he had left behind ? he thought. Was he accounted as long since dead ? Was there one living soul in all England whose thoughts went out to him sometimes ? Slowly he paced along buried in thought. When he reached the end of his walk he sat on a jutting ledge of rock overhanging the boiling surf three hundred feet below, where his eye ranged over the wide expanse of sparkling ocean. Day after day, for years he had looked out thus upon the bosom of the sailless sea, and had seen nothing but the swift flight of the blue-billed *kanápu* and fierce-eyed frigate birds as they sailed to and fro or plunged from aerial heights into the deep ; or far above, the snow-white tropic birds, floating with motionless wing and gazing down at the human figure below. Was it likely, he thought, that his refuge would ever be discovered ? Would——

He started to his feet and with dilated eyes looked at the horizon. There, clearly within view, were the topgallant sails of a ship !

Crouching—he knew not why—upon his knees, he clutched the ledge of rock with shaking hands and watched for nearly a quarter of an hour. The trade-wind was fast bringing the ship nearer, and before long her courses rose to view. A few minutes more he gazed, then, struck by a sudden impulse, he ran along the ledge till he reached the pathway to Bounty Bay. He bounded down the steep and fearful descent to where the *Bounty's* boat was hauled up upon rough skids laid down by Young and Smith many months before. Old as she was, the boat was not now unseaworthy, as she had been when Nahi and the other Tahitian women attempted to escape in her; for Smith had put her in a fair state of repair, so that she might be used for fishing when the surf did not break too heavily upon the shores of the little bay.

Christian tugged vainly at the boat and rocked her from side to side in an endeavour to start her down the skids; but his strength was not equal to the task.

He ceased his efforts, and then looked seaward, but the ship was not visible from where he stood.

" Oh ! for some help," he muttered," " but that I cannot, dare not seek ; neither Young nor Smith must see me." He thought for a moment, then with excitement, began again to ascend the path to his cave. Panting with his exertions he soon gained the top of the cliffs, and ran along the dangerous path till he reached the cavern. He darted inside and quickly reappeared with his musket and a block and tackle, which he had often used to drag weights to his retreat. With this he hoped to launch the boat by making one end of the tackle fast to a point of rock just at the water's edge, and the other to her stern ringbolt.

The musket he intended to fire to attract notice from the ship should other means fail.

Returning to the beach he was soon exerting all his strength to start the heavy little boat down to the water.

CHAPTER XXXV

BY this time the ship was within three or four miles of the island, and had been seen by one of the Tahitian women. She ran back to the settlement, and roused the little community to a state of wild excitement by her loud cries of "A ship! a ship! A ship is coming."

Soon Young and Smith reached the cliffs, and one glance at the ocean showed them the vessel—a ship of war, they were quick to perceive, by the cut of her canvas and her lofty spars.

Young was scarcely able to walk, and his excitement at first prevented him from speaking, but when he could control himself he held a hurried consultation with Smith, who then set off for Christian's cave to inform him of the ship's approach, while Young returned to the settlement and told Mahina to prepare to leave the house and, with the other women, be ready to hide herself if necessary.

They had resolved, as a first step towards safety, that every person on the island should assemble near the cavern. The difficulty of access and the remoteness of its situation, they thought, would afford them all a safe retreat from such people as might land. It was hoped by Young and Smith that, unless the vessel was a King's ship specially sent to search for the missing mutineers, those who placed foot on shore would not easily discover that the island was inhabited. As a first precaution, however, some of the women were sent to remove all traces of human occupancy from the two little beaches, and to cover up the *Bounty's* boat with dead coconut branches and bushes.

Four of them departed to do this, while Mahina and her children, with the remaining women, set out for Christian's cave.

But when they reached the cavern they found it deserted by both Christian and Smith, and saw that no preparations had been made to defend the narrow path leading to the stronghold.

Frightened at the absence of the two men, the terrified women ran hither and thither, calling loudly, and seeking for traces of them; till presently Mahina, wildly excited, sped down the path and looked over the edge of the cliffs to the beach below. Then a cry of alarm broke from her.

Beckoning to the others, she flew down the perilous path to the shore. Half-way she stumbled and, but for a projecting pinnacle of rock, would have pitched headlong to the beach. Before she recovered herself the other women overtook her, and were peering down to discover what it was that had so agitated her. But from where they clustered together they could see only the billows bursting in foam upon the black rocks below ; and while they waited for Mahina to explain there came the report of a musket from beneath.

Too far down on their way to turn back, as their rears dictated, Mahina's companions stood trembling and hesitating, their hearts filled with an undefined apprehension that some fresh tragedy had occurred.

*   *   *   *   *

Smith, filled with anxiety for his leader, had hurried along the rocky track to Christian's cave. The dreaded hour had arrived at last—the hour that he and the other mutineers had so often feared. A King's ship ! Yes, she could be no other ! His seaman's eye told him she was a ship of war. Perhaps she was a Frenchman ? That was not likely. She was English—sent to search for them; and even if she were not, she evidently intended to send a boat ashore. Once a landing party from the ship ascended the cliffs they could not fail to see the houses, and would not take long to find those who lived in them. Then would come discovery and a disgraceful death.

But, thought he, Christian will never be taken alive ; and even if the presence of white men upon the island should be discovered, the cave was hard to find. And still, even if the ship were in search of Christian and his companions, the identity of the inhabitants might not perhaps be suspected. If the worst came to the worst, they could make a fight of it to the death in such a place as Christian's stronghold.

So ran the quick current of his thoughts as he

panted up the ridge to the cave—then, with an exclamation of dismay, he saw that it was untenanted.

As loudly as possible he called Christian's name, but
only the countless reverberation of his cries answered
him from the desolate solitude. A hurried glance
down the path which he had just ascended showed no
human being in sight. Surely Christian could not be
far off? He must either be coming along the ridge
and hidden from view, or lying asleep somewhere
along the edge of the cliffs. Perhaps he had gone to
the beach?

Hastily descending again, Smith struck across to the
eastern side of the island, till he came to a spot which
overlooked Bounty Bay. He knew that Christian, in
his lonely wanderings, sometimes visited the place, and
sat for hours upon the wreckage of the *Bounty's* spars.
A thick, stunted growth of matted scrub and vines
grew to the very edge of the cliffs, but hastily pushing
through it, the seaman looked down. There, far below,
he saw the man he sought, bending his tackle to launch
the *Bounty's* boat!

The next moment, too anxious even to lose time
by descending the regular path Smith, at the hazard of
his life, began to scramble down the almost precipitous
face of the cliff. At last, with bleeding feet and hands,
he reached the shore.

"In God's name, Mr. Christian, what are you
trying to do?" he demanded, breathlessly.

"What am I trying to do?" repeated Christian
fiercely—"I am about to end it all. That is a King's
ship, and I am going to give myself up."

"You must be mad to talk like this. Come away at once and let us get back to the cave, or we shall all be discovered."

"It will be your own fault if you are ; you and those with you may do as you please, but I will board that ship," answered Christian wildly, and Smith saw that he was nearly mad with excitement. As he spoke he still strained with all his might on the tackle, and the boat, once started, slid down the skids till her stern touched the pebbly beach.

"By God, you shan't do this ! Our lives as well as yours depend upon your hiding with us "; and Smith laid his hand on the fall of the tackle so as to prevent Christian from unshipping the hook.

"Stand back, Smith ! Stand back, I say. I swear that no longer shall justice go unsatisfied. I *will* go !" As a wave dashed up, the boat lifted and floated ; he sprang past Smith, jumped in and cast off the tackle.

Seizing hold of the gunwale, Smith exerted all his strength and drew the boat broadside on to the beach.

"Beware, man, beware !" and Christian's eyes blazed with sudden fury—"let go your hold, I say. I am dangerous !" Smith recognised it was no time for words ; he released his hold, jumped into the boat, and threw himself upon the desperate man. They went down together, and the boat rocked from side to side with the violence of their struggle. No word was spoken, but there was in Christian's face such a look of savage determination to overcome his friend, that Smith at last aimed a blow at his head, thinking to stun him for a time.

Nerved with a madman's strength, the blow only seemed to rouse him to greater fury ; with a mighty effort he freed himself from Smith's left arm, which was wound about his waist, and in another moment his hand grasped the barrel of the loaded musket, which he drew towards him by the muzzle.

Then Smith again threw himself upon him. There was a short, fierce struggle, a report, and Fletcher Christian sank back with a groan—the ball had passed through his chest.

Sick with horror, Smith staggered to his feet and raised the dying man in his arms. He lifted him out of the boat and carried him to the beach, where he placed him in a sitting posture ; then tearing off his shirt he sought to stanch the fearful rush of blood.

" My God, sir ! my God, sir ! you don't think 'twas my doing ? " he asked in anguished tones.

" No, no, my good fellow," gasped Christian, " you are not to blame. My foot must have touched the trigger. . . . I was mad."

Smith knelt beside him, overcome with grief and blinded by tears. He took his leader's hand in his and tried to speak, but one look at the gaping wound told him that the end was near.

And then there echoed from the cliffs a cry of heart-broken agony. Mahina, springing from rock to rock, had reached the overhanging ledge under which her husband lay, and, looking down, saw him.

Leaping to the ground, she turned upon Smith. " Thou murderer ; thou hast slain him ! " she cried, and pushing him away, threw herself upon her knees beside her husband.

"Nay, nay, Mahina," he said; "not so. My foot struck the gun. . . . He hath ever been my friend. . . . Listen to me . . . for in a little time I die."

Slowly and gaspingly the words came, and Mahina, with a sob of misery, saw the grey shadows of death dimming the eyes of him she loved so well.

"He shall not die; he shall not die!" she cried wildly to Smith and Young, who had now joined them, and was overcome at the scene before him. "Save him, save him, lest ye both die accursed!" then burst into anguished weeping, as she bent her face upon her husband's knees.

"Is that you, Young?" asked Christian faintly—"my time is nearly run, old friend," and he put out his brown, sun-tanned hand. "But, quick; listen to me. . . . Save yourselves while there is yet time. . . . The ship must be near now."

"No," said Young, pressing his hand, "she kept off quite suddenly when within a mile of the land. I saw her stand away again to the westward. In another hour she'll be hull down."

"Thank God!" he murmured. "Mahina . wife . . . come closer to me, . . . and you, Young and Smith, give me your hands. Promise me that no one but yourselves shall ever know where I lie. Let no other white man point to my grave and say, 'Fletcher Christian . . . mutineer.'"

He ceased, then by a dying effort, opened his arms wide.

"Mahina! My wife! Mother of my children!
· · · it is all over now," he sighed with his last breath,
as his arms closed gently round her neck.

She pressed her cheek to his; his head sank upon
her shoulder, and then lay there in the quietness of
death.

*   *   *   *   *

Years later, when Pitcairn was "discovered," the
venerable man, loved and revered by the children of
the mutineers under the name of John Adams, revealed
his identity with Alexander Smith, and tremblingly
waited to hear his fate from the lips of the naval
officers who had landed on the island. The story of
the death of Young from consumption soon after that
of Christian, as well as the deaths of the others of the
ill-starred company, was told by him; though, faithful
to his promise, he refused to show his leader's last
resting-place; and the listeners heard for the first time
the fate of the *Bounty* mutineers.

THE END.

UNWIN BROTHERS, PRINTERS, WOKING AND LONDON.

www.ingramcontent.com/pod-product-compliance
Lightning Source LLC
Chambersburg PA
CBHW060555030726
47498CB00005B/1405